W9-AMC-581

JOURNEYING

BARBARA FLEMING

FIVE STAR
A part of Gale, Cengage Learning

Detroit • New York • San Francisco • New Haven, Conn • Waterville, Maine • London

Y07-2533

GALE
CENGAGE Learning™

Set in 11 pt. Plantin.
Printed on permanent paper.

LIBRARY OF CONGRESS CATALOGING-IN-PUBLICATION DATA

Fleming, Barbara Allbrandt, 1963-
    Journeying / Barbara Fleming.
      p. cm.
    ISBN-13: 978-1-59414-790-6 (alk. paper)
    ISBN-10: 1-59414-790-6 (alk. paper)
      1. Women—Fiction. 2. Diaries—Authorship—Fiction. 3. Wagon trains—Fiction. 4. Frontier and pioneer life—Fiction. 5. Colorado—History—19th century—Fiction. I. Title.
    PS3606.L459J68 2009
    813'.6—dc22   2009013824

First Edition. First Printing: August 2009.
Published in 2009 in conjunction with Tekno Books.

Printed in the United States of America
1 2 3 4 5 6 7 13 12 11 10 09

This book is dedicated to my father, the late Lester H. Stimmel, who gave me a love of reading and of writing that has sustained me all my life.

ACKNOWLEDGMENTS

How can anyone write without the aid, comfort and support of a critique group? I know I could not. This novel never would have happened without my two friends and critiquers, Rev. Sylvia Falconer and Cheryl Ravenschlag, and my writing partner, Barbara Sherrod. My gratitude knows no bounds.

I deeply appreciate my editor, Alice Duncan, who is sensitive and astute. Many thanks, Alice.

I also thank my daughter, Alison Day, and my husband, Tom Fleming, for being there when I needed them, and just for being there. Friends, family and community are what hold us up; I am very fortunate to have such special ones. And I am lucky to live where I do. The rich history of my hometown engaged my interest in history years ago and has sustained it ever since.

While writing this novel I made extensive use of the Fort Collins Public Library and the Fort Collins Museum Archive. The archivist, Lesley Drayton, and her predecessor at the Fort Collins Public Library, Rheba Massey, went way beyond the call of duty to help me with my research, as did Lesley's two assistants, Pat Walker and Susan Harness. My profound thanks to them all.

Finally, this novel honors the legions of women who settled the American West more than a century ago. How marvelous they were! I am awestruck by their strength, their courage, their independence and their determination. We owe them more than this book could ever express. Hannah Morris Bowman is my tribute to them all.

1872

April 13

I boarded the train early this morning, with no one to see me off.

I left Mama and Karl a note saying that I was going to visit Cousin Carrie in Kentucky. I am of legal age; they cannot prevent me. But I told a lie, and I took something which did not belong to me. I should be burning up with guilt, but I find that I am, rather, full of excitement and joy.

In truth, I am heading west on this bouncing, noisy train. I sold Grandmother Evans's brooch, which I spirited out of Mama's room last night, to get the money for my ticket. We have agreed that Lucas will meet me in St. Louis, where we will try to find a wagon train. Then we must ferry to Council Bluffs. He is coming on the afternoon train. We will marry at the end of our journey.

Why should it be that two people who love each other cannot marry as they choose? Why must society be so blind?

Lucas is an honorable man. He has promised that we will not consummate our union until we are legally wed. We can claim 160 acres for our own if we can stay five years on them. Not many do, I am told. That seems such a vast expanse of land. I do not even know how much an acre is. It's not an easy life, they say. But we will succeed! *We will!*

We must farm the land so as to have a home, but it is my fond hope that we will then be able to move somewhere that

9

will allow Lucas to practice his profession and me to teach music, as I have always dreamed of doing.

Once we join the wagon train he must take the role of my servant. I am to be a widowed woman who is fulfilling her dead husband's dream of settling in the West. In a wagón we can take provisions and bring livestock with us, ready to set up house-keeping when we find the right place. I think he has a bit of the romantic in him, for he seemed quite excited about our adventure. Are we at the edge of a precipice, about to fall off into the abyss, or at the entrance to Paradise, about to find our happiness at last?

April 15

At the end of this interminable journey, I got off the train and went to the hotel to wait for Lucas. But the train has come today—and Lucas did not get off! I scoured and scoured the platform, looking up and down, and could not see him anywhere. Oh, if only we'd been able to leave in a more orderly fashion! Where is he? Was I wrong to embark on this mad adventure?

We would not have left so suddenly had not Karl announced at dinner last night that he had found me a husband.

"Karl," Mama said in her quiet, serious voice, the one I remember from my childhood, "Hannah has reached her major-ity. You cannot force her to marry." I was amazed to hear Mama defy Karl, for she had not done so in my presence before.

My stepfather kept on as if there were only a gnat in the room, not my mother. "His name is Wilhelm Hessler," he said. "He's an elder in the church, widowed, with three children who need a mother. He's had his eye on Hannah for some time, and last night he offered for her. She should be grateful!" he roared.

Mama tried once more. "Hannah is not a piece of merchan-dise like those at your store. You cannot just give her away."

He glared at her. "She will do as I say," he shouted, thumping his hand on the table and turning to leave the kitchen. As he walked out he said, "Wilhelm will be here tomorrow night for dinner, Hannah will welcome him, and the arrangements can be made. We will have her married by the end of the month."

Mama sighed, a gesture I recognized all too well as her capitulation, once again, to my stepfather. Her brief, daring spark of defiance had burned out.

But I remained defiant. "Mama, I will not marry this man or any man Karl chooses for me."

"How can you not do as he says?" she replied. "He provides for us. He saved your father's store. Some day it will be yours. All we have to do is wait and be patient."

I put my hand on her arm. My poor, weak mother, who cannot imagine herself, her life, without a man in charge of it. . . . "Mama, I will not marry Wilhelm Hessler, not to save the store, not to please you, not for any reason whatsoever."

She slumped down in her chair and began to weep. In the past, her tears had often succeeded in my surrender, but not this time. Marriage to that man—his image had come to me by then, a dark, small, brooding fellow with unkempt, sniveling children—was impossible.

I left the kitchen and went to my room, hastening to pack my portmanteau. I slipped into Mama's room and took the brooch. Then I sat up at the window until dawn, when I hurried out of the house—while Mama and Karl still slept—and went to find Lucas.

It was only a short walk to where I knew he would be at that hour—at the small café across the street from his rooming house, eating breakfast and preparing for his day. And indeed he was there, but of course I could not talk to him or sit with him then. Instead, I found a small boy outside of the café and promised him a five-cent piece if he would deliver a note for me. I watched from the window as he took the note to Lucas. I watched Lucas read it and get up, hastily, to leave the café. As soon as he stood, I quickly walked away.

We met at our usual spot in the hospital, the linen closet, where we knew we would not be disturbed. When I told him of the dire situation, he agreed that we must leave Cincinnati at once. We made our plans—I would take the train that left later that morning, and he would follow the next day. As both of us are painfully aware of the difficulties that lie ahead because of his dark skin, we fixed on the plan for him to play my servant. We would seek a wagon train, or go west alone in a wagon if none was to be had. There are not so many these days, what with the railroad stretching clear across the continent.

I was thankful to arrive in St. Louis. The train was hot and dusty, and there was no refreshment offered. Luckily, I had thought to bring food with me. It fit nicely into my portmanteau, and I had brought a vessel of water, but the journey lasted longer than the food and drink. There was no opportunity to relieve myself until we stopped at a station along the way. I became very weary of the men who kept trying to occupy the empty seat next to mine. They all seemed to think that I, a woman alone, could not manage without their "protection." I had to tell the last one, who was very persistent, that I was on my way to a convent in California (a very Catholic state, I am told) to begin my life as a nun, and that I wished to pray in peace, before he moved away from me.

But Lucas is not here! There is nothing to do but return to the hotel and wait, hoping and praying that I was not wrong. I love him, and he loves me. *I cannot be wrong. I cannot.*

Now I have sat in this dingy hotel room for hours, writing in this journal, waiting. What if Karl finds out where I have gone and comes after me before Lucas arrives? I will not go with him. I will scream for help and get away, somehow.

My Lucas—what an extraordinary man he is. He has told me something of his history (though no one else knows the truth). He was born in New Orleans to a house slave who had been forced by the young master. Only a short while after his birth, his mother, known to me only as Roxie, and he were spirited away from the plantation and put on a ship bound for France. Who saved them? Lucas believes it was his grandfather, the patriarch.

Roxie must have been a remarkable woman indeed. Not long after they arrived in Paris she found a benefactor, and she and Lucas lived well thanks to him. Lucas attended the best schools, learned several languages, and had ambitions to become a diplomat, until his mother died when he was but sixteen. He decided then to become a physician, in hopes of finding a cure for the consumption that killed his mother. Young as he was, he apprenticed with a famous Paris man and had struck out on his own by the time he was twenty. Is that not amazing and wonderful?

How blessed for me that he came to our country just before the war, at the behest of an American surgeon he met in Greece when he was studying there, invited here to share his knowledge and skill with the man's colleagues in Cincinnati. And further blessed that he did not return to France when the war started. Had we not met, he tells me, he would have returned, but I held him here. I am so grateful that I had decided, during the war, to give the poor soldiers what comfort and cheer I could. I went to the hospital twice a week, sometimes more often, to write letters, to help with other chores, and once in a while to play for them. Had I not chosen that path, Lucas and I would never have met. And now he has come with me to create a new life together.

April 16

My darling has arrived at last. The desk clerk at the hotel sent someone up to my room at ten o'clock this morning to announce that my servant had arrived. I went down to the lobby to see him. There he was—dirty, unshaven, looking exhausted.

We had to be very cautious in our greetings. He merely said, "Sorry to be late, Miz Hannah," and was careful to avert his eyes. I know how it hurts him to be perceived in this way, humble and ignorant, but we both know that it is necessary.

Shall I ever *not* thrill at the sight of him? He is not an excessively tall man but is sturdily built, with broad shoulders and long arms. But it is his hands and his face that I love the most. He has long, slender fingers, and his palm is broad and quite pink, in contrast to the back of his hand. The veins are fine and blue. Had he not become a surgeon, his hands would have been perfect for a concert pianist.

The outstanding feature of his face is his deep black eyes, ringed by impossibly long lashes. With his high cheekbones, narrow nose and dimpled chin, he has an exotic look, as if he were from Arabia or far-off India. In fact, the surgeons at the Cincinnati hospital supposed him to be from Turkey. He has an unusual accent that is hard to place, ensuring that people do not take him for a mulatto. When he smiles, which he does not often do, his eyes light up like candles. In his embrace, I feel safe and secure.

Still, he does have dark skin, and as such is not considered my equal, at least not in this place. Will he ever be? Anywhere? We must proceed with great care now.

The clerk at the hotel said that Lucas could sleep in the back of the hotel with the other servants. I do not like this, but what can I do? After he had deposited his bags, he went to the waterfront to find out about a wagon train.

He learned that there was one heading out in two days. We have to buy provisions. He will arrange for a wagon and horses on my behalf, but he left the provisioning to me.

To me! What do I know about staples and supplies for a wagon journey west? I must consult with someone, perhaps one of the other women who are going. I will go down to the waterfront and see what I can discover. In my new life I need to be bold and courageous, never my habit at home.

April 18

We are on the ferry, being jostled around so that I can hardly write in my journal. I hate this. I am doing my best not to disgrace myself by becoming ill. Once we are on dry land again, I am sure I will be fine.

April 20

The wagon train is underway. The leader, one Mr. Kent, was hesitant about letting us join until I "crossed his palm with silver," as it says in the Bible. However, he placed us last. Lucas noted wryly that if trouble develops on the trail, we will be in the worst position. He drives the wagon with his rifle at his side.

I am astounded at the jolting, the discomfort, of this conveyance! We had a carriage at home, though I walked most places, and never was I bounced about as I have been in this wagon. Lucas explains that it is because the trail is rough and rutted, not smooth or paved with stones as city streets are.

I have not thus far in my life been this close to horses, either. One always mounts the carriage quite a distance from the beast. What huge creatures they are! Though Lucas insists these two are gentle, not to be feared, I keep away from them. Worse, we have acquired a cow and calf. In Cincinnati, milk came to our

15

door daily via the milk wagon, meat from the butcher. I've never been within five miles of a cow. They too are large creatures. Still, this one is quite placid as long as we don't disturb her calf. It is a revelation to me that even dumb creatures have such powerful maternal instincts. I have named her Judy, after a woman I knew at the hospital who bears her a slight resemblance.

Most of the women, I note, walk beside the wagon rather than riding in it. That is no doubt the wisest course. I shall do so from now on. Thank goodness Lucas insisted I purchase these sturdy boots.

April 22

Will I ever learn to cook over an open fire? I burned the biscuits this morning, and last night's potatoes were hard while the beans were mushy. Lucas just laughs. "You'll learn, Hannah," he says. I thought I knew how to cook, from helping Mama and Mary in the kitchen, but we had a stove and oven and ample supplies of cooking utensils. Here, I have one pan, a skillet, and an open fire. Dreadful! Lucas, I note, did not offer to take on the role of cook as well as wagon driver. Quite likely he does not even know how to fry an egg.

I find walking all day, in this heat, arduous but not impossible. I am thankful for all the walking I did at home, to and from the hospital, to and from church. I believe my legs are strong enough to bear this demand on them.

The gnats swarm around us; I can see no way to avoid them. Large flies pester the animals, especially the horses. They flick their tails all day long. By the time darkness falls, I am so weary I can scarcely hold up my head, much less a pencil. And it's too dark to see. I try to write during nooning if I can; once we have eaten, the men and the animals usually rest in the heat of the day before we start on. One day soon I need to write a letter to

Mama, but not yet. When we come to a settlement, perhaps I can find a way to post a letter. I am sure she is anxious about me. Now that we are on our way, it seems safe to tell her what I have done. Karl can never trouble me again—though he might take his anger out on her. Dear Lord, I pray that is not so.

I must beg her forgiveness for taking the brooch and for leaving as I did, but she surely must know that there was no other way. I had told her quite plainly that I would not marry Mr. Hessler, and she knew I would not. Perhaps she wept because she knew that I too, like Lawrence, would leave home rather than endure the fate Karl had planned for us. I had to take the brooch, too. Though I had a small amount of money set aside, it was not enough for the train ticket. Lucas wanted to give me money for the fare, but I did not think that proper since we are not yet wed.

The people in the wagon train appear to have accepted Lucas and me as mistress and servant; indeed, they pay us almost no mind. They seem uninterested in anyone else. They don't seem to want to know why anyone is here, where anyone is going. They ask no questions. They are not for the most part overly friendly, but no one has challenged us. How different from Ohio! There, if Lucas and I had been seen together in any other way except briefly exchanging greetings at the hospital, we would have been the objects of derision and worse.

I well remember the first time Lucas and I kissed. We had talked so often, casually, at the hospital, knowing that others watched. Yet the attraction between us was powerful. We both felt it.

One day I went to the stockroom to get a fresh supply of blankets. I had them in my arms as I turned around, and there he was. We were alone; we fell into each other's arms, the blankets tumbling in a heap onto the floor. I am afraid that I was quite forward; I pressed myself upon him until he could do no less than kiss me.

Lightning struck! My whole body tingled; my loins were afire. I wanted only for that kiss to last forever. I wanted more than that.

But of course the kiss could not last. In a moment we heard footsteps, so he stepped away and disappeared.

From then on, we took every opportunity to be together. I think of those times so often now, as Lucas and I play out this charade. We cannot touch. We cannot be alone. I long for him, but I can do nothing. Not now. If only we could hold hands, let alone exchange a kiss. But if we kissed, we might not be able to restrain ourselves.

April 24

Walking, walking, walking. One foot in front of the other, over and over again. How many miles have I walked since we left? A thousand? A million? I do not know. I thought I was strong enough to manage it; now, I am not at all certain. By day's end my legs ache so I can hardly move them. Lucas advises me to massage my legs. It would not be proper for him to do it, he says. Proper! Did we not abandon "proper" when we left civilization behind?

My feet—oh, my poor, poor feet. They are blistered in every conceivable spot. Lucas has rubbed ointment on them, and advised me to wear two pairs of stockings, which helps, but they still hurt. Lucas says I will soon grow calluses. What would Mama think of that?

I must walk with caution, lest I turn an ankle on a hummock of grass, or encounter an unexpected hole in the ground made by some subterranean creature, or disturb a snake. Mr. Kent has told us to be on the lookout for snakes, as they are numerous here, and for holes. I do not want to suffer the fate of one poor woman, who turned her ankle the second day on the trail. She and her family had to turn back, for she declared she would not spend her days being jostled to death on the seat of the wagon. If she could not walk, they would have to wait until she could.

There are times when I am certain I cannot take another step. I put one foot in front of the other nonetheless, and somehow I continue to move forward. I had not known I could endure so much.

Where are we? I am not sure. Somewhere in Nebraska Territory, someone said. A long, long way to go. We have not discussed a destination. The train is headed to Oregon, but I hope we can find a hospitable place soon. I don't want to go that far.

April 26

Lucinda Smith is large with child. I think she will be having the infant very soon, though I know little about such things. At the hospital I did not work in the area where children were born. Mrs. Smith already has three other children, and her husband, a small, unpleasant man from New York State, is quite cross with her.

Their wagon is but two in front of us. Yesterday, she lay down in their wagon after the noon respite, and her husband shouted at her ferociously. He may even have struck her, for I heard her cry out once. She stayed in the wagon despite his treatment of her; I think she does not feel well. She has not emerged again, leaving the oldest child, a boy of about seven I estimate, to cook the evening meal and look after his younger brother and sister.

I do not envy her at all. Nor do I imagine she is eager to add another little one to her brood. But what can we women do? In spite of Karl's and Mama's attempts to keep me away from the world, I do know how babies are conceived, and I do know that

19

women have little choice in the matter, for there are few ways to prevent becoming with child—and men, says Mama, must have their rights. How frequently I heard that said in Cincinnati! But I *know* Lucas is different. He will not demand. We will come to each other in joy and love, and I shall be as willing as he.

I wonder that the Smiths came on this journey at all, knowing how imminently she would have her child. How can a woman manage an infant in these circumstances? They have other children, but they are very young, too young, I think, to be of much help to her.

Still, I have found rewards from this experience which are not to be found in any city. Stars—millions of stars! I did not know there were so many in the sky. And space, more space around us than one could ever imagine in dreams or fairy tales. At night, the sky is immense, full of twinkling lights. The moon, when it comes up, seems larger and brighter than it did in Ohio, though I can't think why.

Last night we gathered around the campfire. One of the men has brought his fiddle, and he played for us. The music was haunting, sad, evoking thoughts of death and loss, but I found it comforting all the same. For the first time, I felt myself part of the group. I have not become much acquainted with the other women; we are all so busy all the time, or so tired.

Then we began to sing, old, comfortable hymns that everyone knows. Rather to my surprise, I enjoyed the singing. After that, one man began to pray, and others joined him. I went back to our wagon. I do not wish to have religious views imposed on me, however well intentioned, after so long a time of listening to Karl berate Mama and me for our lack of faith night after night. He prayed for our "evil" souls, so he said, but he himself is evil incarnate, even though Mama appears not to know that.

April 27

As we were rolling west this morning, I heard the most ungodly shrieks coming from one of the wagons. Soon we knew it was the Smiths' wagon, and the cries were coming from Lucinda. One of the older women went to Mr. Kent, the wagon master, and asked him to stop. I did not hear the exchange but learned later that he told her Mrs. Smith would just have to have her baby as the wagons were moving. "If she can't wait till nooning, we can't stop for her," he is reported to have said.

I believe that he said it as reported; he is a hard taskmaster. He has narrow, squinting eyes and a very loud voice. The tone is harsh and commanding. That's what's needed, I suppose. Still, I could wish for a more amenable wagon master.

Moment by moment things were getting worse in the Smith wagon. No one could escape hearing Lucinda's screams of agony. Mr. Smith finally pulled off the trail and stopped. Then about twenty women descended on Mr. Kent and insisted that he circle the wagons until the labor was finished. Some of them carried their iron cook pans or knives. They were determined!

Wanting to avoid a rebellion, I expect, Mr. Kent acceded. The wagons were circled, and the women got down to business.

Lucas made a move toward the Smith wagon. He wanted to help Mrs. Smith bring forth her child.

But I stepped in front of him. "Lucas, we cannot reveal who you are. Not here, not now. Some of the men in this train would be very angry if you helped her. And Mr. Smith, such an unpleasant man—he might even try to shoot you!"

He said nothing. I could see the strain and frustration in his face.

"Did you ever assist with birthing children since you came to the United States?" I asked, walking away from the circle of wagons.

He shook his head, his lips tight. "No. Dr. Roth advised

against it. He said biases were too deep."

"Then please, please come with me. I cannot bear to hear the poor woman scream, and I long for a cool dip in the stream. You can keep watch to make sure no one comes upon me while I am disrobed." Lucinda sounded like a wounded animal. I could not bear to listen.

With one more glance at the Smiths' wagon, Lucas turned and followed me down to the water. I knew that his deep instinct to help, all his training, was at war with his common sense, and I am thankful that common sense won out.

I was glad that the high bank muted the sound. When I got into the water and began splashing around, I could no longer hear the screams of pain.

How lovely it was to slip into the cool water and wash my body, my hair (poor hair—how it suffers!), my undergarments. Lucas sat high up on the bank, watching for intruders. Did he steal a glance at me? I don't know, but I would not mind if he did. (Oh, Mama! Only a short time away from your dictates and I am already growing reckless.) I was quite refreshed when we returned to the wagons some time later to find that the difficult time was past; Mrs. Smith was delivered of her baby, a fine, big boy, they said, the train ready to move on. We missed the noon-ing, but Lucas and I lunched on johnny cake (which tasted of the grit blown into the batter by the wind) and molasses as we traveled and were quite content. It is too hot for one to be very hungry.

I had drawn some water from the creek to put in my drinking jug, but Lucas insisted that I boil it first. We cannot have a fire until we stop at dusk, so I was quite thirsty by the time we stopped for supper.

My lips have grown dry and caked in this heat. Lucas advises me not to lick them, as he says that only makes it worse. He has given me a solution which tastes rather unpleasant but seems to help the flaking skin. He told me to use it every night. I think I will have no trouble remembering to do so. I wonder why he is so much less bothered by the dryness and the heat than I. Does his dark skin protect him?

In the heat and with only the wagon to offer privacy, I have abandoned my corset. Who could lace it for me, as Mary used to do? I did not bring the right clothing for this journey. My Ohio clothes are too delicate and frilly. These women wear simple cotton frocks with no lace or any such excesses on them. The dresses just touch the tops of their shoes so they do not drag and get dirty at the hem. I have started to sew myself a dress like theirs, with the help of Martha Andersen, whose wagon is just ahead of ours and who is very kind. We have begun to exchange small conversation as we walk along during the hot and dusty day. She has told me her story: her husband lost their farm in a drought and wanted to go west and start over again. She agreed, but with the promise that they would never move again once they had settled somewhere. She is afraid of being attacked by Indians and carries an ax with her as she walks.

On her advice, I am tearing up two of my frocks and sewing them together so as to create one sturdier gown. Foolish me, not to have thought of that! Of course, I could not carry too much in my portmanteau, and Mama would have become suspicious had I started to make myself such a practical gown—even had I supposed I would need it. I thought it more important to bring a few books, writing materials, some music, in case I ever see a piano again.

How different this experience is from what I imagined it would be! When Lucas and I were making our plans, I envisioned a romantic adventure with beautiful moonlight and cool breezes at night, ample time for delicious, thoughtful conversations and of course for romance. I was thinking only of freedom, not of the practicalities. Who would prepare the meals? Mary has always done that in the Morris and Schussman households. Who would launder the clothes? Mary again. But alas, I did not bring Mary along in my valise. There is no one but Hannah Morris to do this work, and so much more than was required in Cincinnati. And Hannah has much to learn.

I did, thankfully, while in Council Bluffs purchase a bonnet like those the other women wear. Mama would be scandalized that I am out in the sun all day with only a bonnet for protection. I can hear her: "Where is your parasol, Hannah? The sun will ruin your skin."

April 29

It is already hot, though it is still April. The nights are cool, but by midday, with the sun beating down, I am perspiring profusely and feeling the heat most grievously. I imagine I do not smell too nice. Lucas does not complain. (We cannot, of course, come close enough to each other to be too much offended.) He, too, perspires profusely. His shirt gets very damp and clings to his body, a sight I find quite pleasing.

I am glad for the nooning, when we can sit in the shade of the wagon. It is hard to get up and walk again after we eat. I am finding, though, that my legs have grown stronger, my feet more accustomed to walking all day. I do not mind it as much as I did.

Some of the men went hunting while Lucinda was in labor. Mr. Andersen, our nearest neighbor, brought back three fat rabbits, and Martha skinned them and made a delicious stew for supper, which she kindly shared with us.

Shall I ever learn to do such a distasteful thing as skin an animal? I shall have to, I suppose. Once it is dead, it does not matter what one does to it. She thought to teach me, invited me to watch. I nearly gagged. I did not take the knife, though she offered it to me, but I watched closely. When Lucas's and my lives depend on it, I shall be able to do it, I am sure.

Again last night I dreamed about Karl. I was in the kitchen, helping Mama with supper. She stepped into the larder for a moment, leaving me alone with him. He came up behind me and put his hands on my breasts and squeezed, hard. I jabbed him with my elbow, to force him away from me. He grew angry and began to hit me on the back, his fists clenched, just as I have seen him hit her. When he hits her, she hunches over so as to protect her breasts. I can imagine what her back looks like, full of bruises. I was powerless to stop the beatings. I am but a woman, not strong, and he is a large, powerful man with practiced fists. But he stopped hitting me when she came back into the kitchen. He stepped away.

Mama gave me a long look, then looked at Karl. She was silent, going about her business, stepping around her husband so he could not reach her without moving himself. He snorted, a most unappealing sound, and stomped from the room.

It is the same dream I have had many times. But sometimes, in the dream, he comes to my bed instead of assaulting me before I have retired. I struggle and resist, but he lays his heavy body down on top of mine and forces himself on me. I scream and kick, but I cannot escape his evil presence. I feel smothered and afraid, and the pain is unbearable.

Did these things really happen? Or are they merely dreams, born of my revulsion and fear? I do not know. I do know that I shall never see him again. Lucas and I will marry, and these bad dreams will go away.

April 30

Some of the travelers held a formal worship service around the campfire last night. They sang hymns and prayed extensively, asking God for protection along the way. Several of them were quite fervent. It was not possible to sleep until they were finished, and the service continued for a very long time.

A few of the worshippers, men and women alike, clutched their Bibles and danced around in a strangely erratic way. They became very agitated in their movements, some of them moving quite suggestively. I am curious as to what form of Christianity they practice, but I do not think I will inquire.

For myself, I prefer a quieter form of worship, a more sedate one. To me, communion with the Almighty is very personal, and I am not comfortable sharing my experience with others. We can worship here, in this vastness, with the stars above us in the heavens, and I feel as though I have been to church. I say a silent prayer every night for our safety, for Mama, and for Lawrence. This is more religion than I knew when Papa was alive, when we spent our evenings talking about Enlightenment ideas and philosophies and speculating as to the existence of God. But here, in this wilderness, I find myself believing in a Higher Power, indeed, needing that comfort. Still, I don't want religion forced on me.

Too many times, while living with Mama and Karl, I was taken to church against my will. I preferred not to go and often told Mama so, but she persisted nonetheless, and I knew Karl's wrath would descend on her if I did not go. On occasion, I feigned illness so as to be allowed to stay home, but I knew I could not do that often after what happened to Lawrence.

Lawrence hated going to church. I recall especially that terrible Sunday when we were to attend morning and evening services, with Karl preaching both times. He is not a pastor, but, in his church, members of the congregation are frequently invited to speak, and as Karl is a dramatic speaker, with much arm-waving and finger-pointing, he is often asked to fill the pulpit.

Lawrence told Mama he did not feel well; something he had eaten had disagreed with him and he thought he ought to stay home. The tears came to her eyes as they usually did when we went against her will. "Please come, Lawrence. It will be so much pleasanter for all of us if you do."

He was pale and his eyes were ringed with dark shadows. It was clear to me that he truly felt ill. Karl walked in at that moment, dressed for church. He looked so dignified and stern, my heart leapt into my throat.

"What is wrong, Margaret?"

"Lawrence says he does not feel well and wishes to stay home."

My brother is a small person, slight in build, not tall. He was then but fourteen years old, no match for Karl, who tops him by at least five inches and outweighs him by perhaps fifty pounds. Karl turned toward Lawrence, put his huge hand on my brother's neck, and squeezed. "Lawrence feels fine, don't you, boy?" he said.

I was watching Mama intently. She did not even wince to see her son treated so, though I saw a flash of fear in her eyes. Instead she put her hand on Lawrence's arm and said, "I'm sure he feels better now, don't you, son?"

Lawrence silently accompanied us to church. Somehow, he managed to stay seated and quiet during the service, but that night he became deathly ill. Mama had to call the doctor, who gave him some evil-smelling potion to drink and said it must have been something he had eaten which his body rejected; he should be better in a day or two.

He did get better, in about three days as I recall, and the first day he was well and went back to school, he did not come home. When Mama inquired of the teacher, he told her that Lawrence had left the school with the other students and walked in the usual direction, toward home.

He never arrived. Mama searched all night, riding around in the carriage, for once risking Karl's anger, but she did not find him.

A few days later, a letter arrived for me at the hospital. It was from Lawrence and was very brief, informing me that he had gone to Memphis to seek a job on a riverboat. I knew his secret dream of becoming a pilot like Mark Twain (as Mr. Clemens is known), as he had often spoken to me of it privately.

Mama's plan for Lawrence was that he would work in the mercantile with Karl and someday take it over, since Karl has no son of his own. Considering it all from this distance of time and space, I understand now how impossible that would have been for my poor brother. He had no choice but to leave; the future that he faced in Cincinnati was far more than merely unpleasant, a living hell for my sensitive, musical brother. I did not show the letter to Mama but told her I had heard from him, and what he had said. I have the letter with me still.

Lawrence never wrote to me again. It's been seven years now. If he is alive, he has attained his majority. I am certain that he would have written if he were able. I greatly fear that he was set upon on the way and injured or killed. He is not well able to defend himself. I have held out the hope that he is somehow alive, but as time passes it seems less and less likely. If he went to the cruel war, or got in the way of a battle, he would never survive. Dear Lawrence—how I love him. I am sure Mama does too, in her way, but her behavior does not often reflect her feelings.

May 1

We have come so far! Everywhere around us there is prairie grass, tall as I am. We seldom see a tree. The sky is vast and blue. All day I walk, in the heat, and grow thirsty. I am so tired.

The dust rises as we walk along the trail, though the grass

around us is still green. There are some trees, occasionally a house in the distance, and in some places rolling hills. But even though the grass is still green, Mr. Kent said last night we could only have one fire in the center of the circle for fear of setting it alight. It is hard to believe such lush grass could catch fire.

So all we women gathered around the fire to cook our meals. Though crowded, it was rather pleasant. But I was embarrassed by my poor efforts; these other women are so much more skilled at the domestic arts than I. What good is knowing how to embroider and play the piano or sketch a portrait, amid this harsh life? I must remember the difficulties I left behind, and my deep love for Lucas, and take heart.

I miss conversation the most, I think. In spite of the home Karl created, I loved talking with Mama's friends and with mine, exchanging thoughts and ideas. How I miss my dear friends Laura and Julia. Often we would gather at someone's home (never mine) on the excuse that we were rolling bandages for the wounded. We did roll bandages, but we talked much more—about suffrage, about slavery, about the war, about books we had read. After the war ended, we gathered to make clothing for all those left homeless and destitute because of that terrible time.

No one here has any thought for the intellectual life—except my darling, of course, and he is far too busy and tired just now to talk about anything beyond the necessities of survival. Had we been able to marry in Ohio, I would have gladly stayed there (though not in Cincinnati). There have to be compelling reasons for women to choose this primitive life. I wonder what they are. Of all the women on this journey, only Martha has spoken to me.

Late this afternoon, I encountered a snake slithering through the grass as I stepped off the trail to seek privacy for a few moments. I screamed, not being accustomed to such creatures.

Dogs and cats are the extent of my experience with animals.

Lucas came running.

"What's wrong, Hannah?" he cried, forgetting to address me as "Miss Hannah."

I could not speak, but only pointed to the thing just then moving past my feet.

Lucas laughed. "It's only a garter snake," he said. "Perfectly harmless. Stay still." I am not willing to believe any snake harmless, but I did as he said and moved not a muscle until it had disappeared.

"If you see a larger snake that makes a rattling sound, do just as you did and stand quietly. Hope it will go away. For its bite is poison and we know of no antidote."

And indeed, early this evening the oldest Smith boy came howling toward the camp yelling that he'd been "snake bit." This time I could not restrain Lucas; he ran over to the boy, scooped him up, and brought him to our wagon. With the boy, he got into the wagon so they would not be seen. I heard him ask, "Where's the bite, my boy?"

Then, "I pray it's not too late," Lucas muttered. I could see him take his sharpest scalpel and open the bite so that it bled freely, then lean down and suck and spit, suck and spit, for quite some time, the boy crying over and over, "Am I gonna die?"

At length, Lucas straightened up and reached into his medical bag. He took out one of his herb concoctions, cleaned the wound carefully with carbolic, wrapped the leg tightly with one of his boiled white cloths, and said, "What's your name, son?"

The boy swallowed hard and said, "George."

"Well, George, I think you'll be right as rain now. But you must promise me not to remove that bandaging, and to come see me again tomorrow so I can dress the wound again. Promise?"

George nodded. Lucas set him out on the ground.

"Now let's see if you can stand up."

George sat, then stood on his two sturdy, dirty little legs. Lucas patted his shoulder. "Run along now."

After the boy had run back to his wagon I began to worry. Lucas had forgotten to speak in the ignorant, uneducated way of a servant. Would George have noticed?

I knew Lucas was a wonderful doctor, for I had seen him treat the wounded before. In fact, that's how we met—I was reading to patients, writing letters for them or just talking to them at the hospital where he worked as a surgeon. Many of the patients were veterans with grievous wounds, missing limbs and such. I started going to the hospital with my friend Julia during the war, partly so as not to be home with Karl when Mama was not there. After the war was over I kept on going, for I could see that I was doing some good. The men liked me and were cheered by my visits. Long after the war had ended there were still many wounded soldiers, from both sides, in the hospital.

Lucas and I grew fond of each other over time. I am now six and twenty, a spinster by anyone's standard, and it had seemed to me for some time that I would never escape my home, and Karl. Then I met Lucas and came to love him so deeply that I knew we must overcome the obstacles and marry. He was reluctant, not I.

"I do love you, Hannah," he told me over and over. "But I do not want to destroy your life by becoming your husband."

It took me a long, long time to convince him that my life would be destroyed only if he did *not* become my husband. We had talked for months of leaving Ohio and coming west, where we would be able to start our lives anew. But neither of us supposed we would leave so precipitously.

Difficult though this journey is, there has never been one

second of regret for my part. I would follow Lucas anywhere. I am watching him now as he beds down the animals—his muscled, lean body, his wonderful, gentle hands, so competent and deft. His head is bent over so I can see his strong, long neck. How I love him! How I long to come to him! But we must wait.

It cannot be easy for him; I know it is not easy for me. Waiting is *so* difficult. At night he sleeps on the ground in a bedroll, while I sleep in the wagon. I would join him where he sleeps. . . .

May 2

The night silence here on the prairie is quite astounding. In the city, day and night, there is noise—horses' hooves on the pavement, people talking outdoors, wheels crunching along, sellers of various goods hawking their wares. Even in the depths of night the city is not entirely silent. It seems to produce sound of some kind twenty-four hours a day. But here! Once the people and the animals settle down for the night, the stillness is profound. Occasionally, one hears a wild beast in the distance, or the swish of the wings of a large owl or other bird, hunting food, or the rustle of the grasses in the wind. I am awed and amazed by the vastness of it. When an owl calls in the night, it seems to echo for miles around.

May 3

Is Mama searching for me as she did for Lawrence? Did she go to the hospital and learn that Dr. Bowman is also gone? She knew of our friendship. Pray God she knows in her mother's heart that we are together, and that I am happy. *Please,* Mama, understand that I could not stay with Karl any longer! And that I could never have married that odious man.

Please, Mama, do not weep for me.

May 4

It has begun to rain, sheets and sheets of it. Lightning split the sky, thunder roared, frightening the animals, and the rain leaked into our wagon. Fortunately, Lucas had with much forethought stored our perishable goods in sturdy barrels and crocks which water cannot penetrate, but the bedding is soaked, and our clothing, and everything else. It will take days to dry it all out—if it ever stops raining. I am sitting on the back of the wagon, holding a piece of canvas over my head, as I write. (Small blessing: my journal was safely tucked away under a board so did not get wet.)

I cannot walk in the rain, and the animals slog along very slowly. The downpour is turning everything into mud, slippery and so hard to get a foothold. I wonder Mr. Kent does not stop. But most of the wagons are headed for California or Oregon, and they must cross the mountains before the snow falls, so I suppose we will keep going.

Lucas and I still have not discussed our final destination. We left so hastily that we did not speak of where we would stop. I for one do not desire to cross the mountains and go all the way to California. Stories I've heard say that women are scarce there and the few that have gone are not of the highly moral kind. Most people go to California for the gold even now, I'm told, although there is rich farmland to the south.

As we are not Mormons, Utah Territory would not be a good stopping place for us. We need soon to decide what we are going to do.

People say that a wagon that has come this far must either stop in the territories of Colorado, Wyoming or Utah—or cross the desert all the way to California, for it is not possible to make a home in the arid land between the mountains and that fabled place. Some in this wagon train plan to go to Oregon and will turn north at the Platte River to join the Oregon Trail.

There are many families settling in Oregon, but there are still mountains to cross, and hostile Indian lands, before safe arrival. Where are *we* going?

May 5

We have finally been forced to stop because so many of the wagons are stuck. I think we shall have to wait until the sun comes out and dries the trail somewhat. Mr. Kent is pacing back and forth. He must be furious.

Lucinda Smith came to our wagon today, carrying her tiny infant in an ingenious sling across her breast. I must remember the design.

She looked perfectly dreadful. Her hair fell in limp strands from her head; her eyes were bleak and ringed with dark circles. She was so thin I did not see how she could hold herself upright. The birth must have been a fearsome ordeal for her.

Yet she brought cornbread she had made (how?) and a precious jar of her blackberry preserves. She is from Kentucky, where they grow wild, she said. I imagine she can ill spare them, but she insisted. She said George had told her that Miss Hannah's servant had treated his snake bite.

"George tol' me what you did. Thankee for savin' my boy's life," she said.

"How be he?" asked Lucas. "He hain't come back to have his dressing changed." Inwardly I cringed to hear Lucas talking so. How did he learn this speech, I wonder. Perhaps from the black servants he stayed with in Kansas City while we were getting ready to depart, or from those at the hospital.

"Perky as ever," she told him. "I dasn't let him come here agin; Ezra wouldn't like it at all."

Except when he is playing a Negro servant now, talking like an uneducated black man, Lucas's speech is so careful, so correct, while Lucinda's accent, which I have tried to reproduce here as faithfully as I can, is so thick, her grammar so careless, that I could hardly understand her. The contrast between them struck me sharply—yet where she comes from, Lucas would be considered her inferior, less than human! Not long ago he might even have been her slave. Curiously, she does not seem to be disturbed by his dark skin but treats him politely. Perhaps that is because he provided her with a service, as she is accustomed to having dark-skinned people do.

She puzzles me, being married to that angry little man from New York. How did they meet? Why did they marry? Some things we are destined never to know, yet I am ever curious about people and want to know their stories. Perhaps her circumstances were similar to mine—her father forced her to marry against her will. I shall fashion that story for her since I do not know the real one.

She trudged back to her wagon, which was stuck fast in the mud, lifting her skirt high to keep it from getting any dirtier. I think my life difficult just now; then I picture hers and feel blessed indeed. For some reason, seeing her called to mind an encounter I saw at the hospital not long before we left, with a sullen woman who was berating Lucas for not having saved her husband's right arm. He tried to tell her that the arm had been removed in the field, long before the man arrived at the hospital, but she would not listen. Her manner toward Lucas was ar-rogant and patronizing, yet she was an ignorant backwoods woman with not one-tenth of the education he has had, nor the skill or the knowledge he possesses.

I am not by nature a violent person; indeed, I abhor violence, but I found myself wanting to strike that woman across the face. The episode caused me to wonder how often Lucas has encountered such slights simply because of the color of his skin, especially since he came to America from France, and it strengthened my resolve to become his wife.

May 8

We have moved on beyond the mud at last. The rain stopped in the night, and by the middle of the morning the sun, so much more intense than in Ohio, had dried the trail enough so that we could move forward, though it took some time to get all of the wagons loose. The Andersens had to unburden theirs, leaving some of their treasures on the trail. Their furniture was not the first I had seen; indeed, at times the trail seems strewn with chairs and chests and bedsteads and such. Sometimes, if we have paused for a meal or to rest, some of the men go and break up the furniture for firewood, carrying away only the lighter pieces.

What will *we* do for furnishings? I had not thought to ask. We loaded our wagon lightly, with food and clothing, kitchen items, bedding, and medical supplies, for of course I came away with only my valise, which held mostly books and my music. Without furniture and household goods, our wagon is much lighter than the others. We did not get stuck.

How blithely I embarked on this journey, this great adventure! So many questions I did not think to ask: How long will we be traveling? What will we do when we get there? How will we furnish a home? What will the place be like? I simply left all of it to Lucas's care and thought only about leaving the dreary, uncomfortable place my home had become and getting away from the evil man who lives there. Lucas thought of a good many things, but it does not seem to have occurred to either of us that I might have needed different clothing, or that we will need furniture.

As for him, he is well dressed for the occasion, having purchased some sturdy overalls and shirts of rough, durable material before we left. He wears a large straw hat and big boots. He looks every inch the servant.

Two burly men had a fight after the evening meal tonight. I did not know the cause of it. I saw them scrapping in the center of the circle, and I heard people shouting encouragement to one man or the other. I saw money change hands. Lucas told me later that it was a staged fight on which people had wagered money. I cannot imagine such foolishness. But Lucas tended the bruised hands of the man who lost, and I think he made a friend. We may need friends along the way.

I was dismayed at the fighting and said I felt it wrong, especially since they were gambling on the outcome.

Gambling is wrong, Mama always said, and Karl railed against it frequently. But Lucas pointed out that fisticuffs such as we saw tonight do no harm really and may even help the men release some of their high feelings. As for gambling, he lived in France, where it was as common as drinking wine. "Why is it so bad?" he says. I expect Lucas and I are bound to disagree about some things, but it is a bit dismaying finally to come upon our first serious difference in viewpoint.

I, however, did not advance my point of view further. This disagreement is at present mainly in my heart and mind.

May 15

It has struck me several times, but forcefully today, how *communal* this situation is for us fellow travelers. Privacy is a luxury no one among us can have during this journey. We are all so close together, and the wagons are so open, that anyone nearby knows what others are doing, intimate or otherwise.

In the beginning, I was perturbed by such closeness. It reminded me of the most unpleasant part of my hospital work, the large, noisy, very public wards that housed the patients, sometimes as many as thirty of them in a single room. No man could do anything without all of the rest—those who were aware of their surroundings, at least—knowing what he had done. I used to go home at night and close my door just to savor the peace, the quiet, the privacy.

To ensure solitude in my Cincinnati home I followed Mama's example and pushed a heavy bureau up against my door.

I would give a good deal to be able to close a door now and be alone. Here, even when I am inside the wagon getting ready to settle down for the night I am not truly alone, for I can hear a variety of human noises all around me. Eventually everyone falls quiet and the prairie stillness comes down like a blanket. It puzzles me that the others do not seem to mind the enforced intimacy of this situation.

May 18

Fire! There was a terrifying prairie fire today which leapt from rise to rise with unbelievable swiftness. No one knows how it started. We did not know it was happening until we saw the pronghorns (such beautiful creatures, and how fast they can run!) racing past us. People began to shout and point at the black smoke. Never have I seen anything move so fast, not even a locomotive.

The men had little with which to fight it. We were near a creek; everyone began frantically filling buckets with water and wetting the grass around us. It was utterly disorganized. Then Mr. Kent shouted at them: "Circle the wagons! Then dig, you fools! Dig!"

I did not understand what he wanted them to do until he began to jab a shovel into the earth, still soft from the rains of a few days ago. How had the grass dried so quickly, so ready to burn, and the soil had not?

The men all set to work, digging desperately; some of the women even found what implements they could and began to scoop earth. I did not help, as I thought I would be more hindrance than otherwise.

Soon a half-moon hole around the wagons and a mound of dark earth beside the hole faced the fire. The hungry flames came toward us, still low to the ground because there was very little wind. They licked the edge of the gouge in the earth, then turned east, away from us. If the wind had been high, as it often is on this prairie, digging to China would not have saved us. But as it was, Mr. Kent's quick action was successful. The fire burned itself out, encountering the swampy area we had avoided that very morning. It wanted to go through the wagon train and lick up more grass beyond us, and it could not.

In school, we learned that half of London was once destroyed by fire, and I could not picture it. Now I can. Though we need fire for warmth, how quickly it can bring death and destruction! I shudder to think what might have happened to all of us had the wagon master not been so wise.

May 23

A frightening thing has happened. There was a drunken brawl last night among a few of the men who came in this train without wives. Mr. Smith and others tried to break it up. Where did they acquire the liquor? I did not go near enough to the fighting men to smell them, but Lucas told me that they reeked of whiskey. Mr. Kent had been very firm upon starting out that no one was to carry any liquor in a wagon or on his person; everyone had agreed to this condition (however Lucas does have a small amount of rum in his medical bag to be used medicinally).

This was no staged fight for wagers but a fierce battle between two very angry men, not the same ones who fought earlier. No one knows why they fought, but the results have been consequential for us.

One of them suddenly turned on Lucas and began shouting ugly words at him, words I shall not repeat here. They had to do with Lucas's treating the Smith boy—touching him, sucking his blood—and they were vicious words. How had they found out? Lucas turned his back and started to walk away. Another man leaped at him, pulling him to the ground. Mr. Kent appeared then, having stayed some distance away as long as no one seemed to be getting seriously hurt. Mr. Kent has not liked Lucas from the beginning, no doubt because of his dark skin. (Kent is from Georgia.) He hauled Lucas to his feet and said to me, "You need to control your servant better, Miz Hannah." He pushed Lucas toward me so hard that he staggered and almost fell.

But Lucas had done nothing! I started to protest, then bit back the words.

Some of the men were muttering about "uppity niggers." Lucas still did not speak, only walked back toward our wagon. It began to storm fiercely, and the men dispersed to tend to their wagons and stock.

I could not sleep but lay listening to the crash of the thunder, the lashing rain. I was frightened and worried. Then I heard Lucas speaking to me. He was kneeling at the front end of the wagon.

"We have to leave the train, Hannah," he said, very softly. "Some of the men are angry." I could hear him hitching up Napoleon and Bonaparte (Lucas could not resist bestowing on the horses his French-grown admiration of the little general). "We need to get away, Hannah. Now. Tonight."

I sat up and peered out at him. "Leave the train? Now, in this rain? Continue on our own? Why?"

"Ever since Smith found out that I treated his boy, he's been furious that I dared touch his son. I'm afraid of what they might do if he inflames their passions. Some of them are Southerners."

"Surely they wouldn't do anything to us, to me!"

"I think otherwise," he replied. "In Paris, I have seen angry men turn into mobs. I never want to see anything like that again."

"But won't we be in equal danger traveling on our own?" My throat was tight with anxiety. How could we do such a thing? With no protection from the natives, the wild animals, various other unknown hazards, how could we survive?

"Perhaps," he replied calmly. "But I think it best. If we leave now, while it's storming, we can get away without being noticed."

So we struck out on our own into that awful night. Thank goodness the animals did not put up a fuss; Judy submitted to being tied to the wagon, and the horses plodded along without protest, though they must have been tired.

We could hardly see where we were going. Lucas said we needed to avoid the trail, so we made our way through the prairie grass, Lucas swinging the lantern in front of the wagon and leading the horses, until we came to a sheltered spot where we made camp. He headed south, he said, the opposite direction from the rest of the wagons, which were going north toward Fort Laramie.

To say I was frightened that night would be to seriously understate my feelings. I slept not at all, listening to the sounds of the howling wild dogs (they are called coyotes, Lucas says). We saw a bolt of lightning strike the earth not far from the wagon. I suppressed a scream. We have thunderstorms in Ohio, of course. What was there to be so afraid of, I asked myself? I am not a helpless, simpering female. I will not become one! Yet I could not get the picture of that horrible fire out of my mind. Perhaps lightning started that one; might it not start another?

At length it stopped raining, though the wind shrieked. We huddled inside the wagon, I clutching Lucas with all my might. He held me tightly, and we kissed for the first time in so long. I longed to consummate our love right then and there, but Lucas pulled away. After an eternity, morning came and with it the sun. Thankfully, no one from the wagon train had tried to follow us. Perhaps they were just relieved that we were gone.

May 24
Have we come to the end of the known world? It is so vast here, and so silent except for the call of birds, the trickling water of the stream and the noises of small animals, that it seems we are as far from the civilized world as it is possible to be.

We are a tiny speck in the universe, the merest ants, crawling along an uncertain path to an unknown destination. If man could fly and were to look down upon us from this enormous, endless sky, we would look minuscule indeed. In daylight, I feel small and insignificant but hopeful that we will reach something sometime. In the darkness, I feel helpless, utterly helpless, against whatever forces array themselves in this prairie, in that sky, once the sun has set. The lantern Lucas lights, the candles I use to see so I can write, are as nothing in such darkness.

Today we saw an immense bird flying, swooping, soaring, searching for food. Lucas named it a golden eagle. (How does he know such things?) They are numerous out here on the prairie, he says, for there is a sumptuous banquet to dine on. Seeing that bird was one of the most extraordinary experiences I have ever had, far superior to a night at the opera or a glittery ball, events I once thought the pinnacle of my existence. Though I am frightened and anxious, I am at the same time awestruck by the sights I have seen. No one returning from a sojourn to the West could ever put such sights into adequate words. Even paintings would not tell it all, though some have tried.

May 25

Lucas says he wants to find another wagon train to continue our journey.

"To continue our journey where?" I asked. "I don't want to cross the mountains." I knew my voice showed my fears. I do not admire cowardice in anyone, especially myself, but the last thing I wanted to do was go over—or around—or through—or however one manages it—those mountains and then cross the desert.

"Where would we stop?" he countered.

"I supposed we would claim a homestead before we reached the mountains, somewhere in Kansas or Colorado Territory."

"To settle down, you mean."

"Don't you want to settle down? I thought we would be making a home together somewhere in the West. Are we not in the West now? Besides, it could be snowing by the time we get to the mountains. We can't survive in the cold."

"I had hoped to get over the mountains before the snow flies," he responded, still in that reasonable, patient tone, while I was becoming impatient and angry. "I'd hoped to get to California."

"Lucas, I'm tired of traveling. I want us to find a home and to be married." No doubt I sounded petulant, even childish, at that moment, and I am ashamed of my behavior, but I did not retract the sentiment.

He considered my words for a few minutes. Then he said, "Would you accept a compromise? We could head for a settlement in Wyoming Territory and spend the winter at the first one we come to. Then we can go on in the spring. The mountains are easier to cross in Wyoming, I'm told."

He was so doggedly determined that I saw I could not dissuade him, so I at last agreed. We are heading for Fort Laramie, in Wyoming Territory. We are well behind the wagon train by now, so there should be no trouble. We have not yet spoken of whether we will settle on a homestead.

June 1

We saw the mountains today, rising far in the distance. How beautiful, how majestic, how terrifying they are! They are covered with a blanket of white, even now, in June. They rise to meet the sky in jagged peaks.

I admit to cowardice about our situation. Lucas has his rifle and he can use it, he assures me (although I do not know where he, a physician, learned such a skill), but there are so many menaces—the savages, wild cats, herds of buffalo, outlaws; I shudder to contemplate them all. We must survive now on our skill and wit.

We have seen no buffalo. There are fewer now than there once were, I'm told. We see the pronghorns nearly every day, and sometimes deer, but not much other wildlife, though I'm sure there are small creatures beneath our feet which we do not see. Sometimes, I do see a rabbit scurrying somewhere. I never saw such creatures in Ohio.

Lucas has not shot a creature. We have enough food for a time—dried beef and beans and cornmeal—that we do not need fresh meat just yet, for which I say a small prayer of thanksgiving.

June 7

We have been traveling across the prairie for several days now and have seen no sign of habitation. We are following the river still, Lucas says, so we have water for us and the animals. It is hot. The tributary disintegrated into a tiny creek, so we have begun following the Platte again. To my relief, we have seen no Indians, hostile or otherwise.

I wonder where we are.

The vastness of these plains is overwhelming. This is what the ocean must be like, huge and endless and alike from every direction, with no land in sight. Or perhaps I am thinking of a desert, for this prairie grass seems to wave and shimmer in the sunlight, like African deserts I have read about. Wanderers who get lost in a desert and lack the knowledge to save themselves must feel tiny, so helpless amid the enormity, just as I feel here amid this enormous land. I think it best to submerge thoughts such as these; they do not help me maintain my good cheer.

In this time alone with Lucas I have come to admire him even more. He does not complain, even when I know he must be exceedingly fatigued. He eats sparingly so the food will last. He works hard at each task. But he does not talk much. Sometimes, I see his mouth tightening with tension, yet he will not share his concerns with me.

Last night he held me close and kissed me tenderly; then, gentleman that he is, he retired to his bed with no demands on me. We are alone; no one would know. Still he maintains decorum. I could not sleep, for he had awakened my desire. To my astonishment, this came as an ache deep in my loins. Mama never told me about this.

Were it not for his race, Lucas would have fit perfectly into the Cincinnati society in which I was raised. He has better manners than many "gentlemen" I have seen in parlors and at parties. He neither drinks nor smokes nor chews tobacco, as so many of them do. He never uses a spittoon. He always smells nice (though on our journey, that is less achievable—for me as well). He had the funds, in Cincinnati, to dress quite finely if he chose to do so. How elegant he would look at the theater, at concerts! I can picture him in a fine suit and a hat like Mr. Lincoln's.

I was brought up to become some fine gentleman's wife, and

when I was eighteen I still envisioned such a future. But the war was raging. Most of the young men I had known had gone to fight (some, to my sorrow, for the Confederacy). The eligibles vanished. I had resigned myself to spinsterhood until I met Lucas.

This morning we came to a stream we had to ford. There was no other way. I had not been in the wagon for previous crossings, for while we were in the wagon train the women got out and waded across the shallow streams, while the men led the animals through the water. When we crossed one larger river, there was a ferry for which we had to pay one dollar for each wagon. A profitable day for the ferryman! But this time we were on our own and there was no ferry, so I stayed in the wagon, attempting to guide the horses, while Lucas led Judy and her calf across. The calf bawled the whole way. I have never driven a carriage before, much less a large, cumbersome wagon like this one.

The wagon rocked and swayed so that I felt my heart pounding fiercely. I hung onto the reins. That stream seemed to get wider by the minute. I could not imagine how we would ever get to the other side without tipping over. I prayed and clutched the reins as well as I could. It seemed to take a thousand years, but finally we arrived on the other side. Lucas was smiling. He shouted, "Good, Hannah!" Coming from him, that is high praise. Kind and generous though he is, he is not given to flattery.

I was shaking all over. I had to get down from the wagon and stand very still a few minutes to calm myself enough so that I could go on. But as I walked, I thought, "If I can do this, I can do the rest of it, too."

June 10

I am having my monthlies again. This was hard enough at home, where I had privacy and could wash out my cloths in the big washtub, leaving them to dry in my bedroom out of sight. Now I find I have to wash the cloths out in streams as we pass, or in the river, and hang them inside the wagon to dry. They do not dry thoroughly. They are very stiff and somewhat damp, quite uncomfortable. They rub against my thighs and redden the skin. I do not like to complain, but I long for an easier way!

Mama would think it quite improper and unladylike to mention such a thing, even in this very private journal. Yet monthlies are a fact of a woman's life. Not discussed even among women when men are not present, in my experience, but why not? Why do we not share these most intimate and trying details of our lives, so as to better understand and cope with them?

I recall that when my monthlies began, Mama had not explained to me what to expect. I was frightened out of my wits when I saw blood seeping from my body. Was I dying? Finally, I got up my courage and went to her to ask what was wrong. Then and only then did she take me aside and demonstrate how to handle this "curse," as she calls it. "It is a burden we women must bear for four decades or more," she told me with a sigh.

Yet I know, thanks to Lucas, that this menses is a healthy sign. It is inconvenient, that is true, but it is also an indication that one day, when the time is right, I should be able to bear children. I can't say I rejoice when these cycles begin, but neither do I feel cursed.

By now, Mama and Karl surely know that I did not go to visit Cousin Carrie in Kentucky. They will have had time to send her a letter and receive one in return. I wonder if Mama knows that I have gone off with Lucas. She knew that I had become his friend; I do not think she knew we were in love. In spite of her liberal views toward slavery, she would no doubt be horrified.

Mama came from Oberlin, Ohio, which was on the Underground Railroad route, and she was an abolitionist from the start. I am quite certain she helped slaves escape, although she never spoke of it. She deeply believes it is wrong for one human being to enslave another. Yet I do not think she ever supposed that her only daughter, her dutiful daughter, would herself choose for a husband a man who might have been a slave. I am putting her beliefs to the test, am I not?

How then did she choose such an autocratic man as Karl and become so meek? For he has enslaved her, as surely as if she had an iron collar around her neck. His sanctimonious beliefs are rooted in his religion. His faith is only in abstractions, not realities. Certainly not in people. I cannot imagine him actually touching someone's dusky skin, actually helping someone in need. He is too intent on hellfire and damnation to be concerned with life on earth, except as we all learn to follow his infernal rules so as to save ourselves from such a fate.

"Why are black people held as slaves?" I once asked Mama. I think I was perhaps ten at the time.

"Wrong though it is, slave owners say that they must have the slaves in order to make their plantations profitable. Short of war, which may come in time, I do not think there is any way to change that."

"Do you believe that black people are fully human?" I asked. She turned from her baking and looked at me, looked right through me. "Of course," she replied. "No one is less than anyone else, and no one has the right to enslave another." Her words burned into my soul.

Papa was still alive then. Mama was more open to ideas. After Papa was killed in the war, she changed. Papa was too old to go. Mama told him that over and over, but his convictions drove him to enlist and he was killed, nine years ago this month. He was not even in the battle, his regiment having arrived when dusk had fallen and the fighting was thought to be over. They were ordered out into the field to retrieve the bodies of the dead Union soldiers and to search for wounded, and a Confederate soldier hiding in the trees began shooting at them. Papa was killed instantly, or so the colonel wrote us.

Then Mama married Karl, who had rescued Papa's mercantile, to protect her interests there. She certainly did not marry for love. Had she known that he would "get religion" after the marriage and try to beat his beliefs into Lawrence and me, I like to believe she would not have agreed to become his wife— no, his *slave!*

Not only was Karl a danger to Lawrence and me, he is mean. He gives Mama barely enough money for the household and her servant and expects her to account for all of it. He kept me penniless. Sometimes Mama would give me money as a gift. But then she had to answer to Karl for it, to somehow work it into the household expenses, so I was forced to conceal what little I had. That is why—mostly, anyway—I did not strike out on my own when I reached my majority. Had I been able to afford a room to rent and a piano, I could have given lessons and made enough to survive. I could have taken Lawrence with me. But Karl's parsimonious ways made that impossible; I'm sure he knew that.

Small wonder Lawrence left. He was but fourteen! Now poor Mama has lost both her chicks. Her husband drove them away. Oh, Papa, I miss you so!

My pencil is worn down to a stub. Perhaps Lucas has another one.

June 15

Lucas has several pencils in his medical bag. He also has a pen, which he has lent me along with a good supply of ink. I am grateful; pencil writing does not keep well. Perhaps someday I will want to read this journal again, to remind me of how our new life together began.

Today Boney (we have adopted shortened names for our horses) lost a shoe. We have no way to replace it, and he cannot go far without it, Lucas says. He found the shoe and tapped it back on the best he could, but we knew it would not last for long.

"Just long enough, perhaps," I said, "to get us to that house I see over the horizon." A house! As I spoke the word, emotion overcame me. I thought I might cry at this sign of civilization. Along the trail, we had from time to time seen houses and silos in the distance, but they were few and far between, and the people who lived in them not close enough to be seen, even as little specks on the horizon.

But here in front of us was a house, a small lump on the endless prairie. We headed for it gratefully.

When we got there, we found it abandoned. It is a sod house, small, dirty, windowless. Mice and some other small creatures scurried away when we walked over the threshold. No furnishings. The barn is half finished, and there is a cold cellar.

"No one lives here. Perhaps we can—at least for a while," I said to Lucas.

"Right now we need to find a blacksmith to fix Boney's shoe," he replied. There was another house visible to the northeast; smoke came from the chimney, so it was clearly occupied. Perhaps that person could help us.

"I'll head over there with Napoleon and see," he said.

"Lucas! You'll not leave me here alone!" I cried. My voice must have revealed my fear, for he turned to me and said, gently, "I don't want Boney to go any farther than necessary. I promise I won't be long, Hannah. Just stay with the wagon and the cows

50

and I'll be back as soon as I can."

I waited in the shade of the one small tree in front of the little sod house for what seemed hours. All the time Lucas was gone I strove to maintain calm in the face of the vast unknown. He had left me his rifle, but I had no idea how to use it. Eventually he returned, accompanied by a huge, dark-haired man with a kindly face, riding an equally huge horse.

Lucas leapt down lightly from Nappy. "This is Adam," he said. "We are in luck. He is a blacksmith and will repair Boney's shoe."

"Howdy, ma'am," said the big man. "Alma and me'd like to invite ya to our place for some refreshment. Jest follow 'long behind me." He spoke with a soft Southern accent, his words slightly slurred together. His voice, high and thin, belied his size. I was somewhat reassured. I intend in no way to demean him by faithfully recording his language; it is interesting to me.

So, when Boney was temporarily reshod, we went to Adam's house, wagon, cows and all.

Prairie surrounds everything here. For the first time, released momentarily from my anxiety, I noticed the wild flowers dotting the prairie grass, and the deeply blue sky; never have I seen such blue sky.

"Leave the critters and the wagon here, in the shade," Adam told Lucas, indicating a small, leafy tree near his house.

He led us inside a sod house, rather dark and musty-smelling. There are two rooms, one for living, one for sleeping. It has two glass windows. The floor is moist dirt covered with rag rugs. As we entered, a tall, extremely thin woman stood to greet us. Indeed, I would not have known her for a woman had it not been for her long hair, tied at her neck, and the dress.

"Alma, this be Lucas Bowman and his woman," he told her. She smiled and indicated we should take a seat at her table.

The furniture was clearly handmade, somewhat crude but usable. "Howdy," she said. Her voice, in contrast to her husband's, was deep and gravelly. "Would ya care for lemonade?" We nodded gratefully. How she made lemonade out here in the middle of nowhere I've no idea, but lemonade it was, cool and welcome.

Ducking his head, Adam disappeared through the door to give Boney a proper, permanent new shoe, as he had only done a temporary job earlier. We drank the lemonade. Alma put out a plate of sugar cookies. We sat eating them until her husband returned. "Right as new," he announced.

Then he sat down and tipped his chair back. "Where be ya headed?" he asked.

"We're on our way to California," Lucas replied.

"On yore own?"

"We hoped to find another wagon train."

"Too late this year. They've all gone through," said his wife. "It be mighty late to head across them mountains."

"Where are we now?" I asked. "Are we still in Nebraska Territory?"

"No, ma'am; this is Colorado Territory," said Adam.

"That homestead where you wuz is abandoned," he went on. "Year or so back, a fambly come to settle there. O'Halleran, they was. Straight from Ireland by way of New York. They built the house and started the barn, but then the mister, he bit himself in the leg with his ax. His missus called my Alma, who's mighty handy with healing, but she couldn't do nothin'. Leg turned green and horrible smelly. Warn't too long 'fore the man died. The woman just upped and left. Took her childern—we'd counted six, but there coulda been more—and jest took off in that old wagon. Left the cow, and the goats, and everthang. Headed east, they said. No one has ever heard more of her or her younguns. We took in their animals. You could file for that land, Mister Bowman."

Lucas said nothing for a moment. He looked at me.

"We could stay here for a time at least, Lucas," I said, touching his arm. "Until next spring."

Lucas still did not speak. He studied his hands a long time. Though his face was impassive, I could see the struggle in his eyes. I kept silent; I had expressed my view and was content to let him decide. I have so little experience of men. Karl was so frightening, Lawrence so timid, Papa so lost in his thoughts and his music and his money troubles with the store, that I learned nothing about how to respond to a man like Lucas. I am never certain when to leave the decisions to him and when to speak my mind.

"What's involved in the filing?" he asked at length, with a small sigh.

"Johnson City is near 'bout twenty mile," Adam replied. "Due west. Follow the creek and you'll come to it. They's a land office there."

My heart lifted with hope. Perhaps he would agree to stay here. I much preferred this trackless prairie to any more days on the trail. "If I filed," he said, "we'd have to stay five years to prove up the land, correct?"

"That's how it is," Alma agreed. "One day lessen that time and ya'd lose the land."

"How far are we from Fort Laramie?" asked Lucas.

"A good five, six days anyways," replied Adam.

Lucas was silent for some considerable time. My heart beat fast with hope and fear. If only we could stop right here, stop traveling and make a home together!

"I suppose we could winter here," he said finally. "What do you say, Hannah?"

"I would like to stay, Lucas. I would very much like to stay."

"Homesteading is what you want to do?"

"I want a home, Lucas. *Our* home." Somewhat to my surprise, neither Alma nor Adam turned a hair at my statement, which clearly indicated that we would be making a home together. Lucas had ceased to be my "servant."

Lucas turned to Adam. "I'd need to survey, wouldn't I?"

"Nope—O'Halleran done that. Jest tell 'em yore filin' for the old O'Halleran place."

Lucas stirred in his seat. "But I'm uneasy about leaving Hannah alone there. That trip could take two or three days, back and forth. Our wagon—"

"No Injuns around here for some time," Alma broke in. "Hain't seen none for five year or more. Not many travelers come this way, neither. Yore things'll be safe. But yore welcome to leave the missus and yore wagon and cow here whilst you go. We could milk the cow for ya."

Lucas looked surprised and pleased at that suggestion. Both of us are accustomed to the more formal ways of Ohio society; the city dwellers we know would not be so ready to offer their help or hospitality to strangers. Yet I instinctively trusted these homesteaders. I touched Lucas's hand. "I would be pleased to stay with our new neighbors," I said. "You could get started yet today."

"Not so good headin' west in the afternoon, 'gainst that sun," Adam put in. "You folks kin put up here tonight and y'all kin get a good early start in the mornin'. Time you get that sun in yore face, y'all be pretty close to the town."

Perhaps, I thought, I can learn to milk Judy while Lucas is away. He had done this chore on our trip, and it was one of so many I must master in this new life. Usually there was not much left after the calf was done with his dinner, but there had been enough for the two of us.

"One more question," said Lucas. "Is there a church in Johnson City? Does it have a minister?"

54

"No church," said Alma. "But they's a minister comes round ever two-three months and does a service in town. He'll be round agin purty soon, I 'spect."

June 18

We are back at our new home, *our* homestead. Lucas has filed the claim and gotten papers to prove it. Whether we will stay the five years is still undetermined. Right now I would like to stay, though I know it will mean hard work every day. Lucas did not voice an opinion; he just set to work.

Wood will be needed to put down a floor in the house, to make furniture, to make heat and a fire for cooking, for so many things, and there is so little here. Lucas will have to chop down some cottonwoods by the river bank some distance from here, or buy lumber in the town. We do not have a fortune, as far as I know (though Lucas does not discuss financial matters with me), and we spent a good deal of money outfitting for the journey. But there is fresh water nearby—which Lucas insists be boiled before we drink it—and we certainly have feed for the animals with all the prairie grass around us. Lucas says fire is a constant danger and we must be careful that sparks do not start a blaze.

Thankfully, the one thing the O'Hallerans left behind is a good iron stove. All we need is fuel so I can cook indoors. I am still using the campfire and buffalo chips we had collected on our journey. We have to have wood.

We have few furnishings. I sleep on a straw mattress kindly lent us by Alma, and Lucas still sleeps in the wagon. We have no table or chairs as yet.

Adam said Lucas must get a crop in the ground soon, or it will be too late. But there is so much to do. What should be done first?

The land is not completely flat but has little knolls and valleys. A small, merry creek runs by close to the sod house. It bubbles over rocks and the water it yields is quite cold. The half-completed barn is behind the house, a little to the east of it, and the cold cellar is just across from the barn in the other direction, carefully placed in one of the higher hills.

I can see every direction for miles. From the hill over the cold cellar I can see Adam and Alma's house. There are no other houses nearby. I can see the mountains, far in the distance, and the plain stretching endlessly to the north and east. Our house seems so tiny in this vastness, a mere dot on this enormous landscape.

I find that my longings for Lucas have abated due to my fatigue; we work very hard every day.

A privy has become most important. Lucas dug a trench behind the barn (he was careful to situate it so it will not run into the creek), and we have the chamber pot, so we will manage until he gets the privy constructed. We need wood!

If I had my way, we would build a log house, with windows. But that decision will depend on whether we stay here. We are to be married soon, as Lucas heard that the traveling preacher will be in Johnson City in two weeks. I pray that he will agree to marry us.

We have been several times to dine ("dine"? Do folks say that out here? Perhaps "sup" is more appropriate. I see already that I must learn some new ways with language to live here) with Alma and Adam since Lucas returned. They were very kind and hospitable while he was away. I slept in the bed with Alma, while Adam spent the nights in his barn. When Adam was out in the field, Alma talked to me more freely.

"We come from east Tennessee," she told me. "We wuz run out of town durin' the war because Adam didn't hold with fightin' to keep slavery goin' and folks didn't want us around.

They wuz downright cruel. They torched our house and the blacksmith shop and killed our chickens.

" 'Twas not wise of them folks to run off their only blacksmith, but that's sure 'nuff what they done. We left with little more'n the clothes on our backs."

"But you had lived there peaceably until then?"

"That's so. Adam allus thought he might change folks' minds. He sez to me time and agin, 'Black folk is got a right to live free, Alma.' He spoke of joinin' up with the Union army, but he was afeerd to leave me alone after what happened in our town."

"Why didn't you just move to the north?" I asked, in my naivete. It's always so easy for us to figure out what other people ought to do, isn't it? Especially when we are not so good at figuring out our own lives. What seemed simple to me was not so simple to them. They had roots there, she explained, and property. They did not think they could sell the blacksmith shop, for no one else there knew the trade, and Adam had made a good living until he started speaking too freely once the war began.

Alma admitted to me that she had not known until they had left their town that her husband had been party to helping slaves escape. How fortunate for Lucas and me to have stumbled upon abolitionists for neighbors! And how fortunate for them that their Confederate neighbors had not known of his activities. He had considerable courage, say I, to slip slaves through right there in the South, right under his neighbors' noses. Had they known, he would have been lynched, not merely run out of town.

Nor do Adam and Alma seem perturbed to see Lucas and me together. Being from the South, perhaps they assume (as people sometimes do) that I am also a Negro, for I am not fair-complected and have become even darker with all these weeks in the sun, and my hair is black. It takes only one-eighth dark blood, after all, to be judged Negro in the South. Curious that no one in the wagon train seemed to have thought that of me. I find Adam and Alma fair-minded and progressive. Few people in this age after the War Between the States would take kindly to a couple like Lucas and me as neighbors.

"How did you stake your trip out here?" I asked—not my business, I know, but once again my curiosity overcame my good manners.

"Now that were a strange thing," she said. (She pronounced it "thang.") "We wuz walkin' and havin' nowhere to go, when we got so weary we stopped to rest a spell. Farmer who lived there found us fast asleep. Come outta his house, took one look at us, and took us in. Reckon we looked purty poorly, dirty an' all. Why he helped us we never knew, 'cept he was a good Christian man. Adam worked for him, shoein' and such, for some time. Word got round, and he got more work. We coulda stayed right there." (She said "rat thar." I've tried, in this journal, to reproduce their dialect as closely as I can, for it fascinates me. I hope I am not making them seem foolish or ignorant. They are neither.)

From that time on, she says, she and Adam have often taken in strangers, to repay the kindness that was done to them. Even after the war ended, they helped homeless, wandering people whenever they could.

But they decided to come west so as to get as far away from the war as possible. Adam still feared leaving Alma alone and, when it came right down to it, could not bring himself to join the Northern army and fight against his own people, so heading west seemed the only choice. They could get free land out here, and they would be far enough away from the anger and bitterness to live as they chose.

After about a year they had enough money to start out. They too left a wagon train, though they were not forced out as we were, but had become so tired they did not want to go on. So they stopped. They have prospered, except that Alma confessed that they long for children and have not succeeded so far. They have been married fifteen years. They may not ever have the family they desire.

But I do so hope we can! Once we are married, of course.

June 25

Adam has come to help Lucas plow. Watching them work, I am astounded and dismayed at how hard farming here is. How can mere humans conquer such land? We have only plowed five acres, but they seem to be five thousand. They stretch on endlessly. I cannot see the edges of our claim.

Adam brought his two sturdy oxen to pull the plow. He guides them while Lucas guides the plow, trying to get it to dig into the soil. Half the time he misses, or he trips, or something else goes wrong and they have to stop. It is our good fortune that he is so strong; I can see his muscles ripple as he works. There is nothing so exciting as a beautiful man—and my man is the most beautiful of all.

June 30

Tomorrow is my wedding day. Alma has helped me fashion a gown out of one of the frilly dresses I brought along. Alma and Adam will accompany us to town for the ceremony. The minister has agreed to marry us! He is an itinerant Unitarian minister, it turns out. Unitarians are notably free-thinking in many areas of the social arena, I understand, though I know little of them. I don't know how many converts he has made, for he is certainly not traditional, but since he is the only preacher around, people do attend his services when he holds them.

He arrived two days ago. When Lucas went to town for wood, he learned that the good reverend had come. He holds services in the land office, which is the only space big enough (it is also the post office and general store). People sit on barrels and sacks of grain, sometimes on the floor. He christens babies, marries people, performs funerals if need be, and holds hymn sings, which the townspeople enjoy. He has a mouth organ which he plays very well as the people sing the words. They say he knows hundreds of hymns by heart.

Lucas said the reverend raised an eyebrow when told we intended to change "obey" to "trust" in the ceremony, but he did not protest. (We may be the only couple in the whole nation who do not wish for the wife to vow obedience. Lucas is an exceptional man! It was he who suggested it. No doubt Mama vowed to obey Karl, which may explain her reluctance to defy him.)

I confess to considerable anxiety about the coming nuptials. Will Lucas be gentle with me? Will there be pain? How will I respond to him? I love him so; I want to do and be what he expects, but I don't know how. I must rely on his generosity and patience and must trust that I have made the right decision.

Reverend Williams readily agreed to perform the ceremony. I will say no more in this journal about the nature of our marriage. Once it is done, it is done for good and all.

June 30, 1872

Dearest Mama,

Now that I am about to be married, I want you to know that I am safe and happy with Lucas. We are on a homestead far west of the Mississippi. I hope you will forgive me for leaving as I did, but I saw no other way. We left St. Louis in April and came in a wagon train to our new home.

Mama, I love you, but I could not stay there any longer. I would not marry Wilhelm Hessler. And Karl has become far too domineering with his religious beliefs, thinking that all must believe as he does or go to hell. I am a freethinker, and I will not be told how to believe.

I am sorry for taking your mother's brooch, but I had to have money for my train ticket and did not think it proper for Lucas to provide it until we were married. You know that Karl never allowed me any funds of my own, and I did not have enough from the small amounts you were able to give to me from time to time. Perhaps you can reclaim the brooch if it is still there; I left it at a pawn shop near the train station.

I hope you are well and happy. If you have heard from Lawrence, or if you ever do, please send me a letter in care of the land office in Johnson City, Colorado Territory. I would be pleased to have a letter from you even if you have not heard from my beloved brother. On the eve of my wedding day, I long for your smile, your touch, your blessing.

Your loving daughter,
Hannah

Shall I send this letter to Mama? I am certain Karl would not let her read it. Perhaps I should think of some other way to get word to her. I have composed the letter a thousand times in my mind. I have, for now, folded it carefully into this journal. I could not decide whether or not to tell her about taking the brooch, but I do not want her to accuse Mary of theft, so in this letter I have told her about it. That means I must send the letter soon, so she will know where I am, that I am well and happy, and that her servant is not a thief.

July 7

We have been married now for seven days. I have never been so happy, in spite of the discomforts here. Lucas and Adam built our marriage bed, with rope to hold the mattress of dried straw. It is certainly not a feather bed such as I was used to in Ohio, but it will do, especially since my darling can now share it with me. I am praying every day that our union will bear fruit. I so want to give Lucas a son.

I want to describe my wedding, for it is the only one I will ever have. We were married at the home of the owner of the general store. We stood right in front of his fireplace. Lucas wore his best black suit, with a small tie at the neck, and a beautiful white shirt Alma had sewn for him. My wedding dress is white, with a flowing skirt (no hoops), a bit of lace at the collar and wrists, and tiny lace buttons down the front. I had a garland of flowers in my hair.

Adam and Alma were our witnesses. After the ceremony, we had a tasty dinner at the hotel across the street. At least I suppose it was tasty; I could hardly eat a bite. There was no music, except in my head, but my heart was singing with joy.

Lucas is gentle and respectful yet masculine in every way. I could not have asked for a better husband.

Perhaps in France, it is *de rigueur* (a French phrase he taught me) for women to have experience before marriage, and that is why Lucas said little upon discovering that I seem to have been deflowered, merely commenting that he had noticed. Gentleman that he is, he said no more.

Now I know with absolute certainty that what happened in my bedroom in Ohio was not a dream but a horrible reality. Shall I ever reveal my shameful secret to my husband? I do not think I can bear to talk about it. Lucas is so gentlemanly, so forgiving, that he does not demand to know.

I love him so. For his sake, I will endure the hot, dry winds that sweep across the prairie, the straw mattress, the privy not yet built. My hands have become so horribly callused that I fear I may never play the piano again, and my lips are constantly chapped. My skin is so dry. I must ask Alma about some emollient that will help it stay more moist, if such there be. It's a good thing we do not own a mirror, for I think I might be horrified to see my own reflection.

I write in this journal by candlelight, since we must work until the sun sets. I had first thought to record only my journey west, but once we arrived, I have discovered this journal to be a wonderful companion. Not as comforting as my dear friend Julia, my confidante for many years, but very nearly so. I have also seen in myself a hitherto unknown talent for recalling details of events and conversations after the fact so have been able to record with considerable accuracy what people say and do.

Julia—I have not written to her since she married a Confederate soldier she met at the hospital. Though we were quite close friends once, I am doubtful she would approve of my marriage.

I have no woman friend here in whom to confide, only these pages. Perhaps Alma will become a friend to me, but we are very different and there are so many things I cannot speak of to her.

July 10

Such an extraordinary life I live now—who in Ohio would believe it? I am learning so much, mastering the domestic arts more quickly than I had imagined I could. I can even drive the wagon and ride a horse.

Learning to ride the horse was a very trying experience indeed. To come close enough to the beast, to stand beside it, caused my heart to beat excessively. Still, Lucas had said I must mount Boney, the more docile of the two, and learn to ride.

He bought me a man's saddle. "Sidesaddle is a ridiculous way to manage a horse," he informed me. I had to lift my skirt up over my knees, exposing my limbs, but Lucas was amused rather than shocked. "We must fashion you a riding habit, Hannah," he said with a chuckle.

My first lesson did not go well. The horse paid little attention to me, in fact took off at a dead run, causing me to shriek in terror, but Lucas quickly caught up with him on Nappy and subdued him. With Lucas alongside, we rode around a bit. He showed me how to manage the reins and which commands to use for which action I wanted the horse to take.

"You must be firm, Hannah," he repeated again and again. "Horses need a firm hand. Use your sternest tones." He explained that Boney had decided to run because he had not believed I was in charge. If the horse understands that you are going to tell him what to do, he will do it. Otherwise, he will do as he pleases.

I tried my best. After I got off the horse, I felt as if I had been at sea for a week; I could hardly walk! Sitting was equally uncomfortable. But the next day I was better, and each day it was a little easier. Now I can say with justifiable pride that I can ride a horse as well as need be. I'm certainly no horsewoman equal to the cowhands one hears about, nor even as good as Lucas (where did he learn to ride? I must ask him), but my skill is sufficient unto the day, as they say. I am no longer intimidated by these large animals, for I have learned that they will not intentionally hurt me.

Alma helped me devise a costume suitable for riding. It resembles a skirt except that it is divided and sewn in the middle. My limbs thus are not exposed, and I am comfortable while riding. Alma has two or three skirts of the same kind. She too rides like a man, and very well. When she visits, she always comes on horseback.

We rode the horses to our wedding (I carried my wedding dress in a saddlebag) and home again.

I had my monthlies again only a few days after the wedding, but I remain hopeful. And how grateful I am that my husband the physician will be by my side to care for me while I carry our child and bring him into the world.

July 12

Today was an eventful day. As I was drawing water from the creek, I looked up to see a small dog lapping at the water on the other side. He was black, quite bedraggled. He had floppy ears and a short tail. I knew numerous dogs in Cincinnati, though we did not have a dog ourselves, but did not recognize a breed in this little creature, no bigger than Julia's old tomcat.

Where could he have come from? I spoke softly to him. He jumped across the creek and came to my outstretched hand, looking for food, no doubt. I turned toward the house and he followed me.

When I got to the door, Lucas was just coming out for his day's work. He is still breaking sod. It's too late to plant this year, of course, although we can harvest hay in the fall. We thought to trade some of our precious lumber for vegetables from Alma and Adam this year. Lucas says he must break enough sod this summer for a vegetable garden while the soil is still amenable. If he waits until next spring, it will take too long and we will once again not be able to grow our own food. So the barn and the privy must wait for this more important chore.

He looked down at the little dog. "Where did he come from?"

"He was at the creek, drinking. He followed me."

"He looks pretty sad, Hannah. I'm not sure he's healthy enough to take in. But we could use a dog." My face must have fallen when he said the dog looked sickly, for he reached down and picked the creature up. "Let me look him over, and if I don't see any signs of serious illness, we can try fattening him up and see how he does." I had already decided to keep him; I even had him named. "I shall call him Freedom," I told my husband.

"Where do you suppose he came from?" I wondered. "Adam

and Alma don't have a dog. Unless he's theirs and got lost. . . ."
That notion dismayed me all over again. Then I had a cheerful
thought.

"I don't believe he *is* theirs, Lucas. They never mentioned
having a dog, and they would take better care of an animal than
this. Poor little fellow, he looks as if he's not eaten properly for
weeks."

"He's quite young, I should think," Lucas said. "Not yet a
year old. We will ride over there this evening and ask if they
know of anyone who might have lost a dog." He finished
examining the little fellow and set him down again. "See what
you can find to feed him, and be sure he has plenty of water."

We rode over to visit Alma and Adam. I carried Freedom in
front of me on the horse. He cuddled against me in a most
endearing way. They welcomed us and said they had not heard
of a lost dog. It may have strayed from town, Adam suggested,
but if it did, it was probably ill treated and seeking a new home.

Adam reminisced about a dog he had when a boy, before his
father died. It was small like Freedom, he said, and went
everywhere with him.

"What happened to the dog?" I asked. I am always asking
naïve or intrusive questions! Will I ever grow out of that?

"Mam's new man shot him," he said. Then he told us
something of his history. His father died when he was still
young, about eight, he thinks, though no one kept track of
birthdays or ages much in his part of Tennessee. All his brothers
and sisters had different fathers, each conceived by one of the
succession of men who came and stayed with his mother for a
time. As far as he knew, his mother had never married.

At thirteen Adam struck out on his own, for his mother's
new man was trying to turn him into a drudge in his shoe-
making shop. Moreover, Adam said, this "father" had a still in

the woods behind his home. Often the man would return home late in the evening, drunk from the strong, illegal potion, and beat whichever child was handiest.

We have much in common, he and I. Karl did not beat me as he beat Lawrence—with a whip—but the image of his whipping Lawrence is one that I can never get out of my head and heart. Adam emerged from such treatment stronger; Lawrence ran away. Dearly as I love my brother, I have to concede that he is a person of weak will and not, I fear, a survivor like Adam. He may not even be alive now, sad though that thought makes me.

So Freedom has joined our household. I am glad to have a flesh-and-blood companion, along with my paper one. He is a dear little thing.

July 15

Now that the wedding is over and I can write of other things, I shall describe Johnson City (it seems somewhat inappropriate to label it a city, I note with amusement), a crude frontier town on the high plains east of the mountain range. It has one main street, with boardwalks on either side. The land office/post office/general store is the largest building. The town also boasts two saloons, a barbershop, a livery and blacksmith shop, a bustling lumberyard, a jail, a small hotel with a dining room, and what Lucas says is a bordello. All of the buildings on the main street are of rough wood, with false fronts. The houses in the town, behind the main street on both sides, are mostly clapboard, and small. Some tents sit here and there on the edges of the town.

The town lies on the banks of a river, with houses and businesses on either side and two bridges across its span. It is close to a branch of the Overland Trail.

Mr. Devon, who owns the general store, says there are about 300 people living in the town, only about a dozen of them women (besides the "soiled doves" at the house of ill repute). Most of the men I saw while we were there had pistols in holsters. The street is full of horse manure and clumps of dirt from the horses' hooves. I decided that henceforth I will not accompany Lucas to the town because of the manure and dirt.

August 21

We must get a cat! I have been so busy trying to make a home and help Lucas with the farm that I have not paid enough attention to the mouse droppings that appear all over our house, but last night I actually saw one of the little creatures scurry into a corner. I am not a fainthearted female, the kind who would shriek in terror, but I am most perturbed to find these small invaders in my home. I will ask Adam for one of his barn cats, though he commented once when we were there that they are shy of people and difficult to domesticate. Even so, it might be hungry enough to eat my mice. Freedom shows not the slightest interest in the mice, alas.

September 25

It is some time since I have been free to write in this journal. By nightfall, I am so tired I cannot hold the pen. We have been working from first light until dark to prepare for the coming winter.

Today an unhappy accident occurred. While here helping us, sawing wood for furniture, Adam cut his hand quite badly. Lucas treated the cut immediately and, I am certain, successfully, first washing his own hands with the lye soap, then the wound with carbolic, then applying some of his special healing herbal paste after carefully stitching the wound up. Finally, he wrapped Adam's hand in one of his boiled cloths.

I have long known what a good doctor Lucas is; today I observed him at work again. I saw him work miracles at the hospital back home. (*Home,* I say, but this is home now.) His gentle, skillful hands and caring voice went a long way toward curing the sick, but so did his wide knowledge of the human body. Most physicians scorn the concepts Lucas lives and works by—cleanliness, reducing pain whenever it is possible, engaging the patient in the cure (a concept far ahead of its time, I am certain). Most of the doctors I saw working at the hospital seemed to view the human body as one vast laboratory on which they could experiment, not a living, feeling person. They almost seem to prefer corpses from which they can extract secrets.

Often on the battlefield, Lucas told me, the doctors would want to simply amputate limbs rather than try to save them. The pressure to keep going, to move fast so as to help as many men as possible, was severe. Lucas would do everything he could to save arms and legs, and he often did. He received grateful letters from soldiers he had made whole again.

Lucas is greatly interested in the workings of the body. He has a scientist's unquenchable curiosity. While training in Europe, he explained, he had been introduced to the wonders of the microscope, not much in use yet in the United States, at least not by doctors, who seem to think they already know what there is to know.

"What you see in there, Hannah!" he exclaimed. "Tiny living organisms the naked eye cannot see nor the mind imagine. Who knows what kinds of mischief they may cause?"

At one point in his medical studies, Lucas went to Hungary to learn from Ignaz Semmelweis, who had become famous for his work with antisepsis. Famous and reviled, Lucas told me, for many men in medicine still scoff at his theories of how to prevent childbed fever and other pernicious infections.

Brilliant and irascible, Semmelweis alienated his European colleagues by proving so clearly that cleaning hands before delivering babies saved lives. Lucas's autographed copy of Dr. Semmelweis's book is among his prized possessions. Semmelweis had a few disciples, Lucas among them, but Lucas learned not only from that famous doctor; he also studied ancient Greek and Far Eastern medicine, reading voraciously. That is where he learned about the herbs and pastes that he uses so effectively. He sends for them all the way to China and India. He also studied and became an advocate of Dr. Lister's bacteria theories.

When Lucas was still in his twenties, he was enticed to America by his mentor, who offered him the opportunity to learn about different kinds of medicine. Perhaps Lucas wanted to leave the scene of his mother's sad death or was ready for a new adventure. He has never explained quite why he left Europe to come to a land where dark-skinned people were mistreated and enslaved.

His benefactor promised to pass him off as Persian or Turkish, believing that no one would notice any language deficiencies. He is fluent in German as well as French. He speaks flawless English, with a slight but discernible accent. His mother taught him well.

Why did we not sail for Europe when we knew we wanted to marry? I have often pondered that. Certainly, our lives would have been easier in some ways. In France he could have continued to practice medicine. Here, who knows when or if he will? He spends his day using his wonderful hands to do rough farm tasks. Pray God one day he will be able to use his healing arts again.

September 29, 1872
Dearest Mama,

I am at last with child. I say at last because it seems so long a time to me, although we have only been married three months. For two months my monthlies have not come; Lucas confirmed my suspicions from other symptoms, so I know it is true. I am impatient to start my family. How I wish you could be here to share this experience with me, and to help me bring this so greatly desired child into the world. I pray that you will be able to meet your grandchildren one day.

It is now late September. With fall coming on, Lucas and I have been very busy getting ready to harvest and store the hay, finishing the cold cellar, and making our little house warm and snug for winter. Lucas has purchased what seem to me mountains of wood and spent hours chopping it for our stove.

I wish that you could see our little home. It is very cozy. Lucas and Adam have made a table and chairs and a small chest to hold our clothes. Soon they will start on a cradle for the baby. Thankfully, Adam has the tools they need to do this work; Lucas and I brought only a hammer, a saw and an ax.

Alma is knitting baby clothes. The child is expected in the spring. You needn't worry about me. Since Lucas is a physician, he is taking good care of me. If the baby should be a girl, I will name her Margaret, after you, Mama. If he is a boy, we will call him Adam, in honor of our kind and generous neighbor.

I do not know how we would have managed without the Baumgartens. They have restored my faith in human nature, which I must admit was waning somewhat before I left Ohio.

The day of my birth will soon be here. I will be seven and twenty, as you well know. I will be thinking of you on that day as, of course, I do on every other day.

I hope that you are well and not grieving overly much for your offspring who have left you. I love you, Mama, and I always will.

Your,
Hannah

September 30

Adam has brought us bounty from their harvest. Saying he and Alma had too much for the two of them, he brought vegetables, potatoes, fruit, and grain. I have now discovered how Alma can make lemonade so far from civilization. Against all odds, she has a lemon tree in her orchard! Sheltered by the apple and peach trees, it survives well enough to yield a little bit of fruit each year. What a wonder. (Oh, dear. I must work to subdue that childlike streak Lucas teases me about.)

The food, Adam said, was payment for Lucas's treatment of his injured hand, which he described as nothing short of miraculous. He has full use of the hand again, he says, and he wanted to show his gratitude. This episode gives me great hope for the future. With the increasing settlement, which surely will come here, Lucas might be able to use his medical knowledge, I my musical knowledge, well enough to support us quite nicely in town. Of course, that is some time in the future. First, we must bring this baby safely into the world, achieve a warm and comfortable home, and get this land to produce something besides hay. By the time I get past the nausea in the morning and rest to gather my strength again, it is almost midday. Adam and Alma have come several times to help us prepare for winter and for the baby. This is especially generous of Alma, since she so badly wants children herself and has so far been barren. It takes a large heart to rejoice in someone else's good fortune when one wants so fervently for it to be her own.

We have been harvesting hay. Unlike most men, who would not allow their wives to do manual labor when in delicate condition, Lucas has encouraged me to work beside him. Keeping active is good for both the baby and me, he says. Clearly, he does not intend to coddle me. But never had I imagined *such* hard work.

We swing the scythes back and forth, back and forth, cutting the hay, then load it onto the wagon with pitchforks. It must then be stacked in neat piles in the barn—which structure Lucas and Adam finished only last week. Will there be enough hay to see Judy and her calf and the two horses through the winter? Only time will tell.

My arms ache so that I can hardly hold this pen. I. . . .

October 4

So fatigued was I from harvesting hay that I fell asleep while writing in my journal a few days ago. I think that I will die from exhaustion if this travail does not end soon. Only a few more days, Lucas says. Winter may drive us indoors any day now.

All this hard labor has put me in mind of what slaves must have endured—much harder work, in the heat of the sun, day after day, with no respite and no attention to their welfare. And worst of all, no reward. How can one human being rob another of dignity in such a way? Still, talk of slavery and concern about it seem remote to me now. In Ohio, the war was close, the reports of the battles so frequent and chilling, that it was impossible to put affairs of state out of one's mind. Here we live in a cocoon, utterly remote from the rest of the world. What is going on in the rest of America? In Europe? I do not know. Nor, I find, am I overly concerned. The main, indeed the only, purpose of my days seems now to be staying healthy and strong. I had not thought myself so self-centered.

The life of the mind seems to be completely out of my sphere just now. My most intimate concern is the changes that are happening in my body. Though I cannot yet see any telltale swelling to reveal my condition, I see other changes that Lucas says are definite indicators of expectancy. I am most assuredly in the family way, or "increasing," as Mama used to say. In only a few more months, he says, I shall feel the child move within me. That will surely be the most exciting day of my life since I married Lucas.

On Adam's advice, Lucas has strung rope from the house to the barn and from the house to the privy. It seems unnecessary to me; I am hard put to envision being unable to see as far as the barn in a snowstorm, but Adam knows best. Our house is made more comfortable with covered window openings and shutters to keep out the cold in winter. The door is of sturdy pine planks brought from the town.

October 8

Does one ever become accustomed to the *smells* on a farm? When we first came, I was so busy and taken up in the new adventure that I apparently did not notice them so much. Perhaps I notice the odors more in my current condition. Adam and Alma's farm is so pungent with the smells of the animals' leavings, the hay, the rotting produce for the pigs, that sometimes I can hardly bear to be there. The pigs themselves are particularly odorous, and they love to roll about in the muck.

Our farm does not yet have such strong odors, no doubt because we have not yet acquired the stock that creates most of them.

Among other crops, Adam raises sugar beets; I am amazed at how strong *they* smell. To think that such a rank odor can become the sugar we put in our coffee and our food!

I suppose one day my nose will become inured to these assaults on it. That would seem to be the only way one could remain on a farm for a lifetime.

To be fair, the city has odors, too. In Cincinnati, walking about, I certainly did notice a variety of odors, not all of them pleasant by any means. The water has its own stench. And the hospital! Recalling my days there, I realize that I *had* become oblivious to the strong, mostly disagreeable, odors that assailed one in every corner, except perhaps in the room where the doctors took their occasional rest. (I was in there on a few occasions, having been asked to put fresh linens on the cots. They close the door firmly, open the windows, and the hospital smells do not seep in.)

Yet no odor in the city or the hospital is as penetrating or enduring, it seems to me, as these I encounter on a farm. I smell them inside the house, outside, everywhere.

October 9

October is so *brown* here. The Baumgartens' trees have turned, but the leaves are mostly brown or a rather dull gold. The air is crisp, with a constant breeze. How I miss the beautiful fall colors of Ohio! They are a painter's palette across the horizon. How I miss *trees!* Here, there is only the endless prairie, the grasses waving in the wind.

Lucas says I will feel the child quicken soon. What a thrill that will be for me and for him as well. I have had to adapt my clothing to fit my changing shape. Lucas does not want me to wear the corset. He refuses to lace it for me, even loosely. He believes that women who wear corsets throughout their waiting time can harm the infants and even themselves.

"What shall I do to hold myself up if I don't wear a corset?" I asked him.

He said he would consider it and let me know.

The morning nausea has passed. I live in a state of excitement and anticipation. Margaret or Adam, as the case may be, will be the most welcome child ever to grace this earth.

This afternoon the sky darkened ominously. Adam said that means a snowstorm is coming.

October 10

When we peered out the front door this morning to let Freedom out for his morning constitutional, we saw nothing but swirling white. It never snowed like this in Ohio, especially not in October!

Lucas ran out into the snow with the dog, turning around and around laughing. He tipped his face up to the sky and let the snow cover his face. Just as Adam said, we could not see the barn, so Lucas followed the rope to feed the animals, Freedom staying right at his heels. I expect his nose helped him find his way. When Lucas returned, the snow had completely covered his and Freedom's tracks.

While housebound, Lucas and I had a conversation which Mama would find quite beyond the pale. I asked him what it was like attending expectant mothers when he practiced medicine in Europe. Was it different from here, where women seldom go to doctors for such a condition, but only call them (sometimes) when the child is coming?

Do European physicians attend a woman during her expectancy?

He said it is not much different. Only poor or very sick women go to hospitals to have their children, which is when doctors see them. Wealthier women have the doctors come to their homes, where they are sometimes seen before the delivery—but only fully clothed and always with the husband present. "It's quite difficult to determine a woman's condition in those circumstances," he said.

He told me a surprising thing: "Even at Semmelweis's hospital in Pest, where I went to study, doctors do not touch mothers-to-be, and they certainly never feel the growing child in the womb. You are to be my teacher in this experience, Hannah."

So shall I be. Lucas may examine me from head to toe, to learn what he will. In America, I told him, babies are commonly brought into the world by midwives who have had no formal training beyond an apprenticeship, only experience and, I realize, intimate knowledge of a woman's anatomy. Women who go to hospitals to have their children often do not come out again. "Why should that be?" I asked.

"It's a matter of cleanliness," he replied. "Except in Pest, I did not see doctors scrubbing their hands before attending patients. They wore blood-stained coats. We could not examine women before the birth, yet doctors can and do plunge their hands into their bodies to bring forth a child after having been in the morgue performing an autopsy, and they leave infection behind."

"Not you, surely," I said. "You are constantly cleaning your hands with lye soap."

"I do now. When I began practicing medicine, I followed the example of the other physicians and went from patient to patient, sometimes from autopsy to patient, unclean. A woman died after I had attended her delivery. That's when I went to Semmelweis, to learn a better way." The pain in Lucas's eyes as he spoke of the woman's death was almost unbearable to me.

So I allowed Lucas to examine me in the most intimate way, and I was astounded at how detached he was, seeming to concentrate solely on what he could learn by feeling. There was nothing remotely suggestive in Lucas's manner. I concluded that the modesty of women causes us unnecessary illness and pain. When he completed his examination, he reported that he could feel our infant in my womb, and that all seemed to be well. "You are healthy and strong," he told me. He thanked me for letting him examine me thus. "Your passage is wide enough. You should have an easy delivery."

If any delivery is ever easy, I thought, remembering Lucinda Smith's screams as her labor began. When I heard her cry out, I was so frightened that I thought I would never willingly put myself in such a position—but here I am. Surely, with my dear husband by my side, I will not have such an ordeal as she had, poor soul. No doubt it was made no easier by knowing who had fathered the child and what sort of life lay ahead of the babe.

October 18

Lucas has brought me a kitten, a tiny thing only a few weeks old. It is from one of Alma's barn cats. Since it is so tiny and new, I believe I can train it to live indoors with me and to catch these infernal mice before they take over this house! I am not afraid of them like some silly women I have known, but they are dirty little creatures who carry disease, Lucas says.

Yesterday Lucas got out his precious microscope, transported all the way from Europe. He showed me the organisms, invisible to the naked eye, which live on a mouse's hair. I had found one of the pests, quite dead, by the stove and he carefully removed some of its hair to put under the microscope. That is indeed a wondrous instrument, showing us an entire world we cannot otherwise see. It's important to banish the mice, he explained, so as to make sure that our child is not exposed unnecessarily to disease. It will take the kitten quite a few weeks to grow enough to catch the mice, but they say mice can smell a cat in the house. Perhaps that will induce them to leave. Annoying little rodents!

November 1

Amazing—it is November already. The cold seeps into the house through every pore. I stay huddled by the stove as much as I can. It has not snowed since that early October storm, but we expect more snow any day. Lucas goes out and tends the animals, chops wood, then hurries to the barn again. He is making furniture there. He will not tell me what he is fashioning. I told him, "Be careful of your hands. They are our fortune."

Freedom follows Lucas everywhere. I found him, brought

him home, but he cleaves to his master. That's all right, really; so do I.

Lucas has banished another myth for me. Although it was never spoken of openly, I had learned long ago from overhearing conversations—mostly innuendo—that women who are *enceinte* (another French word I learned from Lucas) are not expected to engage in marital relations with their husbands, lest the babe be harmed.

"Of course I would not ever do anything to harm you or the child," he assured me, "but conjugal relations (that he could speak of it so boldly!) do no harm during pregnancy. In fact," he added with his off-center grin, "you might find you especially enjoy it." Trusting my husband implicitly, I took his word for it, and found that he was right.

November 11

The kitten does well. I have named it Puss-in-Boots, for it looks so like the cat in the story, with its black feet and face and white, silky body. It has grown bigger than the mice I desire it to catch. Lucas says it is a boy cat. If I let him go outdoors at night as he wants to do, he may be eaten by a coyote. I hope Puss will be occupied enough indoors, chasing mice.

November 12

Tonight, as I was putting away the dishes from the evening meal, I felt the child quicken within me. It was but an instant, a brief awakening against my womb, the fluttering of a butterfly. My babe is alive and moving inside me! Today, my condition became completely real to me.

I'm sure it's not "correct," and I'm certain it is not done in Cincinnati or any other civilized place in America, but I told Lucas what had happened. Feigning seriousness, he put on his stethoscope and said, "Just let me listen to see if I can hear the heartbeat." He placed the instrument against my swelling abdomen and listened intently. Then he looked up and smiled mischievously. "I think I hear your dinner rumbling about, Mrs. Bowman, and it's so loud I can't hear the infant just now." We both laughed for a long time at his silliness.

I seldom see Lucas silly. He is usually so intent and serious that at times I have wondered if he knows how to make light of life. Given the existence he has led, I expect it's no surprise that he would be so grave. I intend to see that he laughs much more from now on.

Alma and I have refashioned one of my corsets so that it supports only my bosom and does not impede the growth of the child. It seems to work quite nicely—so well, in fact, that I might well continue using it even after the child is born, for it is far more comfortable than a corset, and I find that my breasts are heavier and need some support.

We have been existing mostly on a vegetarian diet, namely the ever-present beans. Lucas says I need meat to build strength for me and for the baby. He is going to buy a pig from Adam and together they will slaughter it. I think I will not watch—yet I must. This is part of our life together that I must reconcile myself to. In Cincinnati, I never saw the animals from which our meat had come. Now I know what happens.

Lucas is also planning to purchase some chickens. "They will give us both eggs and meat," he says. True, but they are messy, noisy, smelly things—I have gone with Alma to gather eggs in her henhouse. They cluck and peck, and their feathers fly about. Well, Lucas will have to build a henhouse first. Perhaps he cannot do that until spring. And in the spring, will he decide to stay or want to move on? Surely he will stay, with our child on the way.

November 14

Today for some reason I could not get Mama out of my mind. I remember so well the last day we spent together, the day before I left. I shall mail my letters to her soon. One particular day came to my mind as clearly as if I were there, standing in the kitchen of my house again.

We were helping Mary bake bread. Though Mama can afford to have a servant, she loves to cook and is often found in the kitchen alongside Mary. "You go on and take care of the beds," she'd tell Mary. "I'll cook today."

But that day, the three of us were together in the kitchen. Karl was gone to the mercantile. I longed to tell Mama about Karl, my hatred and fear of him. But the words would not come. So instead I said, "Mama, do you believe women should have the vote?" In our town and across the country, women were making considerable fuss about that issue.

As always when it came to issues of the day, she was straightforward with me. "Women should be able to do whatever they want to do, and they should have a voice in the government."

"You do not have that freedom, Mama."

"You are right, Hannah dear. I chose to marry again, so I lost the right to determine my own fate. But I wish it for you. Marry thoughtfully, my darling daughter. Choose your life carefully." There was deep regret and sorrow in her voice, to which I am sensitive only in memory. How soon after she married Karl did she realize her mistake—or has she yet realized it?

I know that she married Karl to save the store for us, her children. I did not know until after his death how badly in debt Papa had been. He had been close to losing the dry-goods store handed down to him from his father. My poor, dear, wonderful father, so impractical and so impossible with money. But why, oh, why did he allow Karl to become his partner? Was there not someone else who would have rescued him from debt, someone more kind and less fanatical? Did Papa not know what Karl was like?

Perhaps not—Papa always saw the best in people. And when Karl came along, professing to be as devoted to music as Papa was himself, and offered to forgive the debt in exchange for a half-interest in the store, Papa was blind enough to trust him. I have always believed that he went off to war in part to escape the dreadful mistake that he'd made, for it could not have been long after Karl came that my father realized what his new partner truly was.

Yet Mama married Karl. I have long wondered what hold Karl had over her, that she could do such a terrible thing. *She did not choose wisely.*

But, as Mama advised, *I* have chosen carefully, although she might not agree. Lucas never tries to dominate me. Moreover, I for one am not going to have my life dictated by bearing one child after another. Lucas and I have talked about that (yet another forbidden topic, in Mama's eyes). I conceived the first child so quickly. He plans to take precautions after this child is born so we do not have another until I am ready, which he leaves it to me to determine.

"How will you do that?" I inquired, in my ignorance. He replied with that mischievous look again. "That's one reason we need the pig." I believe I shall not ponder that statement further.

November 22

It has occurred to me, belatedly I fear, that I have focused overly much on my own sacrifices in making this journey west. What about Lucas? I have not considered what he gave up: the opportunity to continue to practice medicine, for one. To earn admiration and respect. To learn new medical theories and put them into practice. To have enough money to live comfortably.

Why would he, why should he, leave all that behind to come out here and work from dawn to dark merely to survive?

He was reluctant about the romance from the beginning. It was I who approached him, who made opportunities for us to be together, who finally told him of my feelings for him. Perhaps I was overly persistent and he finally gave in, or perhaps he found me irresistible. I prefer to believe the latter.

I will never forget the first time I saw him at the hospital. He was sitting at a table with his head in his hands. It was his hands, those long-fingered, broad, strong hands, that drew me to him. I sat down across from him.

"Can I bring you something?" He looked up at my words. His face stunned me, with its beautiful lines. The marvelous eyes. I ached to sketch him.

"No, but I thank you. What I need most is sleep." His voice! Deep, rich, the timbre like that of an opera singer.

"Are you a physician?"

He nodded. "There are so many wounded boys, and so few of us. We lose so many of them."

He was new to the hospital, having been in the field for some months, I discovered. I soon learned that he usually came to the dining area about five o'clock in the afternoon, and I managed to be there most days at that time. We frequently struck up conversation, discovering a mutual love of poetry and books and music. We never lacked for something to talk about. (However, we were careful not to converse earnestly when others were nearby.) My feelings began with friendship, though I was also physically attracted to him in a most unladylike fashion.

To me he seemed exotic. People said that he was foreign, and that made him mysterious and exciting. But I soon learned that he was a richly rewarding person to be with as well.

He always responded to my talk pleasantly, sometimes eagerly, but he never told me much about himself. I did not ask. I, on the other hand, revealed a good deal about myself, though I never spoke of the difficulties of my home life. I told him of my interests in music and art, of my friendship circle, of my father's death. I spoke about my dear brother, Lawrence, and how like our father he was. I gave freely, as I grew more comfortable in his company, my opinions on all sorts of matters political and social.

When the war was over, only a few months after we met, I thought—feared—he might leave the hospital and the city to return to the country he came from, but he did not. Once I asked him why he stayed. "Partly because I am still needed here," he told me. "And partly, Miss Morris, because of you."

As I recall that particular talk, and the look in his eyes, I suppose I cannot say that this move, this "great adventure," was due entirely to my persuasion. Lucas is a man of four and thirty, after all, and he has free choice. He could have left at any time, and he chose to stay. So I shall not feel guilty any longer. Lucas does not often say it, but I believe to the marrow of my bones that he loves me.

I am not a beautiful woman, far from it, but I am comely enough. My great sorrow is my hair, which I used to keep shiny and soft with preparations of Mary's. Now, I can only wash it with some of Alma's lye soap (horrid stuff!) and brush it out. It flies about every which way and will not stay out of my face.

We both knew that we could not legally marry in Ohio. That meant we had to go far away, somewhere safe from those cruel laws.

Thanksgiving Day

What a joyous Thanksgiving Day we had! Adam and Alma invited us to their home, and somehow Alma managed a pheasant, mince pie, fluffy potatoes—a regular feast. Lucas and I contributed cornbread. Next year we will do much better, once our garden is flourishing.

Adam was in a jovial mood. His crops had done well this year. His livestock is thriving. Adam asked Lucas to say the blessing.

"Dear Lord," Lucas said as we bowed our heads, "thank you for this bounty and for the blessing of wonderful neighbors."

Indeed, I do not know how we would have survived these last few months without the Baumgartens. Not only have they shared their food with us, Adam has helped Lucas in so many ways, and Alma has helped and taught me so much.

Tonight when we returned to our cozy home, Lucas loved me in such a way that I cannot doubt his feelings for me. Later, we heard an eerie howling outside. I burrowed closer to him.

"It's only the coyotes," he told me. "In winter, they get hungry and come closer to the settlements."

We'd heard them before, seen some from a distance in the summer, but I didn't know they would come so close. I have no knowledge of coyotes. We do not have such animals in Cincinnati. "Will our animals be all right?"

"They don't bother large animals," he said. "But we must be very watchful with Freedom and Puss, and we must build our chicken house well. They run in packs and can wipe out a flock in no time."

Even with his reassurances, I felt myself trembling at the thought of these wild creatures hovering just beyond our pastureland.

December 1

Christmas will be here soon. What shall we do? We will have to go to town to buy some gifts. Dare I send a gift to Mama? What would I send her? There is a post office in Johnson City. Perhaps I can mail my letters there.

I shall ask Lucas to take me to town tomorrow. Distasteful

though it is there, it is the only center of commerce within a reasonable distance. I will buy for Alma and Mama plain handkerchiefs which I can embroider (at least I brought that useful skill with me from my former life), and warm gloves for Adam. For Lucas, I hope to find a book. Sometimes the general store has books. Perhaps we can both read the book and talk about it. I so miss the intellectual side of my life.

Lucas returns from his trips with reports that the town is improving. One or two of the saloons have closed since we came here, and a few women have come. Their arrival can only help to civilize the town.

December 7

Tonight, I consider myself blessed to be alive. Lucas and I started to town two days ago. There had been several days of such extraordinarily mild weather (such as never would happen in Ohio) that we were lured into false optimism. When we set out, he on Nappy, I on Boney, Freedom on my lap (I do not like to leave him alone, though Puss does not seem to mind), the weather was still mild, quite warm for December. The sky was blue everywhere we looked.

But as we rode, the sky began to change, growing darker and darker by the moment. The wind, exceedingly cold, whipped around us. Within an hour the first flakes began to float around in the air.

"Oh, Lord," Lucas exclaimed. "We should turn back."

But in five minutes, the sky was filled with swirling snow and we could see nothing. We could hear the creek, but we did not know where it was. On the open prairie there is no shelter. We were bundled warmly enough if we kept moving but not if we got stranded. Lucas had some food and water in his saddlebag, but not much.

We kept going into the blinding snow. The wind grew stronger and stronger. Soon we were bent far forward to shield our bodies from the stinging pellets. The horses were stumbling, walking erratically. "I have no idea where we are, Hannah," Lucas said, and for the first time since I have known him, I heard fear in his voice. It was hard to hear him above the wind. He was shouting but the words barely carried to me. I could feel that he had hold of Boney's bridle. He had dismounted and was leading both the horses.

"Have we turned around?" I called. I could not see him at all, only a blurred shape in the snow.

Suddenly he stopped the horses. I plunged forward, almost dropping Freedom. "What's wrong?" I shouted.

He appeared beside me, very close to my ear. "We have come upon shelter," he told me. I wanted to ask him what he had found, but talking was too much effort. I hunched down in the saddle and hung onto the saddle horn and Freedom for dear life.

He led me into what appeared to be a dugout. It was large, though not large enough for the horses. Lucas tied the horses together by the entrance. "Pray God they will survive," he said. He had brought an oilskin in his saddlebag; he removed the saddles and covered the horses as best he could with the saddle blankets, then the oilskin. Their backs were to the wind. "Now all we can do is wait it out," he said.

We clutched each other, and Freedom, as closely as we could get together and sat in the dugout, just out of the howling wind and snow. That sound was much, much worse than ever the coyotes could be. We could not talk. We used the saddles to pillow our heads. I think I slept. I felt Lucas's hand on my swelling once, checking the child.

After a long time, I woke. Lucas was sitting with his back to the dirt behind us. The howling had diminished considerably.

"I am so sorry, my darling," he said. "I should have known

better than to set out if there was any hint of snow. I have never in my life seen blizzards like these prairie storms." This is what we surely would have encountered in the mountains, too, I thought, had we gone on to California. I did not say that aloud, though. We can see the mountains in the distance on a clear day, snowcapped even in summer. They are so beautiful, but they are also awesome and frightening.

"Nor have I. In Ohio it snows, but not like this. There is more to stop it there."

He told me how he had discovered the dugout, which he supposed to be the start of a settler's cold cellar, though it had no door and was not very deep. He had dismounted and was trudging along, keeping his head down and hanging onto the reins of both horses, when Nappy suddenly stopped and whinnied. Had the animal not stopped, it would have stepped into the dugout and broken its leg. To whatever power gave the beast its instincts at that moment, I am grateful.

I have no doubt the dugout saved our lives. There are no trees on this endless plain except the cottonwoods along the river. There is nothing to stop the wind and snow.

We stayed in the dugout all night. We ate what food Lucas had brought, some dry, hard biscuits and jerky. Sometimes, I heard the horses whinnying outside. I knew they were cold and miserable, but what could we do? I shared my food with Freedom. The food did not warm us much. The dugout was very cold. Though we shared each other's body warmth as best we could, I shivered constantly.

In the morning it was still snowing, but not so hard. We waited some time—I don't know how long. Finally Lucas said he thought he could see the sun peeking through the clouds, giving us our direction. We had to go home again, to care for Judy and her calf (now almost a full-grown bull) and to eat. The Christmas excursion will have to wait until another day.

Though covered with snow and frost, the horses had made it through the night, thank God. They were both upright, blowing frosty breaths into the air, when we emerged. They whinnied at Lucas as if to say, "Take us home, please."

We plodded through the snow. The horses were slow, since they had not been fed or watered, but they seemed to know which way to go. Lucas let them guide us, holding onto the reins. At times the drifting snow came almost to his knees.

It must have been well after noon when we arrived home again. I was chilled to my bones and so was Lucas, though he did not complain but went straight to the barn to tend to the animals. The poor beasts were barely upright, so exhausted and frozen were they, and I knew it would take him some considerable time to rub them down and get them warm enough that he was satisfied with their condition. Lucas is as careful with our animals' health as he is with mine.

I stirred up the fire, which had died down to nothing, of course, and heated some milk (how nice it would have been to have chocolate) and we had warm milk and sourdough bread when he finally came back from the barn.

Never again will I doubt Adam's wisdom about this cursed prairie. The ropes that he recommended to connect the house and the barn do not seem the least bit unnecessary to me now.

Lucas was full of remorse. "If you take ill because of this, Hannah, I will never forgive myself," he said. He brought me some of his medicinal rum and insisted I drink it, then sent me to bed, bundled me up in the covers, and felt my forehead every few minutes until I fell asleep. I woke only a short while ago to find him curled up beside me, sleeping soundly, Puss snuggled up against my back. When we awoke in the morning, the snow had ended and the world was colored a blinding white.

December 24

Christmas Eve. How I long for my piano! Lucas and I sang carols, though I fear we were off key. Lucas sings heartily but with little regard for the correct notes. He learned French carols as a child; I have had to teach him our American ones. We have fashioned a makeshift tree of branches from one of Alma's fruit trees. We hung ribbons and embroidery lace on it and put out our presents. Lucas and Adam went to town with the wagon and fetched the presents I had planned to buy, and I wrapped them with some of my scraps of fabric. I have not mailed Mama's gift yet.

Tomorrow, we will go to the Baumgartens' for dinner and give them our gifts.

The child is very active now. It seems to have more than two arms and legs! I must wait four more months before it puts in an appearance. That seems forever sometimes, although not as interminable as that long night Lucas and I spent in the dugout a few weeks ago. After the child is born, Lucas and I will take him to town when the minister comes so he can be properly christened. I am making a christening dress. We plan to ask Alma and Adam to be his godparents.

There is much to do before April, when the child is expected.

December 25, 1872

Dearest Mama,

Today is Christmas Day. How I miss you and Lawrence! I remember wonderful Christmases when Papa was alive. We would have such a feast, with turkey and all the trimmings, three kinds of pie, and your famous suet pudding, the recipe your mother brought from New England.

I wish with all my heart that I could be there with you, that things could be different, but it cannot be. So I can only write this letter and tell you how happy I am. My child will come in the spring, with the warmth and the flowers. Perhaps I can sketch a portrait of him to send to you.

I'm sure you would think my life harsh and primitive, Mama, and in many ways it is. We live at the whim of nature. We do not have books or music or parties; we only have each other and our good neighbors, the Baumgartens.

I can almost hear you asking, "Do you attend church?" No, we do not go to church. Town is too far away. We will go to town when the minister comes again (he is the traveling minister who married us) to have our child christened. Then his name (or her name) will be entered in my Bible, the Bible that you gave me when I turned thirteen and which I carried west in my valise.

When you think of me, Mama, think that I am well and happy. I hope you are the same.

Love,
Hannah

1873

A new year has begun. We hope and pray that it will be a prosperous and joyous one for us. Though it is very cold, the sky is clear and sharply blue. Would that I could paint that color—it is glorious. We hear the coyotes every night.

Our supply of wood is running low. Lucas will have to go to town again. He and Adam have felled some of the large cotton-woods near the river east of town and hauled them home behind the horses, but even those huge trees will not keep us through the winter.

I do not want him to go, nor do I want to accompany him. My child is due in only a few more months. He has said it is best for me not to ride anymore, so I cannot visit Alma except in the wagon, and he will need that to haul the wood and supplies. I am afraid to be alone here. I do not want Lucas to know that. He thinks I am courageous and strong. How I have deceived him.

Perhaps he can persuade Alma to come and stay with me. No, I must not ask him that. He will have to leave me alone from time to time; I must accustom myself to it.

He is leaving in the morning and will be back in two days, he assures me. I must try to overcome my fears.

January 13

Time seems to go so slowly. I do the few chores that must be done in the house, feed the cows and the dog and the cat, take Freedom out for a brief stroll (not long; it's too cold to go far), and work on my child's layette, and still there are endless hours in the day. Today, I decided to bake bread, which helped while away the hours.

What will our child be like, I wonder. Will he be as dark as Lucas? Will he have my features, or his? What will our blended seed produce? And, most of all, how will the world regard this precious creation of ours? Lucas has suffered much, unjustly, because of his dark skin. Will our child have the same experience of life?

Perhaps, out here, people will be kinder. They have been kind enough to Lucas, seeming not to notice his skin color much. Of course, he has won them over with his quiet ways, lovely manners and many skills—but still, there must be thousands of black people in this country who have gifts to bring to the world but no chance to give them, simply because of their skin. I hope and pray that our son will be regarded by others for what he is and what he has to offer, not for his skin color. I think of this in quiet moments. While Lucas is away, I have much time to ponder.

January 14

Last night I had a terrible dream. Such nightmares have not visited me since I left Ohio. Why now? It frightened me most particularly because I am alone in the house. I know now that I must tell Lucas what happened to me in Karl Schussman's house, or I shall never know peace.

January 15

It is three days now, and Lucas has not returned. I am terribly afraid. We have not had a storm, so it could not be the weather which detains him. Shall I go look for him? Shall I stay here and try to be patient? What shall I do? I cannot go look for him; it is too cold and I might put the child at risk.

If he does not return tomorrow, I will walk to Adam's house unless there is a blizzard.

January 16

Lucas returned home last night, very late. I could see that he was terribly weary; indeed, he was swaying on his feet, but I could summon up no sympathy for his condition. All I could think of was that he had left me alone here, and I was frightened. I could not control myself but lashed out at him.

"Where have you been?" I cried. "I have been so worried about you!"

He stepped back, almost backing into the stove, startled at my outburst. When I saw the stricken look on his face, I was contrite. What came over me?

"I am exhausted, chilled to the bone, and the last thing I need is my wife chastising me," he answered sharply.

Had he responded gently, I'm sure the outcome would have been different. As it was, my patience had been tried to its limit, so I reacted to his angry tone with anger of my own.

"You have no notion how I feel, sitting here alone in the middle of this desolate prairie! You leave, and I do not know what has happened to you—what am I supposed to think?"

"You are excitable because of your condition, Hannah. Sit down and try to calm yourself." I felt the child grow restless in me, as if he could sense my mood.

That infuriated me. Lucas was treating me as if I were a patient, just another hysterical female behaving as women are thought to behave—not his wife. It was not to be borne.

"Do not treat me so!" I shouted.

"Treat you how? I have no idea what you mean." His tone still sounded intolerably paternal to me.

"As if I were one of your patients, to be coddled and soothed. Or a child."

"You are one of my patients," he said. "My only one, at this time."

I began to cry then. He turned away from me, and my heart was sick. Our first quarrel, and it felt terrible. Not only that, but the child within me was moving restlessly, almost as if he knew something was wrong.

He said no more but took off his coat, which had stiffened from the cold, and poured himself some coffee. When I had stopped crying, he cleared his throat and said, "Do you want to know what happened to me, why I was delayed?"

I apologized and went to him, holding out my arms. He embraced me lovingly. Lucas does not nurse his anger or hurt but lets it go and goes forward. "Of course I want to hear what happened," I said, and sat down to listen.

He arrived in town safely, he told me, though the streets seemed very quiet, but when he got to the livery stable the owner whisked him and Nappy inside and said that a gang of robbers had stormed into the town on horseback, guns flashing, and taken over the saloon. The Marshal was expected soon, but would he be able to subdue and arrest them? No one knew. Mr. Marks advised Lucas not to go anywhere until the gang either left or was jailed. Though Johnson City does have a sheriff, it seems he mysteriously disappeared the day the gang came to town. No one has seen him since.

Owen Marks kindly invited Lucas to put up at his place over the stable until the situation was resolved—which could be days. Lucas knew no way to get word to me. Everyone in town was hiding in houses or stores. Noise continually issued from

Paddy's Saloon—gunshots, shouts, laughter, glass breaking. Not even the "ladies of the evening" dared enter the saloon.

The robbers were thought to be the same ones who have recently been holding up stagecoaches or trains by placing impassable obstacles in the road or the track and forcing the driver to stop.

Lucas stayed in the livery stable two days, waiting. Sleep was impossible because of the noise. The second night, he and Owen peered out their upper-story window to see the Marshal and a group of armed men Lucas called a posse ride right down the main street. There must have been twenty men with him, Lucas said.

For once there was no noise coming from the saloon. Lucas and Mr. Marks watched the Marshal and his men go inside. It was as quiet as a graveyard in the town. A few minutes later the lawmen came out, the robbers staggering along at gunpoint, hands tied behind their backs. The Marshal and his men slung the outlaws onto the backs of horses and away they all rode.

Once the invaders had left, the story came out that the robbers had at last become sufficiently drunk in the saloon, having broken open the whiskey supply, to offer no resistance. The Marshal and his men simply walked in, handcuffed them, and informed them they were under arrest.

Lucas concluded his business, but decided to wait until the next morning to start home. How foolish I felt, and how small, for getting so angry. It is so unlike me. I humbly begged my husband's pardon. Perhaps Lucas is right; it is due to my condition. And how foolish the townspeople must feel as well, knowing they could have marched into that saloon themselves and subdued the gang.

I must make an effort to master my fears. If I do not, I will never be able to live here, especially since I must often stay here by myself. What happens when I have a child to care for and protect?

January 30

Adam reports that we have a new neighbor to the south of us. This is quite a surprise, for settlers usually do not arrive in the middle of winter. His name is Jacob Richards, and he has settled down the creek a few miles—without a wife or family, which is equally unusual. If he is half as nice as Adam and Alma, we will be truly blessed.

Today Adam stopped by on his way back from town to say that the sheriff has returned from his hasty trip with news—it seems the robbers are reported to have buried their ill-gotten gains somewhere in the bluffs twenty miles or so west of Johnson City. It is said they stashed their "treasure" there before coming to town to drink and celebrate. They are now jailed in Denver, but they refuse to divulge the exact location of their booty. Several groups of townspeople have gone up to the area to dig for it. That is not wise, in January. We have had another warm spell the last few days, warm enough to hang the wash and air the bedclothes, but a storm could come anytime, as we are learning.

While the weather is warm Lucas has been working outside chopping and stacking the wood he hauled from town. He is sorting out pieces large and strong enough for fence poles; to fulfill our claim, we need to put up a fence and dig a well, as well as to plant at least ten acres. When we succeed in these endeavors, we will certainly have earned our one hundred and sixty acres.

This cheers me considerably, as Lucas was at first only willing to stay until spring. Now it looks as though he is prepared to settle here, for which I am profoundly thankful.

Lucas also brought me a special treat from town, a novel by a

New England writer, Louisa May Alcott. It is charming. Every now and then the general store acquires a book from somewhere. Lucas buys all they have whenever he goes to town.

Back in Cincinnati, I would have had to hide Miss Alcott's books, for Karl would consider them heretical. He allowed only the Bible and religious tracts in the house. He threw out all of Papa's books, despite our pleas and protests. I hid my books from him when I brought them home. Usually, though, I went to the lending library and read books there. The librarian was very kind and understanding, never questioning why I asked her to set the unfinished books aside for me. Now I can read whatever I choose. That freedom alone makes this arduous journey and the life I have now more worthwhile.

The town is growing, Lucas tells me. Half a dozen new residents have come—for what purpose, I am not sure. One, an ambitious and courageous widow, has started a grain mill. I greatly admire her enterprise and strength. Several new houses have been constructed, and there is talk of building a church.

Lucas learns a bit about the history of the town every time he visits. Mr. Devon, one of the original settlers, likes to recount the tales. Lucas remembers well and brings the stories to me.

Only a few years ago, before we came, Johnson City was a wild town. It had been settled originally as an army fort, being on the banks of a wide, clear river near the Overland Trail. When the army post was abandoned after a terrible flood in which one poor man died, some of the soldiers stayed to start a town on higher ground. There were more saloons than houses, and the "ladies" ruled the night. On more than one occasion there was a shoot-out in the middle of Main Street, and all the men owned and carried pistols.

Then one night there was a terrible fire, started by a drunken man who tipped a lantern. Almost every building in the town burned to the ground. There was no firehouse, there were no hoses, and there was no way to fight the fire except to draw water from the river. Everyone carried bucket after bucket of water, but it did no good. The wooden structures, which had not been wisely built, went up like matchsticks. No one died, not even the drunk who started the fire (although he was run out of town), but there was not much left except ashes.

After the fire quite a few people left. But Owen Marks and Robert Devon, owner of the general store, along with a few others, decided to rebuild. It was a good location, they reasoned— near the river but on high enough ground that it was unlikely to flood. The land is fertile. Gradually, they persuaded a few others to settle there, including several families. Robert opened the land office, and the town began to prosper. Except for the robber-gang episode, it has been quiet and law-abiding ever since, though there seem to be no discernible laws in the Territory despite its having a legislature and a governor, and few people feel obliged to obey the laws of the nation in which Colorado is not yet a full partner.

Murder is a crime anywhere, however, as is robbery, especially stagecoaches and cattle. That's what the Marshals are for. Beyond that, it is difficult to determine any system of justice.

The women made the difference in the town. It was they who drove away all but one saloon (quite a few of the women are temperance, I'm told, and want to ban liquor altogether, but many of the men object to that notion), they who insisted on boardwalk planking on the sidewalks, they who brought the itinerant minister. The women have invited the disreputable "ladies" to leave town. All but one group have left. The women plan a new church, and we have heard they are also trying to get a school started.

I wonder why the widowed Mrs. O'Halleran, who left this farm so hastily after her husband died, did not go to town to seek help? That's what I would have done. Surely the people there would have rallied to her aid, although the town was wilder then, mostly men, not noticeably law-abiding from the stories Lucas tells. Perhaps she preferred to risk the open prairie. We are not to know.

Yet the town is still a little wild, considering the incident Lucas and Mr. Marks just endured. Perhaps that sort of thing won't happen again.

February 3

Adam visited today with disturbing news. He was riding to town yesterday when a shot whizzed just over his head. He thought it came from his left. He turned that direction to find the shooter. Standing only a few yards away from him, pointing his rifle at Adam, was the new neighbor, Mr. Richards.

"You are trespassing," he informed Adam angrily.

"This be the road to town," Adam replied. "Folks all come this way."

"This 'road,' as you call it, is on my property. Stay off it or get shot. Next time, I won't miss." Anger laced Adam's voice as he reported this statement.

Adam is a peaceable man, but he does not like being threatened. He dismounted, his weapon in his hand, planted his feet apart, folded his arms across his chest and told the man to put his rifle down.

The man ignored the request, which Adam said he made politely. "Jacob Richards is my name. *Mister* Richards to you," the man replied.

Adam replied to that by stepping back and bringing his weapon to his shoulder. Richards did not flinch.

Adam's description of the man who stood but a few feet away from him is chilling. He said Richards has the coldest eyes he has ever seen. They look like a dead man's eyes, Adam said.

Richards spoke in a snarling tone. Adam said he was reminded of some of the men in his town in Tennessee who were brutal to the Negroes. They had the same look of hatred and fury.

An odd thing—Adam says Mr. Richards wears a Confederate uniform, complete with cap and boots. Does he not know the war is over?

"Purty foolish for two growed men to shoot each other over a trail," Adam said to us.

"What did you do?" I asked. How did Adam get out of this predicament without getting hurt or hurting someone? I asked. Adam is a large man. He did not say so, but I imagine that Mr. Richards might have weighed his chances and decided against any further confrontation.

"Led my horse acrost the crik, but I never turned my back on the man," Adam said. "Kept my rifle in my hand. Asked him if the land on 'tother side were his too."

Richards replied that his property ended at the creek. "Just be sure y'all remember that," he called to Adam as he rode away.

Like Lucas, Adam never ventures away from home unarmed, but except for hunting he does not use his weapon. To be shot at, to be threatened by a neighbor, was a profound shock to him.

"We'll jest hafta make a new trail on 'tother side the creek," he informed Lucas solemnly.

Lucas was incensed, but he agreed that there was nothing to be served by insisting on using the old trail. Still, he commented that Mr. Richards sounds like a dangerous man, one whom Adam or he—or someone—might have to confront one day. "He seems too eager to shoot at people," Lucas said. "He bears watching."

It does not appear that Mr. Richards is going to be the good neighbor we had hoped.

February 22

Another blizzard, only this time Lucas and I are at home. Thanks to the rope, he is able to get to the animals. The world has disappeared. When he opens the door, all I can see is white swirling everywhere. The wind howls and the snow, so hard and dry, batters the house. We can hear it hitting the walls outside. It is quite different from the soft, wet snow I knew in Ohio.

To my distress, I find that the babe causes me to have to relieve myself more often than formerly. I have no choice but to use the chamber pot, which Lucas empties when he goes out to the stock. I am chagrined to discover that marriage removes all barriers. By its very nature, marriage is intimate, and in this small dwelling our marriage has revealed all there is to know about each other's bodies. Married women who are able to maintain modesty about their bodily functions live in much larger houses than I do.

Perhaps it was the intimacy of the situation, or the sense of confinement; I cannot be sure. But I have at last told Lucas about Karl. And in the telling, I know with finality that it is real: how he would come to my bed at night, force himself upon me, grunting and perspiring, and then threaten to kill me if I told Mama. As if I could ever have found the words, or the courage, to describe such an event to her!

"I never told Mama. I have never told anyone before." I told him how I had asked Mama for a lock on my door, and when she asked me why, I was ashamed to tell her.

Lucas was not angry or upset as I had so feared he would be. Instead he said, so kindly, "It was not your fault, Hannah. You must not blame yourself for this."

"It only happened a few times," I replied. "Then I moved my

dressing table in front of the door at night and blocked it so he could not come in."

"Did he try?"

"The very first night I did that, I could hear him outside the door, rattling the knob. He whispered that I must let him in. I did not respond, and finally he went away. He never came again."

"I wonder that your mother didn't hear him and come out to see where the noise came from," Lucas mused.

I could not keep the bitterness from my voice. "My mother is not a sound sleeper, never has been. She must have heard him, and she chose to stay in her bed. Besides, what could she have done? He is large and strong, and she is not. She is very frightened of him."

"Oh, my darling," Lucas said as he pulled me to him. "It will be hard to forget, but I hope you can, someday. And you know that I will never hurt you."

March 12

It has been some time since I wrote in this journal. Part of the reason is that I feel very lethargic. My body has grown large and cumbersome; moving around takes considerable effort. It is all I can do, most days, to complete my essential chores. After I work even a little, I find I need to rest.

Lucas does not chastise me. "Rest is the best thing," he says. During his most recent examination, he announced that I might be having twins. "I can't be certain," he said, "but I seem to feel more limbs than there should be for one child." He could only discern one heartbeat, however, so it might be only one child after all.

Twins! How on earth could I manage them? We are only prepared for one child. I am hoping that what Lucas is encountering in my womb is my one child being very active. Goodness knows, I am aware of the activity. The child does not seem to sleep—which means I do not, either. It is difficult to find a comfortable position, sitting, standing, or lying down.

March 29

Lucas says the child could come at any time. My time of confinement has finally arrived. I am to stay quiet, stay abed, and wait. I have read and reread my books. Puss comes to sit beside me and purrs softly. I look around the room which has come to be home to me: the chest Lucas and Adam built, the small table and low-backed chairs, the stove, the trunk Lucas found one day, returning from town. It was full of someone's fine linens and such, so sadly abandoned like many other pieces of furniture and goods we saw along the trail—useless, I thought at first, then realized they would do nicely for clothes for the child. And they smelled so lovely; they reminded me of home and the fine linens we had there. The shelf he put up to hold my few books, the small cabinet for dishes and utensils, the hooks for the cooking pots. And of course, the cradle, so nicely carved by Adam and Lucas and lovingly prepared by Alma. She sewed tiny clothes for my baby, knitted blankets, even embroidered a little cap. It's hard to imagine that a human being could be small enough to fit into these garments.

This is my home; this is my life. It has no frills or decorations, not even many comforts. How amazed Mama would be that one could live with so few material possessions and be so content. Yet I am. Spring is in the air. I can open the door and let it in, smell it and almost taste its fragrance, and it soothes me. Never did I inhale such scents in the city! The fresh grass just coming up, the delicate smell of newly arrived flowers, the very air carries a soft perfume.

Except that I am restless now, and tired, and *so* uncomfortable. I don't think I would feel any different in the most plush surroundings imaginable. To think that women have been bearing children for centuries upon centuries! One would suppose there would only be a single child for each family if women had the choice. Unfortunately, we do not. Unless one is married to a man such as Lucas, and one has slaughtered a pig to keep baby after baby from being conceived.

April 20

I was delivered of my child one week ago. It is difficult to write about, but I must set it down on paper. The women I have known did not speak of such things, not even to each other, and we ought to. Lucas says, too, writing of it may help me with my grief.

The pains began very early in the morning. Lucas tended to the animals, then set me to walking around the room to ease the pain and hurry the birth along. I walked for quite some time.

In the hospital, I never attended women who had given birth, never was near when birth was occurring. Mama told me nothing about it. All I knew about what to expect is what Lucas has told me, but he is a man and cannot know this pain, no matter how sympathetic he might be to my suffering. It felt as though my body were being torn in two, which in a way I suppose it was.

After a time an unexpected event occurred; a clear fluid gushed out onto the floor. But Lucas was unsurprised. "Normal," he said. "You are progressing nicely."

Then in several more hours, the pains came more frequently, more harshly. I could hardly breathe for the intensity of them. Sometimes, I think I howled like a wild animal.

Lucas was wonderful, so patient and gentle. He explained to me what was happening and encouraged me to participate in the birth. "Push," he told me. "Push as hard as you can. And breathe deeply." Then he told me to pant. I am quite certain his ways of assisting childbirth are revolutionary! I do not know where he learned these methods. He regards birthing a child as a natural occurrence, not some sort of malady as so many doctors do. And his instructions did help as long as I followed his instructions and did not let my panic rise to the surface.

I was soon lying down and had lost all my dignity. I was engulfed by the agony of the event. It seemed never-ending.

There was a time during this ordeal when the overpowering emotion I experienced was rage. I may have shouted out some words I would not dream of recording here.

There was blood, a good deal of blood. Lucas was somewhat concerned. "You are losing more blood than you should," he told me. "And I don't see the infant crowning." Meaning, he explained, that the head should be visible. Yet I felt an irresistible urge to push the child out. I strained with all my being.

Another eternity passed, filled with indescribable pain, and at last the child presented. Lucas shouted with joy. "It's a girl," he said. "A healthy little girl." In a moment I heard her lusty cry. She was small, he said, which concerned him some, but he carefully cleaned her, put her to my breast, where she nuzzled for food. I looked at her carefully, counted her fingers and toes and admired her head of fuzzy, soft hair. "When she starts to eat, I think she will grow. She looks fine. She's beautiful," Lucas said, emotion cracking his voice.

But alas, we were not done, for there was a twin after all. A boy. Lucas brought him into the world and tried, for how long I do not know, to revive him, to no avail. Little Adam left this life as soon as he entered it. He was so small, so perfect; why could he not have had the breath of life?

How can I feel such joy and such grief at the same time? I have my child, my beautiful, wonderful daughter, but my son is dead. We buried him that same day, saying words over his grave from our Bible. Lucas made a tiny coffin for him from a piece of good maple we had left from making furniture. Oh, Adam, why did you not live? What did I do wrong?

Lucas insists that it is not my fault, that sometimes things go awry and no one knows why. But I shall carry this sorrow and guilt with me the rest of my life. And I shall try again, when I am stronger, to give Lucas a son—a living son.

April 21

To my amazement, I was up and about only a few days after Margaret was born, and none the worse for it. In Cincinnati, after a confinement, a woman would stay abed for weeks, as if she were an invalid. I halfway expected that would be the case with me, but Lucas insisted that I get out of bed on the second day, and by the third day I was almost back to my normal activities.

"Giving birth is a natural act," he reminded me. "Animals are on their feet again within hours afterward. Why should humans be different?" Some of his ideas differ sharply from the expectations of society with which I am familiar, but he is always right. What is wrong is to treat giving birth as an illness, an aberration.

April 27

It is two weeks since this new life entered the world, and neither Lucas nor I have slept more than an hour or two at a time. The infant cries—oh, how she cries!—and breaks my heart, for there seems to be nothing that will ease her distress. I walk with her, I try to feed her, I put on a clean cloth; nothing helps. She cries. I cry. At times I cry for Little Adam (I shall never get over that grief), at times for myself, because I do not know what to do for my child. Lucas says it is her digestion. He thinks perhaps my milk does not agree with her. I am in despair.

April 29

Today Adam, bless his heart, came with a gift. It is an old, worn, wonderful rocking chair. He had found it on the trail some time ago and saved it, since he and Alma still hoped to have a child of their own. But he has decided I must have it; the motion might soothe the baby.

Someone abandoned that chair, which was much beloved, I am sure, on the way west. I am sorry for them, but, oh, so grateful, for this rocking chair appears to be just what tiny Margaret Louisa desired. When I sit there and nurse her, she eats contentedly, then sleeps. Joyous day! And she is growing. Lucas says she is healthy and strong; he examines her daily. He is absolutely enchanted with her. He will be a wonderful father. What a fortunate child she is.

I wonder if Papa was so entranced with Lawrence or me. I don't suppose he was. He was not affectionate toward us when we were small. It was only when we grew older and could talk with him about intellectual topics, exchange ideas, discuss politics, that he showed his care for us. Yet I know he loved us both, even though he did not deem it appropriate to say so.

Margaret resembles her father. She has his large, dark eyes, abundant curly black hair and chocolate skin, though hers is lighter, milk chocolate. That skin is like satin. Are all babies so silky soft? Her face is round, her nose broad, her mouth a rosebud. Lucas insists she looks just like me, but I do not see myself in her. She certainly has my temperament, though; she is very persistent even at this young age. She demands her nourishment.

Looking down at her sweet face brought to mind a memory I have tried to suppress—Mama, holding in her arms a dead child, Karl's child, conceived and birthed long past the time when she should have been having children. Mama was forty-seven when this child came stillborn into the world. I had been away when she was giving birth, delayed at the hospital when a large ambulance arrived full of wounded men. I had known that she was *enceinte,* as Lucas says, but I had not shown much interest in her condition. I think now that her expectancy made me very angry, because the babe was Karl's. I did not want a little brother who looked or behaved like him.

She would not release the babe for some time but held him quietly in her arms, tears coursing down her cheeks. I did not know then and still do not know whether she was crying for the child or for herself. She cannot have been so heartbroken to have lost Karl's child! I say so, yet I must admit to the possibility that Mama cared for Karl and genuinely desired to give him a son. Perhaps it was fear for the consequences that elicited her tears. He was angry indeed when he returned, late at night, from a church meeting, so angry that he stormed out of the house and did not return until morning. I sat with Mama and tried to comfort her.

"You are not to blame, Mama," I assured her. "These things just happen sometimes."

"I am too old to be bearing children, Hannah."

She confided to me then a sad secret I had not known— before I was born, she lost three babies, and one more between me and Lawrence. Two were stillborn like this babe; two times she failed to carry the child long enough. With Papa, she conceived six children and kept only two alive.

"How did it happen that you bore this one?" I am always asking such bold, naïve questions. That one spoke itself before I could prevent it. She looked up from the child, gazing into my eyes for the first time. I saw agony in her eyes that haunts me still.

"Do you suppose I had any choice in the matter? Men demand their rights, and women can do little to prevent the results."

"But there must be something you can do, Mama. Surely you cannot have this happen again."

"You are right; I cannot have another child. I had considerable difficulty this time. The labor lasted an unusually long time, and my womb is very weak, the midwife said. Another time might be fatal, she told me."

"Oh, Mama!"

"There is only one way, which Karl will not accept with good grace."

We buried the child early the next morning, with Karl still gone, just she and I and Mary. That night, Mama moved into the bedroom Lawrence had occupied for so long. Late in the night, I heard Karl pounding on her door, shouting. She must have somehow secured the door.

It was after she moved out of his bedroom that my travail with Karl began. Did she know, or suppose, what he might do?

Why, I wonder, did I not conceive then, when I conceived so quickly after Lucas and I married? Karl was able to father children; the dead baby proved that. Or—dare I suppose such a thing—was the child not Karl's but that of Mama's good friend, James Rogers, Papa's accompanist when he played the violin? Would Mama, could Mama, have deceived her husband so? And me as well, implying so clearly that it was Karl's child? Perhaps that is why Karl was so angry, and why Mama cried so desolately.

I should never have had such daring thoughts if I were still in Karl's house, still confined to his narrow view of the world. Coming out west has opened my eyes to so many things I never considered before.

I recall more than one occasion when I came home from the hospital to find James there, visiting in the parlor, after Mama had married Karl. But they always sat well apart from one another, on either side of the fireplace, and Mama served him tea.

Some tiny part of me wishes that Mama had come to know James in the Biblical sense, or better yet that she had married him instead of Karl. He was so like Papa in some ways, gentle, humorous and kind. He would have treated her well, although we might all have died for lack of food and shelter.

Blasphemous thoughts! I should not have even entered them in this journal, though I intend for no one else to see it. Still, I will destroy these pages tomorrow.

June 2

How long it has been since I wrote in this little book! Between the child and the chores, which still must be done, the days simply vanish. I cook and wash and milk the cow, gather the eggs (hateful chore!), fetch wood, air the bedding. Then I carry water. Somewhere in that time I stop and feed Margaret, who has grown so much. She smiles now, chuckles at Lucas and me. She is becoming a distinct individual. I am charmed by her. But there was an incident today which must be recorded.

I was just returning from the creek with water, Margaret in the sling on my chest, when a large, dark horse with a man astride rode up beside me. To say I was startled is an understatement. I jumped so that some of the water spilled.

The man drew his horse back. "Sorry, señora," he said. "I did not mean to frighten you."

He did not merely startle me; he terrified me. His horse was much larger than either of ours, and the creature was snorting fearsomely; the man sat high on the beast, his face concealed beneath his very large hat, and he was armed, a pistol hanging prominently from the holster at his side. The weapon had a jeweled handle. I put one hand to my throat and tried to control myself.

"Who are you? What do you want? My husband is nearby, in the field." My heart was pounding; my throat was dry. I tried to sound calm. I gestured vaguely toward where Lucas was working. He would not have heard me had I called to him, but it made me feel better that I could see him in the distance. We had a bell I could ring if I needed him, but it was some distance from where we stood at that moment.

The man's face was hidden under his large hat. When he dismounted and removed the hat, I saw that his skin was brown, his hair black, and his eyes weary. "I am Hidalgo, at your service, madam," he said, with a deep bow and a sweep of his hat. "I am on my way north, to seek work at a cattle ranch, and I am in need of water for my horse and for me."

I could see that the horse was tired; its flesh was quivering. They must have come a long way.

He was a Mexican, but not in the least like the frightening stories we have heard of them; he was courteous and well behaved. Still, I was frightened. He was a stranger, and I didn't know what he might do.

"Rosita smelled the water and headed for the creek. I could not hold her back. She was very thirsty. We did not know we were on your land. We have come many miles across the prairie with no sign of water." Indeed, the horse had moved to the creek and was drinking noisily.

"Let me show you the horse trough," I said, feeling a little less afraid, "and I will get you some water from the house." I showed him where he could find food and water for his horse. He left her there, her reins dangling loosely on the ground, and strode back over to stand uncomfortably close to me.

I turned and hurried inside, deposited Margaret in her cradle, and got a cup of water, some biscuits (I have finally learned to bake a respectable biscuit), and a slice of ham. I handed the food and water to him and backed away.

"Gracias," he said. He seemed unaware that I was afraid of him and stepped closer to me again.

"Where did you come from?" I asked.

"We have traveled from Texas," he told me. "I worked on a ranch there, but there was a terrible drought and they lost all their cattle. So I have come to try my fortune here." Though his English was excellent, he spoke with a rich Mexican accent, rolling his "r's" and elongating his words slightly. He smiled as he spoke, showing a row of gleaming white, perfect teeth. I could see that he counted on his good looks and charm to make his way in the world. Not for a vast fortune would I have invited him into my house, and I wished heartily that Lucas would return.

Yet I do not think, looking back on it, that I had anything to fear from the man. Though he was tall and broad and formidable, he made no threatening gestures. Perhaps I was unreasonable to be so apprehensive. Still, there was that pistol on his hip. I believe it is my memories of Karl that have caused me to be so cautious of strange men.

Lucas explained to me, when we talked later, that the culture of Mexico is different from ours when it comes to how men behave toward women. In that country, the women expect men to be polite but somehow intimate at the same time. Here, we expect the politeness but also the distance, until we get to know one another.

After he had eaten the food, drunk his fill and returned the cup, the colorful cowboy thanked me once again, profusely, bowed low, mounted his horse and rode away. "Cross the creek," I called after him and hoped he heard me. "Otherwise, our neighbor may shoot you."

I hate weapons. I have seen the harm they can do. Yet the sudden, unexpected appearance of this stranger has taught me that I must learn to use the new rifle that Lucas purchased not long ago and leaves with me when he goes to the fields. I have told him I would never touch it, I have told him that I do not believe in violence, but when there is a possibility that someone might harm my child, I realize that I must know how to defend myself in order to defend her. How one is changed by motherhood!

Tomorrow, my lessons begin.

June 3

How astonished my Cincinnati friends would have been to see me today. Learning to handle and shoot the rifle was much more challenging than learning to ride a horse. No woman I knew there would ever have dreamed of holding such a weapon, much less shooting it. But I did both today.

The weapon, a Winchester Lucas had purchased from a mail-order catalogue, is large and heavy, heavier than Margaret. He bought the rifle for me but had not pressed me to learn to use it since I have been so occupied with our child. After the incident yesterday, he agreed that the time has come.

"The most important thing is not to hurt yourself," he explained as he showed me how to load the rifle. It is a repeating rifle and holds several shells. If I do not load it properly, or if I mishandle it while cleaning or loading, I could be hurt badly. So the first lesson was how to load and unload—open the trap, load the magazine, close the trap again—and how to clean it. He had me repeat both motions several times until he was satisfied that I had mastered the tasks. I cannot say I became proficient, but I learned well enough.

Then I picked it up, very cautiously, the barrel pointing downward, and he placed the stock against my shoulder. "It's harder for a person with a slight build, like you, to hold it straight and still," Lucas explained. We practiced that for some considerable time, until he was assured that I could hold the weapon steady enough to shoot what I intended to shoot.

I had thought my arms marvelously strong from all the lifting and carrying of heavy objects that I do on the farm, but even such strength did not help when it came to holding up that rifle. And to hold it steady!

I found myself wondering how soldiers do this, over and over again, in the heat of battle. My arm and shoulder were aching fearsomely before I ever fired the thing once. Lucas told me that in battle, soldiers usually kneel or lie on the ground or sit, resting the weapon on one knee. "But you wouldn't have time to do that, if you need to defend yourself," he said. "You need to learn to shoot standing up."

He demonstrated how to sight the target, showing me the small object on top of the barrel, the site, to use as a guide. (I have added so many new terms to my vocabulary today!)

Next he showed me how to cock, or prime, the rifle once it is loaded. Pull the lever down, pull the hammer back, replace the lever. The weapon is then primed, ready to fire. By this time I was trembling with anxiety and fatigue, but Lucas pressed on. My fingers ached; my eyes were tired.

Lucas had fashioned a target for me to practice on. The first time I tried to hit it, the shot went wild because the rifle moved—"kicked," he called it—so much that I had no control over the aim. I had carefully sighted down the barrel as he had taught me to do, and I do have excellent vision. I can see small objects at a considerable distance. I secured my target in my sights, aimed, fired, and nearly fell over backwards.

The discharge was so loud that I instinctively covered my ears with one hand, and the rifle flew away from my grip. I did not drop it, but my shot had not gone anywhere near where I intended. Indeed, the bullet landed in a fence post! Lucas had taken me out to a far end of the field where I would do little damage if a shot went astray, so no harm was done. He, wisely, was standing directly behind me so he would not be in danger.

"Why aren't all soldiers completely deafened by such noise?" I asked him.

He looked at me soberly. "I had not remembered it was quite so loud," he admitted. "It's been some time since I shot a rifle."

"When?" I could not contain my curiosity. How did Lucas, my gentle physician husband, learn to use a weapon at all?

"When I was in the field during the war, I was trained to use a rifle. All the surgeons were, in the event a field hospital was overrun or we had otherwise to defend ourselves."

Of course—I had not thought of that. "Did that ever happen to you?"

He grimaced. "No, thank the Lord. We were always well away from the battles. Had I been taken prisoner by the Confederates. . . ." Neither of us wanted to carry that thought to its conclusion. Never for a moment would they have taken my husband for an exotic foreigner.

Lucas went on, "First, let's put some cotton in our ears to dull the sound. As for the soldiers, you are right. I treated more than a few with damaged or ruined eardrums. I used to offer cotton to the ones returning to battle, but I never did it in the hearing of any of the other doctors, who thought such behavior a foolish affectation of the cowardly."

A brave man, in other words, should be willing to damage his hearing, possibly permanently. How shortsighted men can be in the name of pride! I kept those thoughts to myself, for even my dear Lucas sometimes falls prey to this malady.

Once he had stuffed my ears and his own, we spent another quarter of an hour or so practicing my grip on the rifle, and the position, so that I would be less likely to let go again. Then I tried once more to hit the target. Lucas explained that I must learn to hold it steady even though it kicks against my shoulder.

After so many tries I lost count, I did hit the right edge of the target. Lucas declared himself satisfied for the first lesson. He showed me how to hold and carry the rifle, barrel pointing down into the ground (and not at my foot!).

Tonight, as I undressed to put on my nightgown, I discovered that my right shoulder was bruised black and blue. It is exceedingly sore. Lucas put some liniment on the bruises. He agrees that I can wait a few more days for another lesson, but he also says that in time my body will become hardened to the jolt from the butt of the rifle. I thought again of soldiers and pitied them. I am learning how to shoot only because I know I must be able to defend my child should the situation require me to, not because I must use a weapon in battle over and over again, live or die, kill in order to survive. Why would anyone *choose* to be a soldier?

July 4

Independence Day—not a holiday on a farm, though I'm told that they celebrate more in town, with fireworks and a picnic and games. I'd enjoy going sometime, perhaps when Margaret is a little older. Here on the farm we simply went about our work, as did Alma and Adam. No matter what special day people might decide it to be, the livestock must be cared for, the chores must be done, the crops must be tended.

Our new neighbor, Mr. Richards, keeps to himself so far. Alma and I had spoken of taking him some pies as a welcoming gift, thinking it might render him a little more neighborly, but we have heard some unsettling things about him, so we hesitate. It's said that whenever he goes to town he wears his rebel uniform, and that he hangs a rebel flag on the gate at the edge of his ranch. I do not want to get better acquainted with a former defender of slavery. What might he make of Lucas and me?

It is dreadfully hot. Lucas comes in from the field by noon so as to stay out of the worst of the heat. He advises me to stay inside with Margaret. One advantage of sod houses is that they stay cool even in the dead of summer.

It continues to surprise me that, despite the fact that all the buildings are completed for now—the barn, the chicken coop, the privy, the cold cellar—there is still so much work for both of us to do.

Lucas is starting to build fence. (I regard this as a sign that he has given up on going to California, for a fence is part of our homesteading requirement.) Like other tasks, it is backbreaking work. When he can be spared from his own farm, Adam comes and helps. We owe the Baumgartens a debt we can never repay, except by trying to be good neighbors ourselves.

Today Lucas informed me that he must go to town again to purchase supplies. Now that I know how to use the rifle, I am less afraid, but I wish he would not go. He is always excited and cheerful about going to town and seems not to worry much about how I will fare without him. If he is concerned, in any event, he does not express his feelings. I trust we will not have a repeat of his last trip! There is a new sheriff now, we are told, a Mr. Musgrave, who appears to have sufficient stomach for his job. And of course there are more and more upstanding women in the town, a steadying influence. Would that I could go with him, but who would tend to the animals? And how difficult would the trip be for Margaret, bouncing about in the wagon?

The crops are planted; we can but wait for nature to nourish them. So far, we have had little rain. Lucas is concerned that the vegetables will not survive. We may have to draw water from the creek to water the crops, he says.

I have planted a small fruit tree, an apple sapling that Alma spared from her orchard, on Little Adam's grave. I water it every day. I do not expect fruit this year, but perhaps in another year or two it will bear for us. The grave is on a small knoll behind the house, near my kitchen garden, where it is sheltered from the wind and storms. I have marked it with rocks that spell his name.

September 13

A dreadful thing happened today. I do not know how we will recover from it.

No one warned us that cattle ranchers have primacy over private land when they are taking their cattle to market. No one warned us that a large cattle ranch near Laramie, in Wyoming Territory, would be driving their cattle this way as they went south. We woke up this morning to a thundering sound the likes of which I have never heard. Hordes of lowing beasts roared right through our fields, through the crops we were almost ready to harvest, trampling everything in their path!

The sound is indescribable. The cattle bawling, the horsemen shouting and waving their hats, the horses neighing, the hooves pounding on the ground. It was worse than a freight train. It was terrifying. Lucas, Margaret and I stayed in the house, praying the cattle would not turn toward it. The fence Lucas had erected proved useless in the face of this onslaught. He will have to do it all over again, more sturdily. Could not someone have warned us about this?

After the animals had moved through, we surveyed the damage. Nearly all of our carefully tended crop was trampled to bits. The hay field was half ruined. The fence was destroyed. Thankfully, they did not destroy Little Adam's grave and the fruit tree or my small kitchen garden, all behind the house and sheltered by the little knoll there. But my kitchen garden does not have enough in it to feed us for the winter.

We wondered what would happen when the cattle invaded Mr. Richards's land. We speculated that he might try to drive them off with gunfire. But we heard no distant gunshots, only the fading sounds of the animals as they moved on.

For the first time since we left St. Louis, Lucas showed discouragement. He put his head in his hands.

"I can see now why people give this up," he said. "Storms, insects, drought—is that not enough? Now we have cattle trampling our fields."

"What shall we do, then?" I asked, feeling as disheartened as he. "Shall we, like the O'Hallerans, abandon our efforts and go elsewhere, to try again? Shall we go back to Ohio? Or to France, perhaps?" I did not mention the prospect of going to California, although it must have been in his mind.

He did not answer me but stayed with his head bowed for a very long time. We could not seem to find any way to comfort each other, to give each other strength. I do not know what we shall do.

October 1

Once again my natal day arrives. We have three birthdays to mark now—mine on this day, Margaret's on April 13, and Lucas's, August 18. I am writing today early in the morning, before my family rises, because I wish to contemplate this day.

When I was growing up, birthdays were noted and celebrated until Papa went away. The birthday person received gifts and favorite foods and a gaily decorated cake. It was the tradition in our house that the birthday celebrant could choose the menu for the evening meal. My favorite foods, the meal I always chose: roast beef with gravy, mashed potatoes, cornbread, and chocolate cake for dessert. Just thinking about it makes my mouth water. I could manage such a meal here, except for the cake, but does one want to prepare one's own birthday meal?

After Karl, of course, such "blasphemous" activities as celebrating birthdays went by the boards. Poor Lawrence had far fewer joyous celebrations than I.

Lucas has many virtues, but kitchen skill is not one of them. Before we married, he took all his meals at the hospital or the small café across from his rooms, and I fear he ate rather irregularly. He never learned to cook (to my regret; I understand the French cook wonderfully well). As for me, I am learning the art under these challenging circumstances, but I do not wish to cook this meal. So perhaps we will simply have cold ham and some vegetables from the cold cellar.

Reflecting on my circumstances this day, I am noticing a small seed of discontent growing within. At times I feel imprisoned by this house, this land, as if I will never be able to live a more fulfilling life again.

How can I want any more than what I have? My life *is* fulfilling. I have my husband, my child, freedom from Karl. I was not forced to marry Wilhelm Hessler. I have Alma, my good friend. I must not yearn for what I cannot have, since it was my decision to leave that life behind.

Adam says there is now a church in Johnson City. (Of course, there has been a Catholic church for some time, but we did not choose to have our child baptized there, not being Catholics.)

Our good friend the itinerant minister has gone elsewhere, since the new church is staunchly Presbyterian. I think we will take Margaret one day soon, when there is a minister established, to be christened. I must start to work on a christening dress for her. That ceremony would vastly please Adam and Alma, who are to be her godparents. I do not think Lucas cares for such things.

Far more important than pleasing Adam and Alma is that our daughter be accepted by the community where she is to grow up. It is expected that children will be christened, and it is part of what ties one to others, part of how we become true members of the community. It is not in order to show Margaret to God that I want her christened; it is to show her to the people of Johnson City.

Religion is one topic Lucas and I have not discussed much, not even during our lively conversations at the hospital. I asked him once if he had been a Catholic while living in France, and he said only that his mother had not attended any church. I wondered, later, if that was because the churchgoers would not have accepted her presence gracefully. Perhaps even in the very free French society, courtesans are not welcome in houses of worship.

"But did she teach you to believe in God?" I asked him.

"She taught me to have faith," he replied. That was all he would say on the subject. He may think me too sensitive to talk about religion, given what he knew about Karl's fanaticism.

Before Karl came into our lives, the religion in our home was the god of thoughts and ideas. Imbued with Enlightenment philosophies, Papa taught us to think things out for ourselves, to explore and discuss ideas, to revere the wonders of nature and to rejoice in love. Like Lucas, I did not go to church. Papa taught us about Christianity and other religions and said we should choose for ourselves when the time came. He was a man of peace.

October 2

Lucas did remember my birthday, although he did not offer to prepare a meal yesterday. He brought me a new book, one which he had ordered from an eastern publisher. It is *The Gilded Age*, by Mr. Twain. I shall greatly enjoy reading it!

November 4

Adam and Alma visited a few days after the devastation occurred. Adam was profusely apologetic. "I knew they was comin'," he said. "I meant to warn ya. Then I got the flux and next thing I knowed, they was come and gone."

He felt guilty about not telling us about the annual cattle run, he said. He offered us half of his corn crop, which had been bountiful in spite of the drought, and he said he would help Lucas put up hay.

He explained how to build the fence sturdily enough that the cattle would be forced to go around it. We have to leave a path for them, he said, but we can protect the bulk of our property and crops. He said he would come in the spring and help Lucas put up the fence. It will be of barbed wire, a new invention and quite discouraging to cattle, Adam says. He describes it as strands of wire that have sharp, twisted spikes sticking out of them every few inches. If an animal encounters the jagged edge, it will get cut, possibly severely.

He then said something most startling. The cattle, he has learned, belong to Richards! He owns a ranch in Wyoming Territory. Why does he live here then, we wondered. Adam has heard that he plans to buy up all the land he can around ours to grow hay for his cattle, because the land where they are kept is not productive enough; it is too dry, mountainous and windy there.

I am puzzled at his judgment; sometimes, it is exceedingly dry here as well, and the wind blows constantly. But Adam says the wind is much fiercer in Wyoming Territory and tends to dry out the land much more than here. I had not perceived the winds on our plains as gentle breezes, but it would appear that they are mild in comparison to those that whip across the more northern plains.

Mr. Richards will continue to run his cattle through here on their way to market. Lucas does not choose to visit him and talk about any kind of compromise or ask recompense for the damage that was done. My husband, too, prefers not to have dealings with someone who still wears a Confederate uniform. We can anticipate further difficulties with our new neighbor, I fear.

Ever since the cattle run, Lucas had been awash in despair. He had talked of leaving, but somehow *ennui* set in and he did nothing about it. No—more than simply *ennui*. Darkness. He would not smile, even at Margaret. He ate very little, though I tried to prepare tempting foods. He seldom spoke but went about his chores mechanically, like someone in a dream. He showed no interest in marital relations. Sometimes, he sat at the table for a long time, simply staring into space.

He could not decide, it seemed, where to go or what to do. It's the same unwillingness to commit to a decision (except where the practice of medicine is concerned) that I discovered in him while in Ohio. It almost seems that he is leaving the decision to me. I do not feel it is mine to make; we must make it together or not at all. I wonder, looking back, whether Lucas would *ever* have come away with me had not Karl forced his hand.

So now, as Adam made his confession and offered his aid, Lucas looked almost cynical. He seemed to think Adam was simply humoring him.

"Why are you doing this, Adam?" Lucas asked at length. He stood still, saying nothing, for a very long moment. "Why not see us just move on, another failed attempt to homestead?"

In a rare gesture, Adam patted Lucas's shoulder awkwardly. "Alma and me is grown fond of you folks," he said. "Too, we kinda like havin' a doc around. More folks will come and stay, and you'll be needed to do yore doctorin', which yore a whiz at. So we figger least we kin do is help with yore farmin', which you ain't too good at."

For the first time in days, Lucas smiled. Then he clapped Adam on the back. (His moods can change so quickly!) "You, my friend, are the soul of honesty," he said, laughing. "No

wonder I like you so much. Very well—we will hang on and look
to the day when I can make my living practicing my art instead
of farming the soil."

(How I love listening to my husband talk! His accent is different, exotic and foreign, and he has not lost it since coming
here. I could listen to him all day.)

We are still here.

1874

January 2, 1874

Dearest Mama,

It is winter again on the prairie. Your granddaughter is now nine months old. She is her own very distinctive little person, with desires and dislikes. Though small, she is sturdy and has a healthy appetite. And she is so beautiful, Mama. How I wish you could see her.

Lucas and I have come through a hard year but have decided to stay on our homestead in spite of it all. Were we to return to Ohio, we would not be regarded legally as man and wife. Were we to travel to Europe, I would not know the language or the culture. Margaret would not grow up in her native land. Someday, here, we will have a real home.

I have drawn a portrait of Margaret for you. My skill has diminished, I fear, for lack of practice and opportunity. I wonder sometimes if I shall ever be able to play the piano again, should the chance come my way. I miss my music very much, almost as much as I miss you and Lawrence.

You would find my little home, with its handmade furniture, sod walls and dirt floor, quaint and crude, but it is Lucas's and mine, and I love it. We have been so happy here.

I have also made a sketch of Freedom and Puss in Boots for you. They are sweet little creatures. You would adore them.

I trust this finds you in good health.

Your,

Hannah

January 21

How hard it is to absorb that I left all that was familiar to me almost *two years ago!* I have a small house on the prairie, a sweet, bright daughter, a loving husband and dear little pets. We have survived.

But today, the wind howled brutally. Lucas fought against it to get to the barn. Margaret fussed. When Lucas opened the door, I could see debris flying by, little bits of wood, dried weeds, branches. I hope my small apple tree can withstand such a torrent. There was no snow, just the dry, bitter wind. We usually have wind here, but this is far more fierce than usual.

Alma and Adam visited a few days ago. While the men were outside measuring the boundaries for the fence, Alma asked of me a favor, which I am only too happy to grant her.

"Kin ya teach me to read, Hannah?" she said, so softly I almost could not hear her.

"Of course I can, Alma. I'd be delighted," I replied. "But why now?"

She explained that all her life she had longed for an education. Learning to read seemed far out of reach in her poor family. No one in the Appalachian Mountains of her childhood read; few went to school. Girls were considered lacking in intelligence and were destined for marriage in any case, so "book learning" was thought to be wasted on them. Yet she had yearned. Adam doesn't hold much with women learning to read, she says. Women have their place, and it's not in the world of men. To him, education is for those who must make their way in the world other ways, not from the soil.

Alma's primary motive for learning to read is so that she can understand the words in her Bible, which has sat unread in her parlor for many years. A gift from an aunt who lived in the city and once came to visit, it is a cherished possession, she has told me. She longs to be able to read the words in it. She never saw her chance to learn to read until she met me. In my small home, she sees books. She sees me reading books to Margaret. It had been growing on her for some time that perhaps I might find it in my heart to share the great secret with her, and on this day she found the courage to ask.

I could not be more pleased. A chance at last to repay some of the many kindnesses she has shown me. I have begun to think how to go about it. (I never taught anyone to read before, and it occurs to me that what comes easily to me may be excessively difficult to someone else.) It will be practice for me, too, because if there is no school yet for Margaret, I must teach her to read in a few years as well.

So I embark on yet another adventure. Alma has taught me so much; it is a joy to have a skill which I can teach her in return.

February 16

There are many chores required of me that I dislike, though I have come to accept them and be reasonably skilled, but the worst of all, surely, must be laundry. It takes an entire day! I start by boiling the water, then haul it to the tub in the yard, then immerse the clothes in the tub. With a thick, long stick, I move them around in the soapy water until I begin to see the dirt come out. Some I take out and run up and down the scrubbing board. Then I have to lift them out, rinse out the suds in the other tub, and wring them out as best I can with my two hands before I hang them on the clothesline.

My hands grow red and raw and the skin cracks on laundry

day. I never knew what a hard life our maid, Mary, had! The clothes were washed and returned to us clean and sweet smelling, and if I knew of the labors in between, I am afraid I paid no attention. For shame! I should have better appreciated how difficult this work is and been grateful. She should have been better paid.

I do like the clean clothes that have been whipped about by the prairie winds. When I take them off the clothesline and fold them in the basket, I like to put my nose up next to the garments and drink in the smell—but by that time I am so weary that I can scarcely get the basket back into the house without dropping it. How dreadful that would be; I would have to wash them all over again!

My days have taken on patterns. Bake on Monday, sew on Tuesday, wash on Wednesday, iron on Thursday, change the linens on Friday. . . . All this I must accomplish while still doing my regular daily chores, preparing meals, and caring for my child, who grows livelier by the day.

The laundry is my special bane. It takes all day and by the end my hands are hopeless.

Lucas, of course, works as hard as I in different ways. At night he still has interest, sometimes, in romance. I, alas, do not always have as much interest as he does. On some nights, especially after laundry day, I fall asleep as soon as my head touches the pillow.

And to my sorrow, there seems little time or energy for engaging our minds. I miss the enriching conversations we used to have, sometimes even on the trail west and after we first came. But now fatigue has overtaken us and turned our minds to dust.

March 12

Alma is learning very rapidly. I have brought out all the books I think will be easiest for her to master. I have taught her the alphabet and explained how the sounds go together. She is very quick. I believe I could teach others just as I have taught her. It is indescribably exciting to see the light in her eyes when understanding comes. To hear her read is the purest pleasure.

She has not told Adam. Though I am reluctant to keep secrets from my dear husband, I have not divulged this secret to him either. Lucas would not mind, of course, would indeed be pleased. But if I tell him, he might—quite without intending to—let slip the secret to Adam, who would be displeased with me and with his wife, says Alma. I asked her why Adam, who is such a kind and generous man, would mind that his wife had learned to read.

" 'Cuz he cain't," she said simply.

"Could you not teach him? Or could I?"

"He be too proud to have a woman teach him," she replied.

Alas, for all his excellent qualities, it appears Adam is quite old-fashioned when it comes to the place of women. What shall her new knowledge avail her if she cannot share it with her husband?

When Alma comes with Adam, the men go outside and we have our time together in the house. When Lucas next goes to town, I will ask him to bring me some new books, and we will share those. We have read Mr. Dickens and Miss Alcott, Mr. Hawthorne and Mr. Poe. Alma especially liked *A Christmas Carol.*

It is a particular joy to me that, as she masters reading, Alma's grammar improves and her vocabulary grows. She is much more careful in her speech. Surely Adam will notice that, and comment? But perhaps she is only more precise when she is with me.

I have not, however, shared with her my book by Mr. Darwin, which came west with me. Papa was enamored of the concepts

Mr. Darwin presented, and he wrote in the book. When Karl moved in, I hid Papa's Darwin; Karl would have tossed it into the stove. I'm afraid Alma, too, would find it shocking. It is a great controversy of our age, this proposal that man descended from apes. I find it not illogical, however, and I admire Mr. Darwin's courage in presenting his ideas to the world. But Alma, a deeply religious person who believes that the Bible is the word of God, would not accept or understand his premise, I am sure, and I would never willingly offend her.

A significant number of Christians object strongly to man's being linked in any way to apes and maintain stoutly that mankind began with Adam and Eve, as the Bible says. The idea of man's evolving from any lower life-form is repugnant to them. Alma and I have not talked extensively in this vein, but I am quite certain her beliefs are along these lines of thought.

I recall many lively conversations, during brief respites at the hospital, about this very topic. Mr. Darwin stirred up a hornet's nest that is not yet becalmed. Lucas was always deep in the midst of the discussions, as was I. Sometimes several of the doctors joined us, seeming not to mind my presence even though I am a woman. Among us, during those conversations, there were few who doubted Mr. Darwin. Those who did were the Christians who take the Bible as true gospel, like Alma. Most of the doctors, men of science, seemed willing to wait for evidence to come in one way or the other.

Like my father, I take a scientific and inquisitive approach to religion. I do pray. In spite of Karl's image of God, I believe in Him, but my God is benevolent, unlike Karl's. Yet I also believe mankind must be open to new ideas that science presents us. Perhaps, however, it is more difficult for a man of science such as my husband to reconcile the idea of a deity with the discoveries of science. I must talk to Lucas more about this some time when we are more refreshed.

We had snow today, a screaming blizzard that seemed to shake this unshakable house. Lucas says it is good, the snow, because it seeps into the soil and melts into the waterways. It also discourages the locusts which have plagued the settlers in this area for several years. The scourge might end, if the winter is cold enough. We were not unduly troubled by the rapacious little insects last summer because Adam had bought some turkeys to eat them up before they arrived here. But some settlers nearer Johnson City were completely wiped out, we are told. It's said the locusts eat everything in their path—fence posts, clothing on the clothesline, ropes, trees, not to mention anything growing in the fields. They arrive in hordes, like a black cloud, devour all they see, and move on.

Tonight it still snows. Spring does not seem to be a reliable season here on this high plain. One might experience snow, or hail, or rain, or balmy days with bright, warm sunshine and spring flowers. The weather is unpredictable at best.

The house is quite dark. I am writing by candlelight, Margaret sleeping peacefully in the cradle beside me. She has grown so rapidly that she will soon need a larger bed. Where we will put it, I do not know.

In a moment I will set this aside and join my dear husband in the bed, where he awaits me with love in his eyes. On those nights when we both have enough energy for desire, I cannot let the opportunity pass. (Another subject far too delicate for my eastern-bred mother. Conjugal relationships, conjugal joys, are a deep, dark secret, not to be mentioned in polite company. It must be this new place, this isolation and sense of freedom, that move me to express thoughts I would never have allowed to the surface of my mind in my previous life.)

March 31

Spring is making tentative visits now. The wildflowers have started to appear in the fields. Meadowlarks have returned to nest. I hear their beautiful song and it lifts my heart. There is no more ice in the creek. Lucas and Adam will finish the fence this spring, and we will plant more of the fields.

After seeing the raw power of nature these last months, I ponder how it is that farmers can plant, year after year, in the cheerful belief that this time the crops will thrive. Nature will not intervene, the crops will grow, the fruit trees will bear. Lucas and I seem to have been infected by that viewpoint, for here we are. He has said nothing about California for many months.

Margaret is almost one year old. She walks now, rather unsteadily, lurching about the house touching, exploring, crowing over her discoveries. I love watching her walk on her sturdy little legs. What a joy she is!

We plan to go to Johnson City next Sunday for Margaret's christening. If we take the wagon and follow the more direct trail Adam and Lucas have made since the arrival of Mr. Richards, we can get there and home again in daylight. Adam and Alma will accompany us. I find myself quite excited at the prospect.

April 13

We have not gone to Johnson City, for Margaret is ill. She fell ill the day before we had planned to go. Lucas does not know what is wrong, but he suspects typhus. He queried me fiercely: Have I *always* boiled the water? Have I been certain all her food was clean and free of contaminants? She is still nursing. Dear God, did *I* give her this dread disease?

I am certain I have been careful. I have taken great precautions. What could have made her so ill? How can a child be the picture of health one moment and so near death the next? She tosses and cries. Her forehead is burning up. Days have gone by, and she seems no better. I cannot bear it if she dies. Lucas has spent every moment with her that he can spare from chores. There is so little he can do. His special herbs avail nothing. He prepared a brew which he thought might help, but she spat it out again. He has put plasters on her little chest, put a cloth soaked with camphor on her mouth—nothing helps. Nothing changes.

With his stethoscope he listens to her tiny heart beating. He takes her pulse and times it with his pocket watch. Then he turns away, his face a mask. What does he hear? Why does he not tell me?

To listen to my child gasp for breath, to see her whole body heaving as she coughs, is torturous. I clasp her hand, bathe her forehead and her skin, put a wet cloth to her parched lips. I hold her for hours at a time. I can see how hard she is fighting for life. She does not give in to death but struggles constantly against it. I thank God for that, but I do not know if it is enough. She is so small, so helpless.

We have no hope but prayer. I know I must sleep, yet I cannot. I doze in the rocking chair, but when I hear her whimper or cry, I start up and go to her. Today, she is one year old. This cannot, must not, be the last, the only year of her life!

I would give my own life to save hers. I have never known such agony as to see my child so ill, with no remedy in sight. If she dies, I don't think I want to live any longer. I cannot bear to lose her.

Lucas cried today. Though he made no sound, I could see the tears streaming down his cheeks. He must be so disheartened that he can do nothing to save her. Yet he says nothing. She seems no better.

April 14

Margaret lives. One moment she was gasping and thrashing about; the next, she fell into a peaceful sleep, her chest moving up and down as any child's would instead of heaving with effort from each breath. She is still very pale, and I am certain she has lost weight, but she will recover now, her father assures me.

It can only have been the prayers, for all of Lucas's magic and knowledge failed us. She is very weak. Lucas says we must get her to eat as much as she can as often as she will, to build up her strength. I rock her in the chair and tempt her with favorite foods. Would that I could keep her safe in my arms forever. I have no words for my gratitude and relief.

Lucas has named her illness pneumonia, an inflammation of the lungs. Such young children very seldom contract it, he says. Where did the evil miasma come from? Would that it could have been I who attracted it, not she. She is still so pale, yet I can see life in her eyes, and interest in the world around her.

We are late with the planting. He did not go to town to buy seed. He would not leave his daughter. I only hope it is not too late. He will leave tomorrow. We will postpone the christening until Margaret is stronger. Lucas has begun to emerge from wherever he has been. He is talking to me again, and he sounds more like himself.

April 25

Day by day Margaret and I are recovering, I from the exhaustion of tending and nearly losing her, she from her terrible illness. Soon, we will be back to normal again. After I got past the terror of thinking she was going to die, thoughts of Mama came to me. I remembered the first time Lawrence was ill with some frightening ague. Her eyes were ringed with black, she stumbled in her fatigue, but she would not leave his side no matter how Papa pleaded with her to get some rest. At the time, I resented all the attention my little brother was getting, and I fear I behaved rather peevishly. Now, I understand.

June 2

Lucas has not reached for me at night in some time. Our child is well, the planting is done, life has resumed its usual rhythms. What is wrong? Does he find me repulsive?

Why is it so hard for women to ask their husbands, their most intimate companions, such questions? I long to know; I fear the answer. I wait for him to desire me again.

How can I even think of such things when my daughter has been so ill? Perhaps it is the impulse toward life, the relief that death did not cross our threshold this time, that moves us to desire. I don't understand, but I do yearn.

July 1

Today is the anniversary of our marriage two years ago. Lucas is still distant from me. I feel that I must approach the subject soon or see our precious marriage, our love, begin to dissolve. I do not want to live as Mama lives, in a loveless marriage.

It is early morning. He has gone to do the chores. Margaret still sleeps. How beautiful she is when asleep, her lashes brushing her cheeks, now rosy again at last, her breathing so soft and slow. How I love her.

July 2

A situation has arisen, one I never could have envisioned when I married, and I do not know how to respond. It happened again last night, as it has happened the last two times Lucas has turned to me with love in his eyes.

Margaret was sleeping quietly. I got into the bed and put my arms around my husband as I so often do. He sighed and responded by pulling me close. I fully expected matters to proceed as they usually do—but they did not.

"Lucas, what's wrong? Do you not love me anymore? Why don't you . . . ?"

He lay on his back, his arms under his head, and looked at the ceiling instead of at me as he spoke.

"Lucas, do you not love me anymore?"

"I love you very deeply," he said slowly. "I do not know why I am unable to show you my love in the usual way. I wish it; I expect it, and it does not happen."

"Why?" I asked, astonished. He has ever been a virile man.

"I don't know," he said. "I hope that in time—soon—I will return to normal. I don't know the cause of this . . . inability."

I was awash in relief. It was not I, then, who held him back, but some physical problem from which he would surely soon recover. It was mortification, not revulsion, that kept him from me. And I, in my ignorance and greed, had forced him to speak of it. I felt ashamed of my selfishness.

"It happened to me once before, long before I met you," he said. "The doctors in Vienna did not know the cause. They told me that in time I would return to normal. I came to America and buried myself in my work. After a time, I was indeed normal again. I would not have married you otherwise. But now the problem has returned."

(In a flash of anger and jealousy, I was led to wonder just *how* he discovered that he was once again virile, who was the beneficiary of that recovery, but I did not speak that thought.)

He paused, sighing again. "Lack of virility in a man is a subject doctors do not like to discuss and have no idea how to approach. For all my medical knowledge and my years of study, I know no more than any other physician about it. A Greek essay I once read suggested that it may be caused by excessive fatigue and anxiety. Perhaps I have simply used myself up on other efforts."

I said no more but moved close to him so that he would be assured of my continued love.

Now I can only wait for him to let me know when he has regained his manliness. I do so want to give him a son! How ironic that my husband, as skilled a doctor as walks this earth, cannot cure his own inability. Even the unusual remedies of which he is so fond have availed him nothing for this condition, he says.

Once again I have written in this journal of unspeakable things. If Mama's husband had made such a confession to her (although I cannot imagine that happening), she would never have spoken of it to anyone, not even to God in her prayers, much less committed it to paper. I'm afraid her daughter has become far too forward for her taste. (Yet another page I must destroy someday. The cooking fire will make a nice pyre for these daring entries.)

August 5

A preacher is coming to the new community church (different from the Presbyterian one—there are now three churches in Johnson City!) in September, and we will take Margaret to be christened at last. When we were to go before, in April, I had spoken with Lucas about the dangers of taking her to town and having people recoil at seeing her beautiful light-brown skin, the color of milk chocolate. "Perhaps," I said to him, "they will not even allow her to be christened in their church."

Lucas assured me that he had spoken with one of the church leaders, who was certain it would not be a problem. Our plan was to have the christening ceremony following the regular church service so as not to be so conspicuous. We still have the same plan. We will have to sit through the service beforehand, of course. What will these townspeople, especially the women, make of our little family? I confess it makes me uneasy to think

138

of it, but Lucas says we must face whatever will come, for this is the place we have chosen as home, and we want the people to know us. Some may even like us. We have, we realize, been living in an island of illusory kindness out here on the homestead, with only the compassionate Baumgartens for friends, but I know how cruel people can be. I know the ridicule and condemnation we may face. Still, I will try to be hopeful and believe the best of people.

September 11

I write with delight in this journal that Lucas has once again "returned to normal," as he describes it. We may have to slaughter another pig to keep pace with all his activity! Neither of us knows what brought about this welcome change, but both of us are grateful.

Last month Lucas attained the astounding age of six and thirty years. "An old man," I teased him. We have begun to harvest the crops and to prepare once again for winter. Next Sunday, we will take Margaret to church for her christening, at last.

September 25

Margaret Louisa Bowman is now official in the eyes of God and, more importantly, of the people of Johnson City. Would that we had done this on another day, however. We set out on the appointed day at dawn. Using the new trail, which does not follow the creek, we had only twelve miles to go. I drank in the beauty of the prairie as we rode—the waving yellow grass, the wildflowers, the blue, blue sky. Even after all this time, I am still awed by that vast expanse of blue. The silence of the prairie is so profound. I heard the creaking of the wagon, the clomping of the horses, the sighing of the grasses, the conversations of birds, the whisper of small creatures as they moved about. In a city one would never notice such small sounds. I felt as if I were wrapped in a cocoon of serenity and happiness.

We took the wagon so Lucas could get supplies while we were there. (The general store is now open on Sundays, only after noon when church lets out, much against the wishes of many women of the town, but the merchant insists he needs the business.)

I worry about money. Lucas does not talk to me about it, although I have asked him. He merely says, "We have enough." As far as I can determine, we have taken in no money since starting out from St. Louis, and we have spent a considerable amount for lumber, stock and food. Are we not in danger of running out of funds? I have none to contribute. Yet Lucas seems unconcerned about it.

We have been so much partners, not master and servant like Mama and Karl, that I am distressed at his reluctance to take me into his confidence. I know that he had money, left to him by Roxie, brought over from France, but I've no notion how much. For all his modern concepts, Lucas seems to be very old-fashioned when it comes to financial matters.

For myself, I lived with so little money for so long while under the thumb of Karl that I cannot fathom what it is like to have enough, or more than enough. Thriftiness becomes a habit. Oh, there was money in my household. Karl lived well. We ate well, and we had a servant. But I had very little money of my own and grew accustomed to being extremely careful with what funds I had.

When we got to town, church was just starting. We entered and sat in the back, Adam and Alma beside us. Perhaps no one noticed us. The sermon seemed unnecessarily long to me, although by my timepiece it was only forty-five minutes or so. I have not sat through a sermon for some time, however; perhaps my perception is flawed. The Baumgartens were named as Margaret's godparents. The christening ceremony was quite satisfactory, especially since my precious child so recently went through the valley of the shadow. She looked lovely in her white lace christening dress, made by Alma.

As we walked to the front of the church, I saw half a dozen women stand up, turn to give us hateful looks, and leave hastily. One even said to her companion, "Disgusting." My heart tightened, for I know why they left. Indeed, I was surprised they had not left when we entered the church. Their actions seem quite unchristian to me, but I do understand that society has great difficulty accepting love between a woman of my race and a man such as Lucas, dear, kind and handsome though he is.

We got through the christening; that's what is important. I agreed to this mainly because Alma desired it so and felt it would help us be accepted in the town and because, deep in my heart, I knew Mama would wish it.

After church, Alma, Margaret and I took our picnic lunch and found a shady spot under one of the huge cottonwood trees that line the river. We had no sooner sat down than we heard a horrible shrieking. Looking around, we saw a woman running out of a small house across the river. She was screaming, "Help! He's going to kill me!" Lucas and Adam, who had just started toward the general store with the wagon, leaped down and ran to the bridge, the river being too deep to wade across and too swift-running to swim. Meanwhile, Alma and I watched in horror as a man wielding a large knife followed the woman out the door, brandishing the weapon fiercely. The woman ran desperately, but he caught up to her. Lucas and Adam still had not crossed the bridge.

The man grasped the woman by her long hair, drew her head back and slashed her throat. I covered Margaret's eyes. Alma gasped in horror. Lucas and Adam finally reached the house. The woman was on the ground, the man standing over her with the bloody knife still in his hand. Margaret began to whimper. I realized that I was shielding her sight too firmly and let go. She was too young to understand or remember, I thought. Her interest was quickly diverted by a small carved toy I had in my bag. Alma took to praying fervently.

Lucas bent over the woman. We could see blood streaming from her body. In a moment he stood up. Although we could not hear all of what he said, the word "dead" floated across the water. The man had killed her, just as she'd feared, before our very eyes, and no one was able to prevent it.

Gently, Lucas lifted up the woman and began to carry her across the bridge. (It crossed my mind that the townspeople, many of whom had gathered by then, would be upset to see my husband with a white woman in his arms—but the horror and chaos of the scene prevailed, and no one objected. Some of them know that he is a physician. Some believe he comes from some exotic Far Eastern land.)

Pulling the man's arms behind his back and forcing him to walk, Adam restrained the killer, who was standing quite still, looking dazed. He staggered as though inebriated. They crossed the bridge together that way. Once back across the river, they found a large gathering of townspeople waiting, including the sheriff, who promptly handcuffed the murderer and took him to the jail.

Ours is a nation of laws, but Colorado is a territory; some of its inhabitants must believe that they do not have to obey any laws at all. Brutal killer that he was, the man was entitled to a trial by jury, as it says in the Constitution. He did not get one. That very night an angry mob broke into the jail, overpowered the sheriff (who by all accounts tried valiantly to stop them), hauled the killer away and hung him in the dark of night. "Frontier justice," Adam called it when he told us about it a few days later. I call it mob rule, and it frightens me.

I am still having bad dreams about what I saw. In time I am sure they will fade, but just now they continue to haunt me. Poor woman! Why could we not have saved her? It seems the ultimate irony that we had just come from church, where the virtues of a godly life were extolled to the point of fatigue, and yet God allowed this terrible act to occur. It makes me question this new belief in God which has come to me here on the prairie. My faith is not Karl's fanaticism, not a belief in sin and hell, but a belief in the goodness of the Almighty and the potential goodness of human beings who follow His teachings.

At least, I believed in my God when we went to town that day. Now I question what kind of deity allows such brutality. I ask myself: What sort of god do those women who walked out of the church believe in? Does God discriminate among the races? Did He not create them? Why, then, would He allow his people to abhor some of them?

My beliefs are in tatters. That serenity I had found on the way to the town has been lost to me. I do not know whether it will return.

December 24, 1874
Dearest Mama,

Your granddaughter, Margaret Louisa Bowman, has been christened in the new community church in Johnson City. That should please you and Karl. I soon will begin reading Margaret stories from the Bible, though I must be careful, for some of them are not fit for young ears.

I am quite content here, Mama. Should you converse with me in person, I think you would find me much changed— shockingly forward and firm in my opinions, which my husband listens to attentively. He does not ever tell me what I can or cannot do. He is kind and loving and generous. He is good, and he is a wonderful father to Margaret. Because he treats me with respect, I have become more confident.

I am also strong, Mama. The things I can do! Milk a cow, harvest and bale hay, collect eggs from disagreeable chickens, slaughter and skin one of them when necessary, cook over a wood stove (no coal), draw water from the creek. I could go on and on. I thank you, Mama, for teaching me how to cook, though I have had to learn these other skills, and more, since coming to our homestead.

Would you still like me, Mama? I am not dainty and decorous and deferential to the male of the species any longer. Coming west has been the best decision I ever made, except that I had to leave you behind. I trust you are keeping well.

Your loving daughter,
Hannah

December 25

So much time has passed, again, since I had a moment to make an entry in this journal, which has grown now to three notebooks. Lucas kindly provides them for me from the store. It is Christmas once again, and once again we are sharing the day with Adam and Alma. This time, they are coming to our house for a feast. We have dressed a turkey. I have made cornbread dressing and biscuits and potato cakes. I have cooked some corn from our cold cellar.

We have a real Christmas tree this year. Some enterprising soul in the town (which is growing so fast!) cut trees in the mountains and brought them down to town, where he sold them in the lobby of the new hotel, which used to be the brothel, the respectable ladies of the town having driven the loose women away. (It's said they have all gone to Nevada Territory, where they will not be prevented from plying their trade. The ladies are now working to close the one remaining saloon.)

From some of the trunk linens I fashioned and embroidered a cover for Alma's Bible, and I knitted a scarf for Adam. For Lucas I made a beautiful shirt out of plaid fabric which Alma gave me in exchange for some of my lace. A beautiful man should have handsome clothing. (Another of the skills garnered in my former life comes in handy.) For Margaret, Lucas has made a tiny dollhouse and furniture. She will be charmed, and it will keep her entertained for hours. I have made her a pretty little dress; you would never know it once was a flour sack. Such material is quite pretty and sturdy and will help clothe my child.

We have plans, at last, to begin building our new house, our real, log house, in the spring. Lucas insists we can afford the lumber. I am excited beyond words. He seems to have settled in to meet the homesteading agreement. It is one of the things we don't discuss.

But I have saved the biggest news for last. Lucas having recovered his manhood, we somehow did not get around to slaughtering another pig soon enough, and as a result I am now with child again. This one will be the boy I long to give my husband. I know it.

The child is expected in June. Lucas says that all is well so far, and he can only hear one heartbeat. Surely that is good news. Yet being with child again saddens me, for it brings my lost child to mind. Little Adam is buried in the soil of our homestead. I think about him often, resting under the apple tree in his tiny coffin, but I am usually far too occupied to give in to sadness. Mourning is made more difficult when one's day is full of chores and child, although I visit his grave every day that I can.

It is now late at night. Our guests have left, and the babe

sleeps in her new bed, a gift from Adam and Alma. In our new house, we will have room for the bed and the cradle. In this house, we are quite crowded now.

1875

January 1

We begin another year on the homestead. I have come to accept this life, but I am also forced to admit privately that I dislike it, even though I have not told Lucas of my feelings. After all, it was I who wanted to stop here, who pleaded with him to go no further. But oh, the blizzards and the terrible cold in winter, the relentless heat in summer, depending on the whims of nature for our livelihood, caring for animals that smell and create messes, living in this dark, cramped house. . . . Yet I have Lucas, my love, and my darling Margaret, with another child soon to join us. Perhaps it is only the exigencies of my condition that cause me to be discontented.

Not for a vast fortune would I return to my old life in Cincinnati. Much as I miss Lawrence and Mama, there is nothing I miss about *that* life except my piano, my music.

But on reflection, I must confess that I also miss the intellectual conversations Lucy and I and some of our friends would have, most commonly about books we had read but sometimes about politics. Women are supposed to be sheltered from the cares of the world, including the way the world is run (Lucy's father did not even permit her to read the newspaper), but we know far more than men suppose we do. My circle of friends found great stimulation, perhaps even guilty pleasure, from discussing such topics as the progress of the war, the dangers of imperialism, and of course the enfranchisement of women.

Susan B. Anthony came to our town to speak once; all of us managed, with considerable subterfuge, to attend her lecture. She wore her red shawl, as, we're told, she always does. I was inspired! She is a formidable woman of inestimable courage.

But even though there are rare moments like the visit of Miss Anthony, I have left that life behind now. At present I have my husband, my home, and my beautiful, wonderful daughter to fill my mind and soul. The new child, a boy I am sure, will be named Randall in honor of my father. Perhaps he will in some way resemble my dear Papa. . . .

Only two more years and we will claim this land for our own—surely that is worth feeling joyous about. Yet I find that I do long for the civilized life. Does Lucas, I wonder? What does he miss? What does he yearn for? He does not say. He has given up so much so that we can be together.

February 12

I feel so ill with this child. Each day begins with a time of malaise. Food does not taste good, and when I prepare it for Lucas and Margaret I start feeling ill all over again, just from the smell of it. I do not know how I am going to survive this travail. The work still must be done, and there is no one but me to do it. Lucas does all that he possibly can; he works from dawn to dark every day. I can only try to stay on my feet from hour to hour and pray that I will manage somehow.

February 20

What a delight it is to have this inquisitive young soul, our beautiful daughter, in our midst! Seeing the world through her eyes, it looks fresh and new and inviting. She reaches for everything, investigates freely. (Even putting her little hands in the flour bin yesterday. She looked so adorable I could not scold her. Rather, I wanted to paint her. But of course she never stays still long enough.) She is so charming; I could spend my days watching her explore and discover. She has many words now. Lucas was quite filled with masculine delight that "papa" was her first intelligible word.

I can't watch her all day, of course. Sometimes, I have to tie her to the table leg so she won't get under my feet and get hurt while I'm cooking. I carry her in the sling while I do my outdoor chores. I know that if I let her go even for a moment, she might wander off and become prey for a coyote or who knows what others dangers that await her in the wild. Yet soon she will be too heavy for the sling. She is growing so fast. What ever will I do when I have an infant as well to care for?

March 13

I fear I am neglecting this journal, my friend and companion, repository for my thoughts and fears and hopes and dreams. But I have all I can do to endure each day. There is no improvement in my condition. Lucas says this happens to some women quite naturally; it does not "necessarily" indicate a problem with the child. What does he mean?

March 31

The child quickened today—later than I would have thought. I had begun to fear that he, like his brother Little Adam, was not thriving in my womb. But now he becomes quite active. No more nausea, indeed, my appetite is tremendous, but my back hurts almost constantly. My ankles and hands have swollen. Standing up for very long at a time becomes difficult.

I am in desperate need of the God I so want to believe in.

Alma comes, bless her loving heart, twice or three times a week now. She helps me with Margaret, brings baked bread and delicacies to tempt me, assures me all will be well. What would

I do without this dear friend?

May 15
Randall came into the world a week ago, several weeks early according to Lucas. I did not suffer for so long as I did with Margaret; indeed, he came quite quickly, but Lucas says there must be no more children. He does not tell me exactly why, but something seems to have gone awry with my female organs, and he is concerned that if I give birth again neither the child nor I may survive. I don't understand it; it did not seem that troublesome to have this child, though the birth was not easy and as before I lost a good deal of blood. I was so weak that I had to stay in bed for several days after he was born. Today is my first day out of bed. Thank God for Alma, who came to help with Margaret and the chores.

There must be something Lucas is not telling me.

Randall is much smaller than Margaret was. He would fit into a hat box! But he seems healthy. He cries lustily and eats hungrily, although we had to feed him with a milk-soaked cloth for several days, as he was too weak to suck. Lucas says he must be cosseted and treated with extra care—especially, kept warm. He looks so like his father he takes my breath away. His skin is a pale brown, like a deep suntan, and like Margaret he was born with a shock of thick black hair.

Margaret is by turns torn with jealousy and delighted to have an infant in the house. I have had to explain to her that Randall is not a doll but a living, breathing child and she must be so very careful of him. She is barely two; I do not know how much she comprehends—though she has observed, wide-eyed and silent on the matter, that her brother looks different from her in one significant aspect. I have watched her looking down at herself after seeing me change him. This will have to be explained to her one day.

It is very difficult to care for both of them at once; Lucas, of course, must be at the chores. It is planting time. Nothing must disrupt that. My recovery has been slower than I expected. I asked Lucas last night what went wrong, why I cannot have more children (although at this moment, I do not think I want any more!).

He explained that my womb is tipped in the wrong position and has become very weakened by bearing two children. Because of the tipping, he says, I might not even be able to conceive at all, but if I were to, the child would not stay in my womb for the full term. Moreover, the tipping has affected my other internal organs as well. Another pregnancy might cause other kinds of damage.

"Why did I bleed so much more than with Margaret?" I asked.

He looked at me with pain in his eyes. "I wish I knew more," he said. "We physicians know so very little about how and why a woman's body is as it is, and how it should be, and why things sometimes go wrong. I believe that your uterus"—he used that medical term—"tore during the delivery, and it may or may not repair itself. You must not have more children, Hannah."

He paused and took a deep breath. "The swelling in your feet and ankles also indicated that something had gone wrong. We know of this condition but know no treatment for it. Bearing another child could kill you."

With those sobering words, he drew me into his arms.

May 27

Alma has come again to help, for I am still weak. She adores Margaret and has entertained her, to my relief. She reads to my little girl! I am so pleased and happy that Alma has mastered this skill so readily and so well.

I asked Alma whether she had yet told Adam of her newly learned ability. She told me she has not; she fears causing him unhappiness. "Why should he object to having such a clever wife?" I asked her. She replied that where she comes from, men do not like for their wives to outshine them in any way.

Yet her quick mastery of a difficult skill is further proof to me that the generally held male view of female capacity and intelligence—that we are inferior to men intellectually—is simply wrong. We are capable, intelligent, talented people and should not be left to molder in our houses doing nothing but caring for children and doing household chores.

There now, I have relieved myself of that discontented thought.

July 1

Lucas and I married three years ago today. As I reflect on this time, so full of events and changes, I realize that in spite of the discomforts and problems, I would have done nothing different from what I did. When I became Lucas's wife, I surrendered my soul to him, but he would not steal my spirit, and for that I shall love him unto death. I can no longer imagine a life without him; I love him as much as I did the day we left Kansas City together.

People here do not tend to mark such events with celebration—even birthdays—everyone is too busy. But at night, Lucas and I observed this special day in the best of all possible ways.

July 3

There are rumors that Colorado is seeking statehood. When that happens, I wonder whether the laws against marriage between the races that exist in so many other states will be enacted here. If they are, what will happen to Lucas and me? We can only hope that these cruel, shortsighted laws will not be enacted, or if they are, not enforced. I shudder to recall the trouble at the church when Margaret was christened. Will my children be subject to more such unkindness? Will Lucas and I?

My fears have led me to decide not to christen Randall in town. With Richards here, spreading his ugly message of hate, I fear what might happen. Even though people seem to have accepted Lucas, I don't know how they will react to our children, such tangible proof of the nature of our union. Randall more and more resembles his handsome father. Lucas says he has my eyes, but I don't think so.

Society broadly holds that a union such as ours is immoral, illegal and dangerous to the propagation of the supposedly superior white race. No one can tell me that my husband is inferior to anyone! Nor are my children mongrels, as some cruel writings have proclaimed. How many children are there in the South who, like Lucas, are the offspring of a relationship forced upon Negro women by their owners? Are they considered mongrels? No, indeed; they are regarded as Negroes, therefore inferior, even though white blood flows in their veins. It is flawed logic. Who ever decided that to have light skin makes one superior to those with darker skin? It makes me furious, but at the same time I feel utterly powerless to change the laws, or the practices of our society.

Lucas has told me the story of his birth and childhood. His mother, Roxie, a house slave, was forced by her master and gave birth to Lucas. One night soon after he was born, the main house caught on fire. In the resulting melee, Roxie and her infant escaped, apparently with the complicity of someone on the estate, for no one went after them. They went to the dock and somehow she persuaded a captain who was on his way to France to take them aboard.

He had to have known the risk; helping slaves escape was against the law. I suspect Roxie offered him her favors. Or perhaps, as Lucas believes, the patriarch arranged her passage. From what Lucas says, Roxie was spirited and beautiful, and men flocked to her. She spoke French fluently, for that was the language of the Beaumont plantation.

Roxie was lovely—exotic, like Lucas—and quickly became a much-sought-after courtesan in Paris. Lucas said he and his mother always had comfortable, sometimes even luxurious, quarters to live in, and Lucas had tutors. He learned to ride and to behave like a gentleman. Using the considerable funds she left to him, he decided to study medicine after his mother died of consumption when he was only sixteen years of age.

Always ready for new experiences and seeing advantages in leaving France, which was in political turmoil, Lucas came to the United States in '61, only a few weeks before the war broke out. He was by then well trained in doctoring, so when the war began he volunteered his services as a field doctor. He said he would not leave the country again, abandoning those who were fighting to end slavery. He didn't stay in the battlefield long because he was considered too slow, too meticulous, so he came to the hospital in Cincinnati. After the war, seeing there was much he could do to help, he stayed on at the hospital, where we met. Once we fell in love, his fate was sealed, I fear.

Before Lucas came to America he had not known the deep racial hatreds that divide this country. He left while an infant and lived in a country where he was regarded as a curiosity but accepted nonetheless. Though his features do not readily identify him as belonging to the dark-skinned race, his profile is Negroid, and his skin is as dark as a walnut shell. He has a Negro's woolly hair. Anyone who came to know him well would see those distinguishing features, but in the hectic fields of battle or the overcrowded wards of a military hospital, no one looked that closely. While in Ohio, he had on the advice of his benefactor shaved his head; when I met him, he was entirely bald. Now that we are in Colorado Territory, he has let his hair grow out again. It suits him well, makes him even more handsome. In Cincinnati, he was accepted as foreign-born and allowed to practice in the army hospital. He took care then to exaggerate his French accent, which I never notice at all now. Here, no one seems quite sure what he is, but to the people who have come to know him, it does not seem to matter.

Lucas and I can only hope that our children will not suffer unduly because of their parentage. And that no one will question the legality of our marriage.

August 1

Randall thrives. He is alert and curious, his bright eyes seeing everything around him. He is slower to progress than Margaret was, but Lucas says that is because he did not fully develop in the womb.

My dissatisfaction with this life has not lessened with the advent of children. Rather, it has increased, for I see ever more clearly that if we stay on this homestead we will deprive them of the opportunity to become what they are capable of. What kind of education can I provide for them? We are too far from town for them to walk to school. I will have to teach them myself. How can I do that adequately? There is so much *I* do not know.

August 18

Lucas has attained the grand age of thirty-seven. He is starting to turn gray at the edges of his hair. I think it makes him quite distinguished. He does not like it and sometimes plucks out the hairs in front of the mirror we recently acquired (an addition to our household I heartily dislike).

The log house progresses at a snail's pace. Will I live in this sod house forever? There is no privacy! Lucas and I carry out our intimate lives a few feet away from the children—when they are asleep, of course. When they are older, we will have to find ways to be more discreet. This closeness removes much of the joy for me. Even though they are sleeping, I know they are nearby and I feel constrained.

In France, Lucas says, conjugal relations are an everyday part of life, one which causes no embarrassment or discomfort. People do not always seek privacy. He often saw his mother entangled with one of her lovers, both of them what he calls *"en dishabille."* Apparently, people there also feel no compulsion to be legally united before engaging in such intimacy, either.

I asked him, "Did you not find that unsettling?"

He shrugged. "It's a natural act, Hannah. Why should humans be embarrassed about it?"

"This is not France. This is America. In my upbringing, it was never even mentioned that men and women engaged in such acts together. I had no idea, until I was a grown woman, that men were equipped with—with—"

He laughed. "Your upbringing prevents you from using the correct word. You are so proper in some ways, Hannah, yet so free and bold in others. You are an enigma."

Watching our children as they slept, he said, "How will you explain all this to Margaret when the time is right, or will you?" (His assumption being, I believe, that it will be incumbent upon him to explain matters to his son.) "Did your mother not tell you anything?"

I was indignant. "I hope I am becoming a western woman, overcoming my proper Cincinnati ways."

September 13
Adam visited us today. He did not bring good news.

"He means to run us out, Lucas," he said in a mournful tone.

Lucas did not need to ask of whom Adam spoke. We knew it was Mr. Richards.

"What has happened?"

156

Adam recently acquired a small flock of sheep, which he pastures at the far northeastern corner of his property. He sells the wool and the lambs. Sheep-raising is becoming more common in this part of Colorado. The sheep are easy to care for and relatively profitable, more so than cattle.

Adam told a shocking story—two of Richards's large, vicious dogs somehow got into the pasture and killed three ewes before he managed to run them off. All three were due to lamb in a few weeks. He peppered one of the beasts with his shotgun, but they got away before he could kill them.

"It's a good thing you didn't kill them," Lucas said. "Richards would doubtless have come after you. He sets great store by those hounds of his, so I hear."

Adam only nodded his head glumly.

"We'll have to rebuild your fence, Adam, with more barbed wire. What you have kept the cattle away, but it doesn't stop the dogs. We'll fix it so the damned dogs won't be able to get through without tearing themselves up pretty badly."

"Why do you think he means to run us both off?" I asked Adam.

We've heard stories about the cattlemen, how they are unhappy because some ranchers have brought in sheep. The cattlemen don't like the barbed wire, either; they want their cattle to be able to run free. I wondered aloud whether Richards might simply be one of those unhappy cattlemen.

" 'Tain't that simple, Hannah. Wish it was. Richards has a mean streak a mile wide. He's not an honorable man. He's allus doin' things. Changin' the way the ditch goes, turnin' his dogs loose, hirin' hands that'd jest as soon shoot ya as look at ya."

Lucas remained focused on repairing the problem. "We'll go to town tomorrow," he promised. "I can lend you some money if you don't have the funds to buy enough fencing."

Adam shook his head. "Don't need money," he said, a flash

of pride brightening his eyes. "Be grateful fer yore hep, though."

So the plan is to spend the next several days reconstructing Adam's fence—postponing the log house once again. Yet we must help our good neighbor who has helped us so many times, in so many ways.

Does Richards really mean to drive us off our land? Perhaps he wants to increase his spread. We are so close now to gaining ownership, to completing our obligations. Yet I confess I feel conflicting emotions about it. Can Lucas ever be content here, struggling with the land and the forces of nature every day? Does he dream about practicing medicine again? Can I ever be content here, doing chores all day, with no life of the mind or music at all?

Once again I am puzzled, too, that Lucas offered to lend Adam money. Where is that money coming from? Why won't he talk to me about money? I must ask him, soon.

November 10

Adam's new fence is finished. Lucas decided to put new fence around our property as well. We are battened down, so to speak, ready again for winter, which has chosen to delay its appearance this year. Despite the very cold weather, necessitating hats and scarves and gloves, no snow has come. The wind bites sharply as usual across these treeless plains.

Today I decided the time had come for talking about money. When Lucas came in for his lunch and the children were down for their naps, I approached Lucas without preamble, as I am wont to do.

"How much money do we have, Lucas? Where did it come from?"

He sat down at the table and turned his cup of hot tea around and around in his hands. "I didn't think you were interested, Hannah."

"How could I not be, when I see so little money coming in from the few items we are able to sell in town and so much money being spent? Do you have a golden goose somewhere?"

At that he laughed until tears ran down his cheeks. "Would that I did," he finally gasped through the laughter. "What I have, instead, is a gold mine."

"An actual mine? Where they are finding gold?"

"Oh, yes. It is in California. That was my original destination when we left St. Louis; that was why I at first considered going on alone. Back before the war, I met another doctor on the ship to America. He'd been to California and struck gold, and he offered me a chance to buy into his mine. Then one more man came in right after the war. It pays nicely, regularly. Drafts arrive at the post office quarterly. It supports us well."

"But how do you get the money?"

"They sent bank drafts to Denver, and a courier brought it up here once a month. Now we've got a bank in town, so they send it directly there."

"All that time we were on the trail, they were sending bank drafts." I was astounded, to put it kindly. My husband had been withholding this vital information from me. Why? "When were you going to tell me about this, Lucas? Why didn't you tell me long ago?"

He dropped his eyes. "I planned originally to go to California, earn enough money to buy out the other partners, and make sure the laborers are well-enough paid and well treated. If we had been able to go all the way to California, I would have told you before we got there. You would not have liked the mine, though."

"Why not?" I know my tone was sharp. I was angry.

"Because, Hannah, most of the laborers at the mine are Chinese. They earn very little money for very long, hard days of work. This was not something I knew before I bought my shares.

I knew you would not approve."

"You are entirely correct! I do not approve!" I know my anger was showing then. "Yet when Boney lost his shoe and we met Adam and Alma, you decided to stay, and you have not once mentioned California since, not even after the cattle run."

"The trip this far was much more difficult for you than I had dreamed, Hannah. I could see your strength and spirit draining away day by day. I had no idea, before we set out, how much harder such travel is for women than for men. I could see how much you wanted to stay here, especially with Alma and Adam nearby. I did not feel I could reasonably ask you to accompany me across the Rocky Mountains and through the desert to get to my mine, and I did not want to leave you behind. I began to see my desire to get there as selfish."

Silently I agreed that would have been selfish. Yet his motive was pure. . . .

"Can you not persuade your partners to do something about the laborers now? Who are they? Are they there, in California?"

"I have offered repeatedly to buy them out, and they refuse. The mine is very productive, and they are getting rich. When we all bought in, we had an agreement drawn up at a bank in New York. They went west, and I went to Cincinnati. I thought no more about it for some time, and about five years ago I began getting bank drafts from the mine. I was astonished. And I didn't know about the Chinese workers until a few weeks before we left Cincinnati."

"They send you your share. They could cheat you out of it."

"They are honest enough, and if they are cheating me it does not matter, because I am still getting a considerable sum from the mine. They simply are not as bothered by the conditions as I am."

"Did you ever plan to tell me about the mine, if I had not asked?"

He looked down at his hands, those wonderful, strong hands. "I don't know, Hannah. Perhaps. I am embarrassed about the whole episode and didn't want you to be disappointed in me. I suppose I hoped the mine would play out and I would never have to explain. I have been investing the money, wisely I hope, so we really do not need the income anymore. We are not rich, not like Karl, but we are more than comfortable."

"Then sell out to them!" It seemed such an obvious solution to me.

"I am seriously contemplating that," he replied. "Since I have finally concluded that I can do nothing to change conditions, I might as well sell."

Knowing my husband as I do, I realize it may take him some time to move from contemplation to decision to action. Nonetheless, it was a relief to have this information out in the open between us, and to know where the money is coming from.

November 24

Lucas is teaching Margaret to speak French. Young though she is, she comprehends the language well. Words and phrases that I stumble over come easily to her. He says he will teach Randall, when he gets older.

There's been no more difficulty with Richards. Do we dare to hope he will trouble us no more?

When the weather is fair, Alma often comes to take Margaret for the day. She is quite good with her, and willful little Margaret is clay in her hands. I remarked to Alma one day about her ease with children. It is a shame she does not have any of her own.

"When we were in Tennessee," she replied, "I took care of the children in one of those rich families." Alma's speech and grammar have improved remarkably since she learned to read, at least when she's with me, but she sometimes falls back on her backwoods style of speech. I do not ever correct her. As she becomes more literate, I am convinced she will become more careful. She told me that there were four children in the family, from an infant to a seven-year-old, and she had full charge of them all day long. "They weren't always good," she commented dryly.

Not having children of her own has been the sorrow of her life, I know. She takes great joy and pride in being the godmother of my little girl, and I take pleasure in having been able to give her that gift. How fortunate Margaret is—her father teaching her French and Alma teaching her the domestic arts!

December 1

Why am I not more content? Men say women are intended to keep a home and bear children, no more. The Bible says woman was created from a man's rib. Men say we are weak and mindless.

To them I say, *I* have a mind, although it is not being put to much use now. *I* have a skill, which I cannot employ. *I* have strength I never supposed that I possessed. How I hope that my daughter will be more fortunate than I in her life, free to live as she chooses, to apply her mind well, perhaps even to attend college.

Life without Lucas is unimaginable. I love him. I want to be with him, and it gives me infinite joy that I was able to bear his child. But I cannot live only through him and our children. I need more.

December 7

I wrote too optimistically about Mr. Richards. There has been more trouble, bad trouble.

Lucas and I left the children with their godparents yesterday and set out to town to shop for Christmas gifts. This time we were certain the weather was clear; there were no clouds visible for miles, and Adam said it would not snow for several more days—too dry.

I had stepped into the grocery store for a few items I had forgotten and Lucas was walking towards me down Main Street, his arms full of parcels, when I saw Mr. Richards coming toward him. I had never seen the man before, but from the way Lucas tightened his lips and narrowed his eyes, I knew.

Richards is a rather short man, stocky, with graying hair that sticks out in an unwieldy fashion from beneath his rebel hat. He has a short neck and small, mean black eyes. His boots were obviously built up several inches to make him appear taller.

The man was not blessed by God when it came to appearances. Not only is his face unappealing, his shoulders are hunched and his body seems out of proportion somehow, the chest too large for the legs, the arms seeming to be too long for his body. He reminds me of a large ape. I felt my heart pounding as he approached. I hoped he would pass by without saying anything to us. But it was not to be. He had a pistol on his hip, even though the sheriff of Johnson City had recently decreed that weapons cannot be worn in town but must be left at his office upon arrival. Our rifle was there.

He walked up to Lucas, blocking his path.

"Nigger, I seen you walkin' 'longside that white woman. You walk *behind* her," he said. He spoke, through clenched teeth, in the sort of slow Southern drawl I heard so often in Cincinnati.

I started to protest, but Lucas looked toward me to silence me and warn me not to move. He stepped out into the street so as to go around Richards.

"You hear what I said, nigger?" Richards growled. "She ain't your wife, cain't be, 'cause that's agin the law. So you got to be her slave. And slaves walk behind their masters."

My husband tops Richards by several inches and is the younger and stronger man. He could easily have subdued his tormenter, but he chose not to, nobly behaving as though he had not heard a word.

Evidently, Richards didn't believe the Emancipation Proclamation and had chosen not to recall that the South lost the War Between the States. It seemed, indeed, that he was still fighting the war! I was boiling with fury by this time, but Lucas still said nothing. Then without warning or provocation, Richards reached out with one beefy hand and shoved Lucas's chest, knocking him down into the muddy street. Lucas was taken unawares and fell heavily, the parcels going all over. I ran to help him up. By then Richards had swaggered on down the street, his back to us on his way to the saloon.

From across the street, the new community church minister came out of the parsonage and ran toward us. He must have been watching from his doorway but had said or done nothing until Lucas fell. He reached down to help Lucas up. Turning to me, he said, "Please go get the sheriff, Mrs. Bowman." But Lucas shook his head. "No sheriff," he said as he stood up. "The man hurt nothing but my dignity, and that is easily restored."

Reverend Chadwick helped us retrieve our packages, muttering the while about some people not being very Christian. "Come into my house for a hot drink," he said, "before you start back home."

We had not been much acquainted with the reverend except for Margaret's christening, and since I have decided not to bring Randall to town, I didn't think it likely we would encounter him often. He is a young, unmarried man, lonely I suspect, and I thought he might appreciate our company for a little while, so we accepted his kind invitation. Moreover, we were certainly ready for a respite after this unpleasantness.

"I personally do not hold with marriage between whites and

Negroes," he said at one point as we conversed in his warm but cheerless parlor, "but I also believe that people have a God-given right to the pursuit of happiness, so I do not think it should be against the law for people to marry whom they choose." He said it all so matter-of-factly that I could not resent his prejudicial opening remark and the contradictions that followed it.

"Why do you object to such a marriage?" I asked, my besetting sin undoing me again.

"It does not seem natural," he replied. "And God has decreed that it should not be permitted. But I admit to some confusion on the matter. Since you have settled here, I have prayed about it often."

Lucas had said nothing during this exchange. I watched his face for signs of annoyance or anger but saw none.

"Do you believe, then, that dark-skinned people are inferior?" I asked. I leaned forward, my chin on my hand, excited. It had been so long since I had exchanged intellectual conversation with anyone!

He shook his head. "No. Certainly not. Look at your husband! It's just that the dark-skinned people are so different! How can there be compatibility? And what about children? Where will they belong?"

Lucas rose then. "Our children are fine," he said. "We must go now. I thank you for your hospitality." He bowed slightly, picked up his hat, and headed for the door.

How naïve I was, how foolish, to suppose that merely by removing ourselves farther west, away from Cincinnati, which is so close to the South, we would be leaving behind the narrow, prejudicial views about race so common there. It appears this specter will follow us wherever we go. Pray God it will not follow my children as well.

I knew Lucas was terribly upset. I had seen his jaw working

as he contained his anger. The reverend may have meant well, but he could not have said anything more hurtful. I hastily gathered my wrap and the packages and followed him out, forbearing to say anything lest I say something unforgivably rude.

On the way home I was sorely tempted to ask Lucas why he had not resisted Richards's cruelty. For myself, I was so angry still that I could hardly see. And the reverend! Well, he is ignorant, I suppose, and more to be forgiven. But I cannot forgive Richards.

When we got home and told Adam and Alma what had happened, Adam was ready to take his rifle and dispatch Mr. Richards that very day. Fortunately, calmer heads prevailed and he was persuaded not to commit such an unwise act. But Adam was firm that Richards must not be allowed to treat Lucas in this manner.

"He is from the deep South," Lucas noted. "I encountered more than one man with a similar attitude when I was serving as an army physician."

So Lucas had been demeaned and insulted before; he had not told me of it. "I find it best for myself," he went on after a moment, "not to dignify such boorish behavior with a reaction."

"Wonder why he left the South," Adam muttered. "Shoulda stayed there."

After the four of us had talked for a bit, we concluded that the best defense for the present is to make sure we do not give the man any cause for conflict. "He's just itching for a fight," Alma said.

December 10

It poses a dilemma for peace-loving people when their tranquility is threatened by violence. The Bible says to turn the other cheek, but is that always the wisest choice?

I have pondered the reasons for Mr. Richards's behavior. I do not know what makes any man, any person, hate someone else, or for that matter a whole group of people, simply because of the color of their skin.

Mama told me once, after the war had ended, that white people in the South, especially the men, feel angry and confused by the sudden freedom and ascendancy of the black people whom they had so recently totally controlled. She said good Christians should feel pity and compassion for them while they find their way in the new society. Yet I cannot summon any compassion for a man who pushes my husband into the dirt! She explained that many Southerners had great difficulty accepting the outcome of the war and the imposing of Reconstruction on the South, in a way Mr. Lincoln would never have done it. (What a tragedy that he was killed.)

Lucas refused to discuss the incident any further after our talk with Adam and Alma. And why, I wonder, is Mr. Richards so determined to drive Alma and Adam away? They are not dark-skinned. They have done nothing to earn his enmity except that they are friends of ours. And of course, Adam has the sheep.

Does Richards have any redeeming qualities? I have thus far learned of none. Yet my dear Papa told Lawrence and me once, after he had been accosted and robbed coming home from the store, that no one is all good or all bad. I certainly know I am not all good! Nor, I have discovered over the years, is my dear husband. So we must assume that this man from Mississippi is not wholly bad.

Still, to me he seems evil. Evil exists in all parts of the globe and in all kinds of people. But I must try to see Mr. Richards as a human being with good and bad in him, not the embodiment of evil. Yet he hates, and his hatred has endangered me and people whom I love.

Still I find, after much scrutinizing of my soul, that I cannot be charitable toward Jacob Richards.

December 26

We learned a few days ago why Richards left his home in Mississippi, and the news was not cheering. He fled as a fugitive from a murder charge. Sheriff Musgrave came to call a few days after the episode in town and told us that Richards had killed a woman in Mississippi. He had admitted the act; indeed, he boasted of it. He caught her stealing from him, he claimed, so he was forced to kill her. She was a poor woman, widow of a sharecropper, who left three children for the county to care for. Poor babes no doubt went into an orphanage. Richards was the owner of a gambling house and tavern in the town.

The sheriff in that town was more forward-thinking than most; the usual situation would be that the law would turn a blind eye. But this woman had evidently been related to the sheriff's housekeeper, so he decided to pursue the matter. Richards sold his establishment and left the state after learning that an indictment was pending. That's where he got the money to buy cattle land in Wyoming. Why he came here to Colorado no one seems to know, though Lucas has speculated that he might have been seeking a place where the law is more loosely enforced. We are still only a territory, after all.

Sheriff Musgrave learned all this from a reply to letters he'd sent to several sheriffs in Mississippi after complaints began to come to him about Jacob Richards, Lucas not being the only object of his attacks. Old Betsy, who runs a laundry on the edge of town, has been threatened by him more than once, we've heard, though what she has done to offend we have no notion. She is neither Negro nor associated with any Negroes.

The sheriff who replied to Mr. Musgrave told a story learned from his predecessor, the sheriff who indicted Richards.

(Unfortunately, that enlightened man was voted out of office shortly after that incident.) Mr. Musgrave said the story sounded believable to him. The postscript, the part Richards evidently does not know, is that the charge was dropped as soon as the offending sheriff lost his job, so Richards *could* go back home. To our regret he may not want to now, since he seems to be getting rich here.

Knowing all this made me even more frightened of the man. Sheriff Musgrave told us that Richards has started fights in the saloon and forced other people off the sidewalk, not just dark-skinned ones. (Indeed, Lucas is the only dark-skinned person in Johnson City that I know of, except for the Indians who come to town sometimes.)

Lucas walked with the sheriff to his horse. Sheriff Musgrave warned us to be vigilant, Lucas reported. "There is nothing manly about that loathsome individual," he told me. "If he should come around here bothering you, don't hesitate. Shoot him."

1876

January 16

Lucas often leaves me alone in the house while he is in the fields and cannot hear my voice. We have agreed that if there is trouble, I will fire one shot into the air to call him to my aid. I have not admitted to him just how frightened I am.

Why do married people, who live in such intimacy, hold back from telling each other that which is most deeply felt? I am certain Lucas has not told me some things important about himself, things that would help me understand him more fully, just as I have refrained from telling him everything that is in my mind and heart. When I imagined being married to this man, whom I love so very much, I thought we would open our hearts to each other without reservation. But it has not been so. Are most husbands and wives reticent with each other in some things? I must ask Alma.

January 21

A new year has not brought much change, much relief from the sameness of our lives. I thank God for the children, who daily bring me joy and entertainment. But what shall I do when they get older? I do not want this to be the only life they know. Perhaps we *should* have gone to California!

Randall is walking already—very early, Lucas says. He is so small and wiry. He has the most delightful smile that creates dimples in his cheeks, and when he laughs, his whole body shakes. He is most enjoyable to observe.

Still, he is such a quiet child; he worries me. So different from Margaret! Is it usual for a child not yet a year old to sit in the same place for hours, cooing and making soft little noises? I have not had children before and have no one to talk to about it, so I do not know. Even though he walks, he has not yet uttered an intelligible word, yet I recall that Margaret was chattering like a magpie by this age.

Lucas says I indulge Margaret too much. "She must be thwarted from time to time," he said to me. "She must learn that she cannot always have her own way. When she is an adult, she will often encounter obstacles to her will. She needs to learn now how to handle them."

He does not punish her physically, but he is firmer with her than I am. When she insists, when she cries, he simply sets her down in a corner and leaves her there until she gets over her bad temper. I know he is right, but to do that is more difficult for me. Still, I will try.

They have started a school in Johnson City, bringing a teacher from Illinois, a young woman who has gone to college in the East and has, it's said, many progressive ideas about education. Her name is Georgina Norton and she is boarding with Mr. and Mrs. Marks. (Yes, he recently took a wife! But she did not want to live above the livery he owns so they built a house which, fortunately, has ample room for the schoolteacher.) I mean to go to town soon and meet her. Perhaps we can have a conversation about something besides children and cooking and chickens.

April 13

Margaret is three years old today. We fled Cincinnati four years ago on this date. Alma made Margaret an elegant lemon cake and brought her a lovely rag doll, which she had made. How clever she is! Those two adore each other. I sometimes think Margaret loves Alma more than she loves me. Uncharitable thought! Why should I not be willing to share my wonderful little child with Alma, who has none of her own?

Margaret smiled at the gift of the doll and said, "Merci." Alma chuckled. She is very proud of her godchild, who is learning a second language at her young age. And well she should be proud—Margaret's French advances daily. She is very bright, and I say that with all due modesty.

"Don't boast," Mama always used to say. Once when I came home from school with a particularly high mark on a test, I said, "Look! I got the highest mark in the class!" Mama turned on me quite sharply and admonished me for boasting. For so long after that, I not only never spoke of my accomplishments, I no longer sought them. With that one remark, which I should not have taken so much to heart (except I was but fourteen), she suppressed in me any desire to rise above the ordinary for a very long time, until I immigrated to the West.

I left school when I was sixteen. How I regret that now! I could not have gone on to college, as it turns out (though some women are doing so these days), because the war had started and everyone was immersed in more important matters—but I know now that I would have succeeded. Indeed, I believe now that I could succeed at almost anything I might undertake.

Despite my lack of education, I do have music. Even though I have as yet no piano, I have my music books, my memory, and my voice. I shall start teaching Margaret to sing, and in a few years to read music. Perhaps I will have a piano by then.

Lucas is working on the log house at last! I shall devote every spare moment to assisting him in whatever ways I can. I know it will be sporadic for him, as he has so many other chores to attend to, but he has the foundation laid and has brought logs from town. Adam will also come and work on it when he can.

Lucas has become so muscular and strong; his arms look like those of the river men we saw in St. Louis, loading the boats. The very sight of him, shirtless, intent on his chores, thrills me still.

April 20

Randall has begun to speak. He has decided "Margaret" is too much for him, so he calls his sister "Meggie." It was his very first word, to Lucas's chagrin. I suppose we shall all be calling her that soon enough. He is such a dear child, so placid and easy to please. He does love his sister; he smiles broadly whenever she comes near. She does not bully or tease him, for which I am grateful. He has decided that he wishes to talk and is suddenly advanced in language for his years, I believe. Lucas says he was studying the words until he had mastered them in his mind before trying them out loud.

It is wondrous to me that two children who came from the same parents can be so very different.

May 23

I took the wagon to town yesterday, alone, to get supplies. Lucas was busy with the planting, and Alma came to take the children home with her for a day or two, so I was free to venture into town, the rifle beside me on the seat. At the store I met Mary Austin, who is new in town, and she invited me home for tea. I stayed far longer than I intended; when I looked out, I saw that it had begun to get dark, so Mary suggested that I stay overnight. "You can't head home now," she told me, and I agreed. "But I must walk down to the livery and tell Owen," I replied. I worried about Lucas. I had no way to inform him of my decision and could only hope that he would understand, when I had not returned home before dark, that it had become too late for me to start out.

Mary agreed that I should tell the owner of the livery stable, as it was just a short distance from her house to the stable, so I set out alone, Mr. Austin being away from home at the time. Mary is a timid soul and preferred not to accompany me, as she dislikes being out in the dark, even with her husband.

It was full dark when I started back to Mary's house. Owen wanted to walk with me, but I assured him I would be fine, and I had no reason to think otherwise.

I was almost at Mary's door when someone bumped into me. The smell of liquor on his breath nearly knocked me over. I could see well enough to make out the Confederate uniform. I pushed Richards away.

But he had grasped my arm with his hands, perhaps to keep himself from falling, and when he realized that he had hold of a woman, he tightened his grip on me. His words slurred, he said, "You're that Bowman's tart. Livin' with a black man, y'all hain't be nothin' but a whore. Got some for me?"

He leaned closer to me, breathing hard into my face. I coughed, and he lurched backward slightly. It was enough to allow me to loosen one hand from my arm, but it did little good, because he reached over and began to fondle my breast.

That was enough for me. For an instant, he became Karl in my eyes, and I had vowed no one would ever do that to me again. In that moment I discovered how strong I have become with all that work on the farm, for I was able to free myself and push him firmly far enough away that I could ensure my escape. He fell heavily against the side of a building, then slumped to the ground, momentarily unconscious, I suppose. I did not stay to investigate but hurried on to Mary's house a few doors away.

I chose not to tell Mary what had just transpired. I decided, through a sleepless night, not to tell Lucas or Adam either, because I am certain they would rush out with their rifles and try to kill the man.

Mama has often told me how chivalrous and courteous "Southern gentlemen," of whom she met many in her younger days, are toward women. But only if they respect them. In Richards's mind, it appears that I am a loose woman living illegally with a Negro; thus he does not respect me.

What the man did is inexcusable; worse is what he said, but I have to allow for the fact that he was inebriated and to be grateful for my own strength. Would that I had been so strong years ago when Karl was attacking me. I cannot forgive Mr. Richards, and I cannot forget, but I shall do my best to push it aside and not dwell on it. That does no good.

July 3

I have become more cautious. I do not go outside alone after dark now. I have not slept well since that encounter in town.

We are going to a barn dance tomorrow! I am so looking forward to it. There are more and more settlers here now, and the Schmidts are celebrating July 4 with a pig roast and a barn dance. Everyone is going. I hope Richards won't be there.

July 5

The barn dance was wonderful. There were enough people to form three squares, and it turns out Mr. Schmidt (a very nice man) is a fiddler and a caller. We learned several patterns, then swung and swirled until almost ten o'clock—very late for farmers. There were some older women there, grandmothers who offered to care for the little ones so we could enjoy ourselves without worry. It was so satisfying to see Lucas laughing and clapping and singing. No evil intruded on that night.

The fiddle music was such a delight. Once more I know, sharply and painfully, just how much I miss my music. Now that we have moved into the log house at last, perhaps Lucas can find a piano for me.

Riding home, the night sky so thick with stars that it seemed almost day-bright, a wisp of wind in our faces and the air so cool, I thought how blessed we are to be here, on this high prairie, with each other and our children. God is good.

I have been so busy settling in that I have neglected to record here the joyous occasion of moving into the log house—with glass windows. It has two large rooms, one for sleeping, one for living, and a small curtained alcove next to the living area for the children. At last, they are not just inches away from us at night. More rooms can be added later, Lucas says, or we can add a loft. He raised a high roof with that thought in mind. He maintains it is not good for Margaret and Randall to share a room when they get older. He's right, I know; my brother, Lawrence, and I certainly never shared a room. Once I had matured, I guarded my privacy. Lawrence, of course, was so contained within himself that it would not have mattered to him where he slept or with whom. But it mattered to me.

The children are still so young. There can't be harm in it just yet.

The house seems positively luxurious to me. It has a wooden floor, a sturdy door, and room for all the furniture. Alma, who recently became the proud owner of a new sewing machine, made brightly colored curtains for the windows, and Adam's housewarming present was a bookcase for all my books. There is decidedly room for an upright piano in the parlor. I hope to have one soon.

Being in this house has cheered me immensely. I wish I could say that it has dissolved my discontent, but that is not true. I can truthfully say that I am *less* discontented than I was, but I am still not wholly content with my current circumstances. Happy diversions like the barn dance are rare, temporary. Nothing compensates for the lack of intellectual stimulation and music in my life. I love Lucas as much as I ever did, but I have come to understand that he cannot fill all my needs.

July 21

My terrible dreams have returned. I thought I had banished them when Lucas and I married, but it seems that Richards's treatment of me has reawakened that which had lain dormant for so long. I wake with my face wet, my body trembling, my eyes wide with fear—from a dream. Lucas sleeps so deeply that he has not heard me yet, but he may. In my dreams, I see Richards coming toward me, and I find myself frozen with fear, unable to move, to run away.

August 1

Celebrations! Colorado attained statehood today. Much remains to be resolved, of course, but it is surely a step forward. The union of these United States grows larger and stronger each year. I worry, and wonder, about how this change might affect our marriage, but if that should happen, we will find some way to stay together. I fear inquiring, lest we call attention to ourselves.

We heard about this event while in town. Lucas had at my request taken me to meet the new schoolteacher. We left the children with Alma and rode to town. (I am becoming quite a respectable horsewoman. Mama would say I am boasting, but it is true nonetheless.) Of course we had to rise earlier than usual to do all the chores before departing, but it was worth it.

Georgina is small, slender, with red hair and green eyes that seem to bore through whatever they gaze upon. She looks like a schoolteacher, with her hair pinned into a neat bun and eyeglasses resting partway down her nose. I was a little taken aback at first, but then she smiled. When she smiles, it warms her whole face. I think she will be able to keep the students well in line if she does not smile too much.

Georgina and I met at the horse fountain in the center of Main Street and sat in the shade of the oak tree, which has grown stately over the years, spreading its branches for some distance in every direction. It was quite hot—I felt very much like shedding my clothes! Of course I did not. But why must women be constricted so?

She comes from Indiana, she told me. She came to Johnson City at the invitation of her cousin, the wife of one of the town's newer residents and the mother of two children who need schooling. I asked her about those progressive educational ideas I have heard about.

"It isn't really revolutionary," she said with a smile. "Just that not all learning need be by rote, and that treating children harshly, punishing them for *not* learning, accomplishes little. Children who are engaged in their learning retain their knowledge much better than those who are taught by the rod. Kindness goes much farther."

"But you can't be too kind," I replied, remembering my grade school days. The teachers were always stern, seldom smiled, and rarely showed themselves to be human. We saw them as persons of authority. Anyone who misbehaved received several sharp whacks with the ruler, the boys not infrequently having to bend over, a singular indignity. The girls were struck on the open palm. Sometimes, children were made to stand in the corner for hours. Though I thought the punishments harsh, all of us children knew we were only a few ruler smacks away from anarchy. Without authority, without control, how can a teacher maintain order?

"No," she said, frowning slightly. "But I do not believe in physical punishment. Hitting children accomplishes only resentment and rebellion."

As for me, I have never hit Meggie or Randall, nor has Lucas. I cannot imagine bringing myself to do so. Meggie is a willful child, determined and stubborn, but she will yield to authority when she sees no other way. Randall is so compliant I sometimes worry about him. It does not seem natural. Lawrence and I were not raised with the paddle either, which is why Karl's brutish approach was such a shock to us.

"I wish you well," I told our new teacher. "Some of the boys who plan to attend the school are probably as tall as you are, and from what I've heard they may be coming just to challenge you and to start trouble."

"I'd not be surprised," she acknowledged. "I think they will find they have met their match. Mr. Marks is willing to support whatever I do, he says." She certainly piqued my curiosity. I am quite eager to see how she manages. School does not start until the harvests are in, of course, and will only continue through early spring, when the children are needed on the farms.

"Will your school have a piano?" I asked her. The building is still in process, with all of the men in the town helping out as often as they can.

"It will if I have my way. I believe music is a very important part of a child's education."

"I could come and play for the children sometimes."

Her eyes lit up. "Would you? That would be splendid."

So now I have something to look forward to. Georgina and I agreed we would try to meet from time to time. I feel I have met a kindred spirit.

Not that I do not love Alma dearly, and treasure her friendship, but we are far, far apart when it comes to the life of the mind. Georgina, on the other hand, is a worldly, intelligent woman who has been among civilized society recently. There is so much we can share!

We talked until Lucas returned. Today was a happy day for me.

August 18

Lucas is thirty-eight years old today and has yet to resume the practice of medicine as his main vocation, though his fame as a healer has spread and people do come to the farm from time to time to ask for his help. He has tended to bullet wounds and injuries from plows or hatchets. One man chopped three of his fingers off! When called to the farm, Lucas very calmly sewed them back on somehow, and bandaged the hand. He tended it frequently for some time after the incident. The man still has the fingers, all attached, though he says they are stiff and have diminished sensation. I believe my husband is far ahead of his time in his medical ideas and practices. He says he learned many of these techniques when he studied in Greece, for in ancient Greece their methods were far advanced of their time. Lucas uses herbs to diminish pain and prevent infection, and it seems to work amazingly well.

Still, at present Lucas is a farmer who occasionally treats people with injuries or illnesses, not a doctor who farms for pleasure, at his leisure. This farm ties us down so! We have only one more year before we can claim the homestead; then we can sell it. I hope Adam will buy it so I will not have to completely abandon Little Adam's gravesite. Lucas and I must talk about this soon.

I have several times told him of my desire to relocate to the town, to sell the farm, and each time he says he wants to wait until we claim the homestead before we talk about the future. I no longer yearn to go abroad, and I am certain Lucas has put aside all thoughts of California; our future is here, on the high plains of Colorado. But not on this farm.

Serious conversation with my husband is proving quite difficult amid this life we lead. We are both so weary by nightfall; we work so hard all day that words with any meaning at all do not come easily. We want only to go to bed, to ready ourselves for the next day's demands. When can we talk?

September 20

My encounter with Georgina has borne excellent fruit. Choosing her companions with great care, she has formed a Ladies' Circle, which meets once a week to sew (and talk). She invited me to join. I can't go often, of course; I don't get to town more than twice a month at the most, and it isn't always possible for me to attend the circle even then, but what a joy for me when I can be there with them.

I worried at first. How would the ladies respond to me, married to a Negro? Georgina assured me she had discussed that with them and, although some were shocked at first, all agreed that I was welcome and that they would say nothing unkind to me. If anyone did, she and the others would ask them to leave. And indeed, no one has even mentioned it.

Lucas and I heard some terrible stories about wagon trains of former slaves, heading west, which were pillaged and destroyed, the men killed, because the Southern planters wanted to frighten their labor force into returning to the cotton fields. Out here in Colorado, it is easier sometimes to set aside thoughts of how vicious people can be, especially toward those whose skin is a different color. Why? Nothing makes any of us different except our beliefs and our behavior. Lucas is a fine a man as ever walked this earth.

The circle has helped me be less discontented out here on the farm, but my soul is restless. I tell no one, not even Mama in my letters, how much I long to leave this place, though I think in his heart Lucas knows.

December 24, 1876
Dear Mama,

Once again Christmas is almost upon us. I have not written to you for some time. I enclose sketches of your grandchildren, both of them bright and beautiful children. Randall reminds me so much of Lawrence when he was small.

We are still on the farm. It is thriving. We live in a log house with three rooms and a loft, built by Lucas and Adam, our neighbor. Compared to our first house here, it seems like a castle to me. We had a good crop this year so the cold cellar is full. We abound in the riches of the land.

I have made some new friends, women in the town, and I have joined a Ladies' Circle. The men think we meet to chat and sew, and we do both of those things. The members were chosen carefully. All of us are advocates for the vote for women. I recall your saying often, though not in Karl's hearing, that women should be able to vote just like men and own property even though married. You have imbued me with these radical ideas. Why should women be held back from accomplishing whatever we are capable of in life?

I firmly believe that the opening up of the West to settlement will mean a turning point in this cause. We women who live here, in these difficult conditions, are independent, capable and strong. (I know you are saying, "Don't boast, Hannah," but this is a truth I cannot suppress.) We will not endure being oppressed forever! In our meetings, we write letters to legislators and the President, and we study ways to achieve our goal without lying down in front of carriages or going on hunger strikes, as some women have done. We will seek our goal through trying to get the laws changed.

You would be proud of me, Mama.

> *With love and devotion,*
> *Hannah*

1877

January 19

Once again Nature has played her hand, showing us all that she is in charge of the universe. Many people here say her caprices are the hand of God, but I prefer not to believe that, for Nature can be very cruel and I do not want my God to be cruel. We have had a terrible, killing blizzard that has so far lasted four days. Thanks to the rope, Lucas can get to the barn, and we have learned to store water in the house in winter, but the power of this storm is awe-inspiring. The wind blows with mighty force, driving the snow horizontally across the landscape. Lucas says the animals are cringing in their stalls. We cannot sleep for the howling of the storm. The children are frightened.

Since we have lived here, I have seen hail as large as my fist fall from the sky. I have seen weeks on end with no rain, with merciless, shimmering heat like a desert. There has been rain enough to wash away houses on low ground, and the thunder-storms are mighty. Lightning splits the sky. Thunder sounds like cannons. But this storm, which has imprisoned us inside for so many days, is the most forceful demonstration of Nature's raw power that I have seen. I thank God we are inside, and safe. Poor Freedom! He wants to go outside, but when he sticks his little head out, he is forced back in again. Puss just curls up in a corner; coming out only to eat and retreating again. I have laid straw in one corner of the front room for Freedom and made a box of soil for Puss. I will clean up when the storm eases. We will all just have to suffer their stench and our own.

January 27

The natural burst of temper is over at last, and it left a layer of snow so deep that Lucas cannot walk in it but has to shovel a path through it. The snow is crusty; when someone does step in it, it makes a deep, narrow hole. The sun has come out and is shining thinly. I had hoped it would soon melt the snow, but Adam and Lucas say that will take many days of warmth and sun. Adam lost most of his sheep. He will have to start over again to build his flock.

I hope the snow melts soon, at least enough for travel, because I want to go to town to visit with Georgina and see the school.

February 7

It is most enlightening to watch Lucas with his small son. He is gentle with him, and kind, but he pushes him to achieve. Even at this young age, when Randall is walking with the uncertain gait of a small child, Lucas will not ever carry his son. He was not this way with our daughter. What is the difference, I wonder? Is it because Randall is his son, and he thus expects so much more of him?

March 21

It is still fiercely cold, although spring is upon us. In this place, it seems it can be hot in winter and cold in summer. We exist at the whim of the weather.

On a balmy, spring-like day last month (such amazing weather here!) I did get to town and visited the school. It was quite an enlightening experience. Georgina says she has no need of physical punishment to control her classroom, and I now understand why.

The day I was there, three good-sized boys from farms near town came to the school, insisting they wanted to attend the class. Small though she is, she walked right up to them and asked their names and what grade level they supposed they had achieved.

"Why, ma'am," said the biggest boy, "I ain't been to school at all 'fore now. Reckon I'm in first grade." And he headed for the desk of the smallest child in the school, the youngest Schmidt boy, and started to sit, clearly meaning to shove little Joey off the seat. Georgina walked over to the desk and fixed upon him the fiercest glare I have ever seen. Who would have supposed her capable of it? As I was sitting quietly in the back of the room, I had a very good view of her face but could only see the back of the boy.

"If you really mean to start in first grade," she said, her sweet tone belying the look in her eyes, "you must sit in that corner and study this reader. In due time, I will come and help you." So saying, she handed him a book and pointed toward a corner of the schoolroom. All of the children turned to stare at him expectantly. To my amazement, he walked over there and sat down.

She then turned to the other two boys. "If you are truly here to learn," she said to them, "I am here to help you. If you are here to make trouble, I will send someone for Mr. Devon. He will be here quite quickly, for his store is just across the street. He will enlist the aid of the sheriff to see that you are ejected promptly. So what will it be?"

Both boys turned around and left the room. Will they be back? I doubt it. But the boy who had gone to the corner stayed, much to everyone's surprise, and by the end of the day admitted to Miss Norton that he can read, write, and cipher credibly well. What he really wants to learn, he told her, is geography. She seems to have subdued him quite capably!

After all the children had left we went to the Marks house where Georgina is boarding, and where I was to stay the night, it being too dark by the time school let out for me to start home again. By now Lucas and I have an understanding that if I have not arrived home by dusk, I will stay in town, so he won't worry about me. I spent a delightful evening with our Ladies' Circle in the Marks's parlor, Mr. Marks having politely gone out for the evening. I had peace of mind, for I had deposited the children with Alma before coming to town.

Knowing Georgina and the other women in the circle helps make my life on the farm more tolerable. There are four others, Mary Austin, Clara Devon, Victoria Marks and Dorothea Brock. In our conversation, we do not talk of cooking, or gardening, or raising chickens or children. No indeed! We talk of politics on the national scene—how the railroad is changing industry and what will happen once federal troops leave the conquered South. We talk of the status of the women's rights campaign, with Susan B. Anthony and others stepping up their efforts. Mary told us about a sort of comic opera she'd heard about, called "Trial by Jury," written by a British composer and librettist named Gilbert and Sullivan. Most delightfully, we talk of books. A new Henry James had just been published and was the subject of much discussion. One either likes Mr. James very much or despises him.

We do sew; we are making a quilt in the rather complicated star pattern. I am learning the art of quilt-making, although I do not suppose I shall ever be very good. Mary and Clara are admirably skilled. I had not known it was such an art, and I am suitably impressed. Our quilt will be raffled to raise money for the church. I do not take much pleasure in the domestic arts, but I find the quilting quite satisfying, I suppose because it is much more creative than cooking or cleaning.

April 13

Margaret's birthday has come around again. Such a child she is—bright and lively, curious, quick and full of life. I love her so.

April 16

More about my circle friends: Mary and Clara are especially adventurous. They have a commonality—both are mail-order brides. Mary, who comes from Connecticut, ran a small bake shop she inherited from her father. Well launched into her thirties, she was eking out a living as a lonely spinster. One day she saw an advertisement in the newspaper, western bachelors seeking wives. She sent a letter to one of them; he replied with money and a photograph enclosed, and soon she was on the train, heading to Colorado. She felt she had little to lose with such an adventure except her lonely life, and the money she got from the sale of her business financed her travels. She left behind no close friends or family. She says she has found Mr. Austin, as she calls him, quite a satisfactory mate.

Clara, on the other hand, does have family. Plain and quiet, she lived in Virginia with her younger sister and their family, who had suffered considerable deprivations during the war and had not yet fully recovered. I presume from what she said that she was little more than a servant and nursemaid in the household. The children were disrespectful, her brother-in-law resentful of having to support her despite all the work that she did, and her sister too meek to stand up for herself or for Clara (reminding me of Mama). So the chance to come west, with expenses paid, seemed a godsend to her.

An ardent suffragette, Clara admires Miss Anthony tremendously; indeed, she too has heard her speak. I asked her why, given that lady's views on marriage and on men, she had chosen to marry herself. She replied that she believed—and has found it to be true—that women in the West are more independent, less inclined to obey their husbands without question, than ladies back east. She is convinced that the move to obtain votes for women will henceforth be powered by those of us who emigrated westward. Perhaps she is right.

Clara is nearly forty and Mr. Devon is well into his fifth decade, I estimate, so this pair is unlikely to become parents, leaving her free to pursue her interests. She too chose well; Robert is a good man with progressive ideas.

Dorothea is the intrepid widow who operates the grain mill with a partner. She is succeeding admirably at her chosen work, slowly earning the respect of the men who are her customers. Indeed, several have wooed her, but she refuses all suitors. She says she is perfectly content as she is and has no desire to give up her independence again. She is childless; her husband, like my father, died in the War Between the States. She came to Colorado after the war because she wanted a new start in a place which had not been affected by the war, she tells us. She had read about Colorado and seen paintings and photographs. I am not certain why she settled in Johnson City, and I have not asked. But as shrewd as she is, I think she must see good potential here.

Victoria came to Colorado to marry Owen Marks upon his invitation. They had once been betrothed but had quarreled, which was the reason Mr. Marks emigrated to Johnson City. He frequently wrote to her, trying to make amends, and she finally relented and agreed to marry him. She is shy and sweet; I think she shall not become as good a friend to me as the others, for she is not forthcoming.

April 18
Margaret came upon me tending Little Adam's grave today. She

asked me what I was doing, and I told her that I was caring for the grave of her brother, Adam. I decided then that she should know about her twin. I had not told her before. It is still so painful for me, and she hadn't asked. But Margaret is a person who demands the truth.

"He was born the same day you were," I said, "but he died."

"Why did he die?" she asked, those large eyes piercing.

Dear God, what was I to say to her? She understands a great deal, but she is only four!

At last I said, "I don't know why. He was not strong like you, and he just couldn't stay alive long enough to be born."

She continued to gaze at me. "Did I kill him?" she asked.

"Oh, darling girl, no! Never think that!" I cried. "You are strong and he was not, and that's what happened. Papa tried, but he couldn't save him."

"Did Papa kill him?"

That she could even think such a thing! I was horrified. Lucas would never, never kill anyone. I fear my voice trembled a bit when I said, "Your papa heals people, he doesn't kill them. He would never kill anyone."

But my daughter was still not satisfied. She stood before me, small and sturdy, swaying slightly, her thumb in her mouth. "Did God kill him?"

"God loves people, Margaret; He doesn't kill them."

"Where is he now?"

Should I tell her he is in heaven, when I am not sure myself? I thought a moment, then touched my heart and said, "He is here, in my heart, and in your papa's."

I hoped she was content with the information she now had.

She considered for a long moment, then put her hand on her heart. "Then he's here in my heart, too," she said, and went off to play with the cat, happy at last with what she knew. As she grows, I expect she will think of her twin sometimes, but I don't know what her thoughts might be. Will she feel sorrow? Anger? Pain? I wish I could save her from that, but I know I cannot.

July 1

We have met our obligation and can now claim this land. Perhaps it won't be too long before Lucas will agree to sell it and move to town as I so long to do. He can ply his craft, I mine. We will manage. Though the first well Lucas dug dried up, we called upon a water witcher (what a curious endeavor—but it works) Adam knew to find water, and they have dug another successful well. We have put up fence, built a house, and acquired stock. We have planted and harvested crops. It is amazing to contemplate that we have been here five years. Meggie is four, growing sturdy and strong. Lucas has begun teaching her to ride, not wanting her education in that regard to be neglected as mine was.

Lucas bought Meggie a pony, which she promptly dubbed Tulip, after her favorite flower. I watched them today as he began the instruction.

"Papa, let go!" Meggie called as her father led the pony around in a circle. She did not look in the least afraid. She sat straight in the saddle, holding lightly to the pommel with one hand and the reins with the other. "She's a natural," Lucas pronounced. He did not release Tulip, but I am sure he soon will. My daughter looked so precious, with her dark hair flying and her eyes snapping with delight. She shouted with laughter as Lucas encouraged Tulip to trot. I knew not a moment's trepidation. Meggie will be competent at whatever she undertakes, but her derring-do worries me.

Randall at two years is a sweet, agreeable child, easy to care for. He seldom speaks, yet he is affectionate and seems happy. He seems perfectly content to allow Meggie to rule the roost and follows her wherever she goes, although he's too young for a pony just yet, so when she rode he stood clinging to my leg and watching, wide-eyed. I don't think he will be willing to take chances, as she is.

I worry sometimes that he is not progressing normally. He seems to live inside his head most of the time, sitting quietly or holding a book without turning the pages. How can I tell? I know that he is very different from his sister and from other children his age that I have seen, but I do not know why.

Alma says it is God's will, that He has created in Randall a special child. When Alma invokes her all-powerful God, as she often does, I find my wavering faith in a deity severely tested. I cannot believe in a god of such consuming, demanding presence, so much like the god Karl imposed on me. I must find my own way to belief. When she talks of her faith, I usually just smile and listen. I love her and don't wish to engage in argument with someone I love.

August 7

Lucas has gone with Adam to Denver to help him buy some ewes and rams so he can rebuild his herd. They will be gone for three or four days. I miss Lucas, but I do not mind being here alone with the children now. Alma will come tomorrow for a visit, and we will harvest beans.

Thanks to Alma, I have mastered the arts of gardening and preserving the produce. I can make quite an admirable jar of strawberry jam or preserves, and Alma says I should enter my apple jelly in the county fair competition this year. Though I take pleasure in tending my garden and putting up the fruit, I do not relish it the way Alma does; it does not bring me fulfillment.

Today is Mother's birthday. She is sixty years old. Does she think of Lawrence and me? Does she wonder what's become of us? I do not think of her much anymore, although sometimes she comes sharply into my mind when I am attempting to instruct my children along a particular path. Her words float into my brain, then come out of my mouth. Am I becoming my mother?

I hope I am stronger than she is, more freethinking, more willing to defend and protect my children than she chose to be. I cannot pretend to comprehend the reasons for her behavior, her reasons for such an unwise marriage, so I shall try to remember only the gifts she gave me, the values and wisdom she passed on, instead of the bitter memories that sometimes come to mind. I shall try to think of her in the happy time before Papa died and she married Karl. When I remember her thus, I miss her still.

August 13

Lucas's birthday is almost upon us. Alma and I have determined to make an occasion of it this year. She is making her special burnt-sugar cake, and Adam has devised a pole with streamers. We have invited the Sorensens to join us for the celebration. We plan to roast a pig.

September 2

Even though I disapprove and have tried to make that clear, Lucas is now determined that Randall will overcome his fear of horses. He has put the boy on Tulip, ignoring his screams of terror and my pleas, and has led the pony around the ring, with Randall's face pale with fear, his little hands clinging for dear life. Twice Lucas has done this!

I became very angry at him the second time. He said to me, "My son must learn to be a western man. We can't start too soon."

" 'My son!' " He is *our* son, born of our love for each other. He does not belong to his father alone. I should have—must have—some say in how he is reared. Why is he so proprietary toward Randall and so undemanding of Margaret?

What does it mean to be a "western man," anyway? One who rides horses, shoots a rifle and wears a broad-brimmed hat?

I will put a stop to this. Randall shall not be terrorized.

October 6

More difficulty with Jacob Richards: last week he shot one of Adam's sheep dogs. He hit the poor creature in the leg, so the dog will no longer be able to herd sheep. Adam is sure the dog did not trespass. We do not know what provoked Richards to shoot a harmless dog. My heart raced with fear. What heinous act is the man not capable of doing?

There are other neighbors now, more and more. Richards was not able to buy any land that touches ours or Adam's. But he is still here, causing trouble. What motivates the man? Adam complained to the sheriff, but as usual Musgrave has no way to prove that it was Richards. But no one else shoots dogs. I shall be even more vigilant about Freedom, though he seldom leaves my side, or Lucas's when his master is at home.

Freedom pays little attention to the children, nor they to him. Randall adores Puss, is always trying to pick him up and carry him around, and for the most part Puss endures patiently. It is so precious to watch. It is touching to see him lavish such love on the little creature, for he seems to live in his own little world most of the time and not notice or care when we are tired or impatient or cross. He seems curiously oblivious to the people in his life.

Yet he is very particular about some things. If we don't have a meal at the usual time, he gets anxious and starts to wail very softly. He is always ready to go to bed at exactly the same time, and he wants to hear the same story over and over again instead of a different one. When I kiss him goodnight, he does not respond to me with a loving hug or kiss as Meggie does.

I don't know what's wrong with my child.

November 10

We are having a mild winter. Lucas is able to work outside nearly every day. He is often far from the house, and I always have the rifle nearby. I still have not told him about the incident with Jacob Richards. I do not believe I ever will. I find that as the days go by and I become more and more accustomed to being here alone with the rifle handy, I am beginning to conquer my fears. I have faith that I can protect myself and my children should the need arise.

We had a sad and curious episode a few days ago. I was at the stove, cooking, when I happened to look toward the window and saw a dusky face peering in. Although I was startled, I was not afraid, for we have often seen Indians in the town. Having been dispossessed of their land by the soldiers, they sometimes come around for jobs or handouts.

I have never seen one so close to our house before, although I have sometimes seen them walking by from a distance. Standing at the window, looking in, he presented an unusual spectacle. He wore a small headdress, one feather in a band around his head, and his hair, long, gray and unkempt, stuck out every direction. One eye was nearly closed and drooped; the other was rheumy. He wore only a loincloth, with moccasins on his feet. He was so thin his bare chest caved inward. Even though the weather is warm for this time of year, it was still too cold to be so scantily clad; he shivered. He swayed back and forth slightly as he stood, as if his body could not quite support itself.

Leaving the children inside, I walked out to talk to him. "What do you want?" I asked, knowing that he might not speak English. But he surprised me. "Hungry," he replied. His voice was raspy and thin. How hungry must such a proud man be before he begs for food? For these Indians are proud people. We have not treated them well.

"I'll get you something to eat," I told him. "Wait here."

He squatted at the trunk of the maple in front of our house, leaning back on his haunches. He seemed unperturbed by the view he was presenting to me.

I wrapped some cornbread and bacon in a cloth. Looking around, I also found some boiled eggs and a piece of pie. I added those items and took them out to him. When he saw the food, he began to eat as if he had not had any sustenance for days, shoveling the food into his mouth with both hands at once. I could see how thin his legs were. Loose flesh hung from his arms, which must once have been very muscular. I am not certain how old he was, but I would venture to guess that he was well advanced in age.

When he had finished eating, he let forth an enormous belch. He turned to walk away. He had gone no more than a few feet when he slumped to the ground. He made no sound as he fell.

I ran into the house, picked up the rifle, ran outside, and fired one shot high into the air. Lucas came on the run. By the time he got to the man, who lay in an ignominious heap on the ground, life had fled. "He's dead," Lucas said quietly.

I had seen death before many times at the hospital but never so unexpectedly. He had just finished consuming my food with a hearty appetite. I could not understand. "What could have caused such a sudden death?"

"I could not be sure unless I cut him open, but I am pretty certain that his heart simply gave out. He must have been starving for some time."

I am trying to eradicate from my memory the image of him falling and dying, but I cannot erase the guilt I feel about the Indians. At least, I tell myself, this one came here and received compassion, instead of wandering onto Richards's place and being killed, or riddled with buckshot like Adam's dog.

Lucas and Adam took the poor man's body to Johnson City for burial, but were denied the church graveyard because he was not a Christian. They left him then with the sheriff, who is going to try to locate his tribe so they can provide him with a burial appropriate to their beliefs. Mr. Musgrave is a decent man, a true Christian, even if lacking gumption in going after wrongdoers. We have had Cheyenne and Arapaho in the area from time to time; I expect the poor dead man is one of those. There is no way for any of us to determine his origins, so we can hope that someone claims him.

This experience calls to mind the many times I tried, and failed, to find out who a dying soldier was, so his family could be notified and his effects sent to them. Sometimes all we could find on the young bodies was a letter from home, signed with just a first name, worn from being read over and over, or a letter the soldier was composing to his wife or sweetheart. Sometimes there was a painting or daguerreotype. It saddened me so not to be able to send it to someone in the soldier's family, since we did not know who they were.

December 31

It is the last day of the dying year. Each year that begins anew brings with it hope and promise, and the reality is always somewhat different. I fear I am indulging in self-pity. I am not helped by the fact that Lucas has gone into one of his silent moods again and will not tell me what is wrong. Perhaps it was the death of the old man. Perhaps it is worry about Richards. More likely, it is frustration at not being able to practice his chosen profession, his life's work. Doctoring is what he was born to do. I am only surmising that this is what has brought on the black mood. He does not talk to me of his worries.

There's news—Georgina and Reverend Chadwick will be

married in the spring. She has insisted she will only marry if she can be allowed to continue teaching at the school, an unheard-of precedent. Fortunately, Robert Devon is sympathetic to her views (no doubt to a considerable degree due to Clara's influence), and he has persuaded the school board to allow it as long as she remains childless. She says she does not wish to become a mother, preferring to mother her little charges at school. Laughing, she said to me, "They go home at night to their parents. I go home to a good book."

I hope she and Herbert have come to an agreement on this subject. Don't most men wish to father children, to carry on the family name? Boldly, I intend to bring up this topic with Georgina one day soon. For one thing, I need to make sure she has access to the information Lucas has provided me about how to keep herself from being with child. It requires Herbert's co-operation, of course, but if he agreed to allow her to continue to work at her chosen profession, he will surely agree to this.

1880

February 12

I have determined that I am going to make Lucas listen to me about selling the farm. My unhappiness has grown, and when I have tried to tell him he has always postponed the conversation until "later." Now, later has come, and we must talk about it.

We can sell out to Adam and move to town. The children must go to school; we live too far from town to take Meggie back and forth every day, and I will not board her in town, not even with my beloved Georgina. I must have music, and stimulation, and something in my life besides this exhausting, constant work. Men say it is the lot of women to make a home, to care for the children, to support their mates. I say it is the misfortune of women to be shackled so. And I will do it no longer.

February 14

Jacob Richards is a man who takes his time in exacting revenge. I am sitting by our bed, watching Lucas fight for his life. Richards has shot him.

Lucas went out yesterday to tend the fences. As time for the evening meal approached and he had not returned, I grew concerned. I prepared the meal and fed the children, then went outside to look for him. I had no sooner stepped out the door than Nappy came into the yard saddled but riderless. I was truly frightened then. Lucas was in trouble, or the horse would not have returned alone.

I considered what to do. If I went to look for him, I would have to leave the children alone. Meggie is only seven, hardly old enough to tend her little brother and herself. I had no notion where he might be, nor what I would do if I found him. I hoped Nappy would lead me to him, but I was not certain of that.

After brief deliberation I decided to ride to the Baumgartens' in the wagon with the children and leave them there while Adam and I went to search for Lucas.

Adam, of course, did not want me to go along, but I was adamant. "Lucas is my husband. I must know what has happened to him," I said.

It had grown dark when we set out. Adam rode Nappy, hoping he would take us to Lucas. I drove the wagon with his team. We rode out to the northern edge of our property, west of where it touches Adam's. We had a lantern which provided some illumination, but it was difficult to see. After an eternity, Nappy headed toward a deep spot in the creek and whinnied.

There lay Lucas, half in and half out of the water. The water was dark with his blood. I suppressed a scream. He was breathing; he was alive, but his breaths were shallow and labored. We managed, between the two of us, to get him into the wagon. He was much heavier than I would have thought, since he is so slim. He was not conscious, just an unresponsive weight. Adam grunted with the effort. I held Lucas's arms and head.

I could not see what was wrong but felt certain he had been shot. I have seen enough wounded soldiers to recognize the wounds.

And that proved to be the case. When we got him home and onto the bed, I could see the hole in his shoulder made by the bullet. I knew that I must tend to him immediately. Adam did not know how, and Alma was caring for the children, who must not be allowed to see their father in such a state. Besides, for all her healing skills, I doubt she has ever tended a bullet wound. Nor had I, and my observations at the hospital during the war were many years ago. But I had only a month or so ago watched Lucas remove a bullet from the leg of a man who accidentally shot himself.

When we got his coat and shirt off, I determined that the bullet had entered his right shoulder just below the shoulder bone, not far from his neck. Slightly different aim would have surely killed him. Dear God, I had to clean and suture the wound.

I checked his pulse as Lucas has taught me to do, thanking him silently for the medical knowledge he has shared with me over the years. The beat was weak but steady—a good sign, I thought. I noted that the blood had clotted, another good indicator.

In his medical bag I found a pair of tweezers that looked to be the right instrument, and a sharp knife to open the wound a little more. Lucas was still unconscious, but I tried to get him to swallow a little laudanum so he would not have pain. As he could not manage it, I proceeded, fearful that waiting any longer could be deadly. After cleaning the tweezers in carbolic, I carefully, slowly opened the wound a little farther in order to see better. Adam held the lantern for me. His hand shook. He was uncharacteristically silent.

I endeavored to keep my own hands steady as I probed with the tweezers to find any remnants the shell might have left and to clean the wound. It seemed to take hours. I was anxious to avoid any possibility of infection, so I stopped often and cleaned the tweezers. When I had the area as clean as I could manage, I poured alcohol into the open wound. Lucas stirred slightly and moaned; I tried to block out the sound. Once I had cleaned the wound, I closed it up carefully with neat, small stitches. Lucas moaned again.

Adam had to help me turn Lucas over so I could clean and bandage the exit wound on his back. The bullet had gone through at a downward angle, exiting a few inches below the entrance wound and leaving a jagged opening. It came very close, I believe, to puncturing a lung but did not. It took another eternity to clean and dress that wound. I stitched it with one of my sewing needles, praying all the while that he would not come to and feel the pain. I wondered, later, if I should have done that first. Indeed, I had almost forgotten about the exit wound until Adam asked me about it.

Having done what I had to do, I proceeded to behave in an unexpectedly womanly fashion and faint dead away. Poor Adam! He eventually left, after he had aroused me and seen that nothing more could be done at present, to tell the news to Alma. He said he would bring some of her healing salves back with him the next time he came, and he assured me that he and Alma would care for the children as long as need be. His parting words were, " 'Twere Richards. Musgrave has to go after him now, or I will." The sheriff had been curiously reluctant to charge Richards with any of his previous crimes, saying he lacked evidence. Of course, we once again have no evidence, but who else could it be?

Now I sit with Lucas, waiting for him to regain consciousness. I wipe his forehead, wet his lips, feel his pulse, and pray. He lay in that cold water, losing blood, for such a long time. I fear for his life.

February 16

Three days, and Lucas has still not come around, although he stirs and moans from time to time. I don't know what else to do for him. He thrashes about in his delirium; I fear he will reopen one of the wounds. Sometimes, he calls "Maman." Once, he called my name as he was moving his body back and forth. I am not strong enough to hold him down. Dear Lord, what shall I do?

I have wrapped him in every blanket I can find to keep him warm, and cleaned around the stitches. I see no sign of infection; the wounds are clean, though red, with no yellow matter around them. He does not seem feverish. Yet he has not awakened. When he calls out, he never opens his eyes. I know he is unconscious still.

What to do? How to help? I am so weary; I sleep from time to time in the chair, but I will hear him when he wakes.

February 17

This morning Lucas opened his eyes and spoke my name. He reached for my hand and held it a moment before falling asleep again. This was a natural sleep, thank goodness. The crisis has passed. I felt his forehead for signs of fever, but there were none. The wounds were healing well. Thank God! I knelt for a prayer of thanks. Let the healing begin.

At noontime, I prepared a light chicken broth and woke him to eat. He managed to swallow a few bites, then slept again. It is a healing sleep. I woke him again later to eat some milk custard. Often at the hospital we fed the patients such bland, soft food, easy for them to swallow while they were recovering from an injury. They frequently complained and asked for "real food," but the doctors insisted they could not have such until they were stronger. Sometimes, I wondered how they would get stronger with the kind of food one might feed an infant, but I kept my silence, and now I am doing the same for Lucas. How glad I will be when he complains of the fare!

Lucas woke again late in the evening. He talked a little then; he asked me what had happened and I told him what I had done. "I cleaned everything very carefully," I assured him.

"You did well," he told me.

"You taught me well," I replied. I have often wondered, indeed, why physicians insist that women are not capable of learning their profession. Did I not perform a surgical procedure? My hands are smaller than a man's; surely that was an advantage in this situation. Perhaps one day more than a very few women will be admitted to medical schools. I did hear once about a woman who was allowed to attend a medical school back east somewhere and went on to practice medicine, but she seems not to have moved the established order very far in our direction. For myself, I never want to do such a thing again, but I have proved to myself that I could!

Adam brought discouraging news. Though the sheriff was deeply regretful about what happened to Lucas and promised to see what he could do to find the culprit, he informed Adam that the bullet could have come from anyone's gun. Most of the men (and women) around here own the same kind of rifle. Since there were no witnesses, even Lucas himself not being able to say for certain that it was Richards who shot him, the sheriff once again could not charge the man with any crime.

February 20

Lucas is sitting up now, eating well, and his color is much better. He thinks the wounds are healing. He told me his recollection about what happened.

"I was riding Nappy along the fence, checking for breaks, when I heard the click of a rifle. I turned in the saddle, looking for the source of the sound, when I felt the bullet hit. I tried to hang onto the saddle horn and start for home, but I must have fallen off the horse and slid into the water. That's the last thing I remember.

"If I had not turned as I did, he would have shot me in the back and surely killed me. That was his intent."

"But you did not see Richards?"

"I saw no one. Wherever he was, he was well concealed, behind a cottonwood, perhaps."

"We don't know, then, that it was Richards."

"*I* know," said Lucas. "I know."

There was some small chance it could have been someone else, for people have come onto our land from time to time. I thought about the Mexican cowpuncher who stopped by for water; I thought about the old Indian. But then I remembered Richards lurching toward me in the dark in town. He is so angry, so full of hate. This is his vengeance on us for being his neighbors and living together as man and wife despite our different skin colors. A cold band of fury enveloped me. I wanted to ride over to his land and shoot him. He tried to kill my husband!

Why, I wondered, did he wait so long? Had Lucas done something that caused him finally to turn his anger into action? I could think of no incident recently—but Lucas does not tell me everything. Many parts of his life are kept hidden from me. He tries to keep me from fretting too much, so he does not often tell me about unpleasant episodes.

"Did something happen to bring this on?" I asked him as we shared the evening meal. (He is eating "real food" quite handily now.)

"I have pondered that question as I lie here," he replied. "All I can recollect is that we encountered one another at the bank a few days ago. I bumped into him by accident as he was entering and I was leaving. I apologized, but no doubt I was not servile enough to suit him."

It is hard for me to fathom that an unintended act such as bumping into someone and apologizing could trigger such a coldhearted action, but Adam has frequently said that Mr. Richards has a heart of stone and would kill his own mother if sufficiently provoked. Apparently, he does not need much provocation to kill. Yet he waited so long! Why?

March 7

Lucas is still very weak, but he is on his feet now and moving about, although carefully. Being a physician, he is acutely aware of his physical condition, so he guards his strength each day. The children have returned home. I told them that their father had been ill but is much better now. Until he is stronger, I have decided to delay my demand that we leave the farm.

Though recovering in his body, he does not seem to be recovering in his mind. He has gone into the dark place again, only this time he pays no attention even to the children. He speaks to me, or to them, not at all except to say that Richards must be made to pay for what he has done. He talks only of the shooting. It tugs at my heart to see the children hurt and puzzled by his neglect. He is beginning to frighten me. I tried, yesterday, to talk with him. This is not the Lucas I know!

"Lucas, you must let the law take care of Richards," I said to him.

"The law will do nothing," he answered. "The sheriff has said there is no proof."

"The Marshal will come soon," I said.

"And how will he respond differently? Do you really think any lawman will try to find out who shot a black man?" Lucas's tone was so sharp, so bitter, that I drew away from him.

"We must not let this destroy us. It is time to leave the farm and move to town, where there are more people and we can start a new life."

He only looked at me with those dark, handsome eyes. He said nothing.

At night, he lies still in our marriage bed, gazing at the ceiling, silent. He does not move away if I touch him; neither does he respond. Saddest is the way he treats the children—he often does not reply when they speak to him. He has not resumed Randall's riding or Meggie's French lessons. He barely touches his meals.

We cannot go on this way.

March 20

Every day I try to talk to Lucas about leaving the farm. Yesterday, Adam visited and offered to buy it outright. Lucas merely looked at him—at his old friend and helper!—with blankness in his eyes, got up, and left the house. He has not started the spring planting. He feeds the stock and does his chores, but he is no companion to me nor father to his children. The man who loved us, whom we loved, has gone away somewhere, and this shell of a man has come in his place.

April 1

I have begged and pleaded with my husband to talk to me, to work the farm, to pay attention to his children. I only get from him the same dead eyes and silence. I love Lucas, and I want desperately to be a good wife to him, but I must think of the children. Last night I found Meggie sobbing in her bed.

"What's wrong?" I asked.

"Papa says he's going to sell Tulip! You can't let him, Mama. You can't!"

For the last several days Lucas has taken to sleeping in the barn, with the horses. He's there most of the day, too. Meggie told me she had come into the barn that afternoon and asked her papa if he would set her up on Tulip, and he told her to take a good look at Tulip, because she would not be seeing the pony again. When she asked him why, he said he was going to sell him. When she began to cry, he told her to leave the barn or he would turn her over his knee.

Turn her over his knee! Neither one of us has ever raised a

hand to our children. They do not know such harshness and never will. Now Lucas is so distraught that he is threatening our children. It will not do.

After the children were bedded down, I went to the barn to seek him out. "Lucas, why have you threatened to sell Tulip?"

He didn't answer me for a long moment. Then he said, "She won't need the pony in town."

"In town? Does that mean you will sell to Adam and move to town with us?"

"Hannah, I want you to take the children and leave the farm."

"But—"

He continued as though I had not spoken. "I need you to leave, Hannah. I don't want you here."

He doesn't want me! He doesn't want me here, or his children! I never imagined I would hear such words from his lips.

"Why?" I cried. "Lucas, my place is with you. I need to be here, by your side. Why are you sending me away?"

He turned and stepped away from me as I reached out to touch him.

"I need to be alone, Hannah. It is not good for you and the children to be here just now. When I work this poison out of my soul, I will come to you."

"But, Lucas—" I protested once more.

"Go," he said. "Leave the farm. I will come to you when I can. I will put money in the bank for you. You can find a house in town. Tell the children I will come, when I can."

He wants me to leave the farm, leave the only home we have known together.

He drew a deep, shuddering breath and looked at me. For the first time in weeks, he seemed to really see me standing there, tears streaming down my face. But he did not move toward me as he once would have done.

"Hannah," he said at last, "I order you to go."

"Order me? In all the years we've been married, you have never ordered me to do anything."

"I am ordering you now. I want you to leave. Tomorrow."

Weary and full of tears, I at last agreed to what he wanted, though I pleaded with him for some time before finally turning toward the house and beginning to pack. How, oh how, will I tell the children? My heart is breaking, but I will take them—and Freedom, Puss and Tulip—and go to Georgina in the morning. I pray that he will come to us soon.

April 13

Meggie's birthday, and the saddest day of my life. We are in town, at Georgina and Herbert's home, and there has been no word from Lucas. Did he watch us drive away in Adam's wagon? I don't know. I couldn't bear to turn my head and look. I'm not sure I could have seen him, or my house, in any case, because my eyes were blurred with tears.

Georgina has tried her best to console me. Lucas will come soon, she says, and he must have had some very good reason for wanting the children and me to leave the farm. I will find out what that reason is when he comes.

Dear Georgina had a small celebration for Meggie, a chocolate cake (her favorite) and a gift for her. I felt terrible; I had neglected to buy a gift for my own daughter. Instead, I wrapped a one-dollar gold piece in some gaily decorated paper. I felt so negligent; it has always been a particular joy for me to watch her open my carefully chosen gifts. But Meggie seemed content with the effort, even appreciative. She asked that I buy her a small bank to keep her money in. I am grateful that she was not upset.

For the children's sake, I have tried to remain as cheerful as I can. They do not know how I cry at night, reaching for the husband who is not there.

At least I can enter them in school, instead of trying to teach them myself with inadequate materials and knowledge. Meggie can read, and Randall knows his numbers and can count to one hundred, but we have not progressed much beyond that. I find I know so little; they need to know so much. And on the farm there is so little time in the day, with all the chores to do, that we cannot devote many hours each day to learning.

Before we left, I went out and said good-bye to Little Adam. I left some daisies on his grave. Pray God Adam will buy the land as Alma and I had planned, and I will be able to come visit my son's resting place.

Lucas is in the grip of some kind of madness. I can call it nothing else. I never feared that he would harm the children or me, rather that he will take some rash action that will bring the wrath of the law down upon him and change our lives irreparably.

April 15

We have settled Tulip at the livery. Freedom and Puss have adjusted well enough to their new home, although Freedom does not like the Chadwicks' small, enclosed yard, and Puss seems to be causing the good reverend to sneeze. We must find our own home soon. I shall prepare it for us, and for Lucas when he comes. Yes, I shall say *when*, not *if*. I can, I must believe that Lucas will recover soon and join us here.

April 21

Georgina and Herbert have welcomed us most cordially. The parsonage is large and comfortable, but I have started looking for a house. Kind though Georgina is, this is not my house. The situation is awkward for both of us. Not to be mistress of my own house after so many years of doing so is disconcerting, and

I do not think it wise for children to live in the same house as their teacher. And dear as Georgina is, she is not fond of dogs, I fear; Freedom is constantly under her feet.

The children are in school. Meggie is in transports of delight; she adores the whole idea. She learns quickly, and her knowledge of French has impressed most of the other children, although I suspect there are some who are resentful and think she is too strongly promoting herself. Randall is, as always, very quiet. If he likes school or does not like it, I cannot determine. I asked him about it and he merely shrugged, as he so often does (and as he has seen his father do more times than I could count). School will let out soon, as so many children are needed on the farms, but Georgina has said she will continue to tutor my two, to help them catch up with other children their age. It appears they were lagging farther behind than I had supposed.

I have discovered yet another daring educational theory of Georgina's—unlike every other teacher I have ever encountered or known of, she does not attempt to train children with the inclination to write with the left hand out of that "bad habit" but instead allows them to put their pencils in whichever hand they prefer. Thus have I learned that my son prefers the left hand. Some say this is a sign of extraordinary intellect. I hope it will not cause him to be teased.

Randall cries himself to sleep at night, sobbing so terribly that I want to cry myself. He eventually falls asleep, but this must be exhausting him. I go to him and he clings to me and sobs and will not tell me what is troubling him. It must be that he misses his papa, and the farm. Or is he being mistreated at school? Some of the children do not know him and may have remarked on his creamy-brown skin (so beautiful to me). If they are being unkind, Georgina has not mentioned it, nor has Meggie, but I wonder.

I know I must be strong for the children. They do not know

the full extent of the tragedy that has come upon our family, and I pray they will never know. I pray every day that Lucas will come to us and end this terrible time.

And yet I find it wondrous and exciting to be in town at last. Of course this is not Cincinnati, with concerts and balls and worldly people, but neither is it the farm, isolated and dull and demanding. I go to the school every day and play for the children after they have had their noon meal. I shop and mingle and visit.

The town has grown tremendously. We have a barbershop (where the men tend to gather), a dry-goods store, two banks, two attorneys' offices, a druggist's and stationer's store, and even a dentist—though I would not patronize him, for I have heard some unsettling stories about his "medicinal" drinking. This town is liquor-free now, thanks to the ladies, but one can still get "medicinal" liquor at the drugstore. Main Street has expanded in both directions, north and south, and there are even businesses on several side streets now. The general store, where the post office is, has started to specialize in staples and produce. A butcher is soon to set up shop, it is said, as is a photographer.

I can easily understand why people would choose to live here. The air is pure, the sky is almost always blue, the sun shines much more often than in Ohio. The town is favorably situated near water but on high ground. The railroad is coming soon. It's said that many people come here for curative purposes, when they have consumption or lumbago. The climate is considered salubrious for recovery from illness, particularly of the lungs. There are more and more goods and services here, and fewer vices. There is even a small college here now—which five women are attending! Would that I could go. . . .

Georgina and I have talked of starting a small lending library. Herbert has a large collection of books he does not have time to read. Surely we could get other folks in the town to contribute. All we need is a building from which to operate the library, and a librarian to staff it. That will not be Hannah Bowman, for I fully intend to start giving piano lessons as soon as I can find a house and buy a piano. But Clara might enjoy such a pursuit, and I do not imagine Robert would object to her operating a library. She will do it well.

May 1

Today I visited the bank, and Mr. Ferris told me that Lucas had sent him a note authorizing me to take as much money from the account as I should need. There is more than enough to buy a house. At least Lucas does care about us enough to see to our financial needs, though I have not heard from him at all, and Adam tells me he does not come to town.

Oh, Lucas. My heart is breaking. Is yours?

Why did you send us away?

May 7

I have found a house! It is perfect for us. It has been standing empty for a number of years. It is the house out of which the woman about to be murdered emerged screaming on Meggie's christening day so long ago. The murderer, her husband, is dead, hanged that very night, and as she had no family the house has sat vacant all these years. I can purchase it from the bank, which had been holding the property, for a very small sum, perfectly legally. Some say it is haunted, but I don't believe in such things so am untroubled by that possibility.

To be sure of the legality, I visited the newly opened law office of Mr. Harold Watkins, Johnson City's first lawyer. He investigated the matter for me and determined that the house could legally change ownership. I can buy it for a mere $150.

I find considerable pleasure in making my own decisions

about such a weighty matter as purchasing a house and to be managing money all by myself. Sometimes, when I am walking about the town, it almost feels as though my feet have left the earth. I suppose I have always had the belief that I can do such things; I have never before had the opportunity. Yet with all my heart, I wish that Lucas were here to share this time with me. I would give up my newfound freedoms in an instant if I could have my darling here with me now.

The house is furnished, left just as the poor murdered woman had arranged it before her untimely death. It is large, larger than it looks from the front, with three bedrooms, a parlor, a kitchen, and a pantry. There is room on one side to add an office for Lucas to practice medicine, if he ever comes to join us.

In the parlor there is a lovely, large stone fireplace which will help keep us warm in winter. The floors are polished wood, the walls of lath and plaster. I will ask Owen to build a bookshelf for me in the parlor. *My* parlor. In my mind, I have already become the new occupant of this charming little house, although the very thought of it is as frightening as it is thrilling.

Of course it needs a thorough cleaning, and some of the furnishings are unusable. No matter. It will do for us. Georgina wondered whether I was troubled by the fact that a murder had taken place here. She offered to ask Herbert to come and bless the house for us, to chase any evil away.

I thanked her, but said, "The murder was not *in* the house. Certainly there was unhappiness in this house, but I do not believe in evil spirits or ghosts, and I know we will be able to make a happy home here." If I had believed that evil events portend continuing evil, I would never have been able to take up residence in the little sod house when we first came here, a house which had known much unhappiness. We lived there for quite some time with no evidence of restless spirits.

May 10

I will spend two or three days cleaning my house inside and out and whitewashing the walls, and then we will move in. Dear and kind as she is, I do not think Georgina will regret our departure. I am as eager to start my new life as I imagine she is to resume hers. And I must confess that I feel very unchristian envy of her and Herbert, so happy and loving together.

With all my heart I long for Lucas to come join us. He must be suffering as much as I, yet he could not tell me of his feelings. His eyes looked so haunted when I last spoke with him!

In the daytime when I am full of energy and ambition, eager to get the new house ready so we can move in, making plans, I do not think about him so much. It is at night, when I lie alone in my bed, that I feel the loss most keenly. I miss him desperately.

May 17

Meggie talked of Little Adam today, to my surprise. She has not spoken of him once since that day long ago that I told her about him. She looked up from her book and said to me, "Do you think my twin brother would be as clever as I am, Mama? What would he look like? Would he play with me?"

"What caused you to think of him now?" I asked her.

"I always carry him in my heart," she told me gravely. "But sometimes, he comes to me in dreams, and I wonder."

"I don't know what he would be like, Meggie, except that he would be as handsome as you are pretty, and as clever as you are, and he would love you."

"I thought so," she replied with considerable self-satisfaction, and turned again to her book.

May 20

When we entered our new home for the first time after it had been scrubbed and polished within an inch of its life with help from my friends in the Ladies' Circle, an amazing surprise awaited me. There stood a piano in the parlor! It had a large red ribbon on it. What a wonderful gift! I shall be forever grateful to my dear friends. Wherever they got the money to buy this treasure for me, I do not know, but I could not imagine a better housewarming gift.

It is a beautiful Spencer upright with a lovely resonance. It came to Johnson City, I have learned, on the train, destined for the Carver mansion on the hill. But Mrs. Carver, whose piano it was to be, never arrived. Tragically, she died of consumption before she could start the journey, so Mr. Carver sold it to my dear, dear friends.

The ivory keys are clean and unchipped, and the finish on the maple case is polished to a mirror glow. I spent an inordinate amount of time just touching it, caressing the wood and the keys. My joy is unbounded.

However, it will take me some time, I fear, to regain the skill my fingers once possessed. When I play little tunes at the school for the children they seem obliging enough, but when I try to play the pieces I once had mastered, they are quite disobedient. Oh, Mr. Mozart! Mr. Beethoven! Mr. Bach! Shall I ever again do you justice? I shall have to practice every day to recover what I have lost. Fortunately, I brought my tuning device from Cincinnati and have kept it all these years, so I can soon get the piano in perfect tune.

Just to play the instrument, stumbling and fumbling as I do, brings such joy to my heart that I cannot find the words to express it. And here's a wonder—Randall has taken immediately to the piano. He sat down, his little legs dangling on the bench, his arms barely able to reach the keys, and began to play a tune by ear. Only "Twinkle, Twinkle, Little Star," but remarkable nonetheless. He shall be my first pupil.

May 21, 1880

Dear Lawrence,

I have moved to town and have acquired a piano. Your nephew adores it and is quite as talented as you.

I cannot help but remember you sitting at the piano, Lawrence. You too had an early affinity for music. Do you recall how well you played from the time you were five, even though you never learned to read music? Perhaps you are even now playing the piano in a dance hall somewhere, though I know that would shock Mama and Karl.

Papa gave you and me our musical gifts. He played the violin so beautifully! Many an evening we spent enjoying his music, until he went off to war. Mama hid his violin so he could not take it. Did she know what his fate would be, I wonder? Yet after you left, she sold it, which caused me to grieve greatly.

Meggie, your niece, does not seem much interested in the piano, but I believe it is excellent discipline to master basic musical skill, so I shall endeavor to teach her as well. In a month or two, I think I'll "hang out my shingle," so to speak, and start teaching piano to the people here in Johnson City. How I wish you could see my lovely instrument.

Oh, Lawrence, where are you? I miss you so!

Your loving sister,

Hannah

June 25

A most amazing innovation in our town is the installation of an electric plant and water works, so those who can afford to can enjoy modern advancements such as piped-in water and electricity in their own homes. I have not yet decided whether or not to spend the money. I like the new electric lights that illuminate Main Street at night, but I confess I find the idea of electricity somewhat unnerving; I'm not sure why. Water, however, is another matter. To be free of drawing water from our well would be a great gift for me. That task feels so like the drudgery I was tied to every day on the farm. Of course, in town there is still the water wagon, for those who are not connected to the new system, but it only comes around once a week, requiring careful conservation of water between visits.

Our house is across the river from the main part of the town, but Johnson City has grown enough that it is now surrounded by streets full of houses; thus we are not as remote as that poor murdered woman was. The river runs full these days; I keep the children away from it. Robert Devon has offered to put up a picket fence in the backyard so the children can play safely. We are on high enough ground that I do not worry about flooding, but the river is an ever-present danger for children. The fence will confine Freedom, too, which is to the good, because he is still curious and adventurous even though his hair is turning gray around his mouth and eyes.

There has been another manifestation of growth in the town, a new railroad track connecting us with larger municipalities farther west and with Denver, so it is much easier to transport goods—and people—to our town. The track is near our house. This is progress, I am assured, but I do not like the railroad so well, because it is noisy and dirty. The train belches black smoke that makes the air dirty, the train whistle permeates the whole town, and the train is dangerous. Small boys dare it daily, placing some object on the tracks and then racing to get away before the train comes. I will not allow Randall to do that, although I doubt he would ever try such a thing. He is not the least bit like his intrepid sister.

July 4

We enjoyed a wonderful Independence Day celebration in the town center today. There was a colorful parade, with a band and some proud horsemen, and a picnic, and fireworks after dark. The children were enchanted.

Meggie asks me every day, where her papa is and why he has not come to live with us.

What can I tell her? Today I said, "Papa is very busy on the farm just now. You know how much there is to do in the summertime."

"We must go to see him and tell him to come live with us," she insisted. (How like my daughter to demand, not ask, compliance with her wishes.)

"Papa will come as soon as he can," I assured her. "I don't want to go to the farm today; besides, we don't have Nappy or Boney or the wagon. How are we to get there?"

"I could ride Tulip and go by myself," she replied. "I want to see my papa!" She began to cry.

She struck fear in my heart that someday she might decide to do that. She is daring enough! I resolved to tell Owen as soon as I can that, should she appear and ask for Tulip, she is not to have him unless I have given my approval and one of the stable boys accompanies her.

Instead of causing me sorrow as it usually does, this small exchange with my daughter made me feel quite angry with Lucas. How can he be so heartless? How can he abandon his wife and children in this way? I fear to take the children there to visit him—will he only shoo us away again? He told me he will come as soon as he can, and I have to believe that he will.

August 1

I have found one domestic art which I quite enjoy nowadays. I have become skilled at cooking, for it offers me many opportunities to exorcise my anguish—I can knead bread with vigor, whip eggs and beat batter, chop vegetables—all very satisfying indeed. To my surprise, the food to which I have applied such energy seems to taste better than when I was on the farm, and it is a harmless way to dissipate my feelings.

On the farm, cooking was merely a chore, one which must be done in order to survive. I always did it hastily, without imagination. Here, it has become almost like sketching or painting. I enjoy what I create and find that it tastes quite palatable. Lucas will be very surprised when he comes.

August 9

I can hardly find words to record this tragic event, yet I cannot pretend that it did not happen. It eases my mind to write about it.

As we were returning home from the stables, after Meggie had gone for a ride on Tulip with one of Owen's stable boys accompanying her, I looked down on the river from the bridge. There I saw a small scrap of cloth which had not been there earlier. My curiosity aroused, I walked down to the bank on the other side and saw, to my horror, the body of a child. Death is not new to me, nor does it frighten me, but to see this! I did not try to reach down and touch the child, a small boy, but instead began to call for help. Then I realized that my children were watching. Hastily I took each by the hand and hurried home. I could not stop the tears.

Surely there is no feeling worse than for a mother to lose a child. One's infant, carried in the womb, is in so many ways an extension of oneself. The sorrow brought on by such a loss never eases but is always there. It is so with my lost son Adam.

It has left a hole in my heart that will never heal. My heart ached for the mother of this lost child.

Some time later, the sheriff knocked on my door. "Mrs. Bowman, please tell me what happened. We don't know who this child was or how he got in the river. Did you see anything at all?"

No, I told him, only the scrap of cloth billowing up and down, and the dead child when we walked down to see what it was. I too have no knowledge of who this child might be. The sheriff said he looked to be about four years old, and he was wearing knickers and a plaid shirt. No one had any notion where he might have come from or how he got into the river.

This incident brought to mind my first experience with death, an event which occurred at the hospital only a few days after Julia and I had begun volunteering. I was wiping the brow of a young soldier who had been shot in the abdomen. The doctors could not seem to stem the flow of his blood as it slowly left his body and hastened his dying. He was feverish and thrashing about in pain.

He reached for my hand and gripped it much more tightly than I would have thought someone so weak capable of doing. He asked me to write a letter for him. "I'll just get a pad and pen," I told him, and hurried away to find something. I was gone no more than ten minutes, but when I returned he had gone perfectly still, and his face was very pale. I was taken aback and began to call "Help! Help!" Soon a doctor came to his bedside. He lifted the boy's wrist and felt his pulse, then pulled the sheet over his face.

"That one's gone," was all he said. His voice conveyed no emotion.

When he had walked away, I pulled the sheet back down and looked at the boy's face. He barely had a growth of hair. How old could he have been—sixteen? No doubt he went off to war expecting a romantic adventure. Instead, he was met by the fourth horseman. So young, so innocent. I wept for him.

A few minutes later an orderly came to bear away the body. "Do we know his name?" I asked the man.

He gave me the boy's small packet of personal items, including a letter he had started on the battlefield. I took the small pile and in so doing found my mission at the hospital, locating the companies and commanders of the dead and writing to the families in an effort to provide some comfort about their final moments. I was told that the officers wrote to the families of men who had died, but their letters may have been brusque and businesslike. Mine were tender and gentle. I made up stories sometimes, but I have no shame about that. From then on, I spent a good portion of my time there seeking out dying men and boys and sitting with them. Someone had to care, to ease them on their way.

August 13

We have learned the name of the small boy who drowned, for his mother came searching for him. His name was Juan Martinez. He wandered off from a wagon which was heading toward Johnson City. The family searched everywhere for him but could not find him and finally decided to go on, stopping in town to inquire if anyone had seen him, although after so many days it seemed doubtful he was still alive.

How did he wander away, I ask myself. Was no one watching him? Then I recalled our days on the trail, when I was so busy cooking and washing and doing other chores; how would I have had time to watch a child?

A large family had come from Mexico, the sheriff said—some on foot, some on donkeys, some with the wagon. They had stopped for the night, and Juan's older sister had been told to watch her brother while the mother prepared the meal, but the little girl had fallen asleep. When she woke, he was gone. The older sister is but seven years old, Meggie's age. Too young to be a nursemaid. I would not leave Meggie alone to care for her little brother.

I was in the general store when Mrs. Martinez came to town. Poor woman. She looked dreadful, her eyes red-rimmed, her hair wild, her face ravaged by grief and worry. I feel such pity for her. She spoke very little English. Luckily, the new store clerk came from Mexico some years ago and could speak to her in her native tongue. She told him her sad tale.

Some people in the town have said that the Mexicans should turn around and go home again. No one seemed too sad about the loss of the child. "They can always have more boys," I heard a man say when I was at the store. Though I quickly turned to find the speaker and tell him what I thought of his cruel remark, I could not determine which one it was; a group of men stood near the counter puffing their cigars and talking among themselves. Instead, I went outside to try to find the mother and offer her what consolation I could, but I was told that the family had already moved on. They were going to go to Denver, someone said. Perhaps, they will be able to find work and some of their own kind there.

August 18

Today is Lucas's birthday. I long to be with him, to share in this day and to tell him how glad I am that he came onto this earth. I love him so, miss him terribly. I am schooling myself in patience, waiting, hoping and praying that he will come soon.

Please, Lucas, please come soon.

September 21

I feel almost guilty for my own joy today. The children are back in school, and I have started giving piano lessons!

My first pupil was, to my surprise, not a child but a grown woman, Clara. She approached me after church last Sunday to say that she had always wanted to learn to play the piano; would I teach her?

"Of course," I replied. "You have done so much for me; this is something I can do for you."

"Oh, I insist on paying you," said Clara. We talked about that a while; finally I agreed to accept a small fee. But how much? What should I charge? After much thought, I settled on fifty cents. It does not seem too much, does it?

She came the next day for her first lesson. After she had left, I walked to the general store and purchased a small picture frame, in which I put the coins she had paid me, and hung the frame on the wall in my bedroom. How foolish, no doubt—but it was the first money I had ever earned by my own talents, and I did not want to spend it.

Clara will soon outstrip my knowledge and need to go to a more advanced teacher, I fear. She shows a natural talent that has lain dormant all these years, and I am woefully out of practice. I have forgotten so much. I shall send for some sheet music which is more challenging for her.

But what a delight to start teaching. She has promised to send more pupils my way, so I shall be kept quite busy teaching piano. Preparing the lessons, instructing, practicing my pieces gives me pleasure such as I have not known since I first came away from Cincinnati and married Lucas. If I only had Lucas here with me, I would be content. Without him, my joy is tempered by loneliness and sorrow, and worry about what's happening to him.

Should he come now, though, we would have some changes to make, for I am learning to be an Independent Woman, and it is a wonderful feeling. Were it not for my love for Lucas, my longing for him, and for the children's need for their father, I believe I could live out my life just as I am, teaching and playing and tending to my children, watching them grow, in perfect happiness.

To add to my joy, I have been asked to play the new organ in the community church. I don't know much about the organ and am having to teach myself, but that provides me a challenge in which I delight. My days are full and rich. It is only the nights that are lonely. The bed seems very large, even though Freedom shares it with me.

October 6

The children are back in school, but Randall is unhappy. He is reluctant to leave for school in the morning, and he hangs back when we arrive. I walk to the school with Margaret and Randall, just to ensure their safe arrival. Every morning, I have to persuade Randall to go inside. He will not divulge the reason for his behavior, however. So like his father!

October 10

When I came to get the children after school today, Georgina invited me inside. "There's a boy in the class who has been bullying Randall," she told me. Randall is smaller than other boys his age, not inclined to defend himself. No wonder he has been unwilling to go to school.

"His name is Hank Yarrow. He's the same age as Randall but big and rough. He pinches Randall and pokes him when he thinks I am not looking. I had mistakenly seated them together, hoping Randall might be able to pass on some of his knowledge and good manners, until I discovered the boy's behavior. I have moved Hank, and I will watch out for Randall when the children are playing outdoors, but I can't promise it won't happen again."

"There's something you're not telling me, Georgina."

She nodded. "I didn't want to hurt you—foolish of me, I know. Hank calls Randall names."

"Because of his dark skin?" As he has become older, Randall's skin has taken on a darker hue. She nodded again. Though she did not tell the words, I can well imagine.

I do not know how to shield my son from such insults. He will face them all his life, I fear. Slavery is no longer legal, but blind hatred cannot be erased by laws. I left the school with a heavy heart. If only his father were here to help me. Lucas would know just the right thing to say to comfort and bolster his son.

October 14

Meggie has brought Helene Ferris home from school with her. Though she is the same age as Meggie she is at least three inches taller and perhaps twenty-five pounds heavier. On her moon-round face she wears equally round spectacles, which do not seem to put her looks to best advantage nor to help her eyesight, as she is constantly bumping into things. Her eyes are slightly slanted and she is rather slow of speech. She has had considerable difficulty in school, so Georgina tells me. She is far behind others her age and seems unable to catch up, even though Georgina has spent extra time tutoring her.

She is the daughter of Mr. Ferris, owner of the First National Bank and a widower who sadly neglects his only offspring, I fear. Poor Helene is left to the not-always-tender ministrations of a succession of housekeepers, who evidently keep her fed and in clean clothes but do little else for her. Affection is what she needs and craves. That, I have in abundance.

Helene is quite a sweet-natured child, and she adores Meggie, who bullies her terribly. Not that she is cruel, just domineering as she has always been with her brother. Helene obligingly goes along with whatever Meggie wants to do. In turn, Meggie helps her with her schoolwork, though it seems not to avail much. Poor Helene is slow-witted, I fear. The two girls play at dolls, or swing in the backyard. (Owen has fixed up a lovely swing from a low tree branch. Randall will not go near it, but Meggie loves it.)

Lucas is right—it is not good for Meggie to always have her own way, though I've no notion how to stop her. I think that is partly why she chose to befriend Helene. She told me quite earnestly that she is the girl's only friend and that she feels sorry for her. I hope she did not take up Helene's cause only to have a sycophant. Helene has many endearing qualities.

But at least the other children do not tease Helene as much as they did before, for Meggie is one of the leaders in the school, and not only among the girls. She already has boys dancing attendance on her. One day I shall have them tripping over each other to knock on our door. I can only pray her father is here to help, for I do not think I can manage such an onslaught by myself. She has grown so lovely, young as she is, with her light chocolate skin, her shimmering black hair, her large, expressive eyes and her full lips. I have done some sketches of her as she grows. I am awestruck by her beauty.

Thank goodness, Meggie's presence seems at last to have discouraged Hank Yarrow, for Georgina tells me he has left Randall alone ever since the day Randall's big sister caught the boy teasing my son with a sharp stick. Meggie is not much bigger than Hank, but she is far more forceful.

November 4

Lately I have been suffused with guilt about Alma. Though I sent a note with Adam when we moved to town, explaining the situation and inviting her to visit me, she has not come. I ask after her whenever Adam visits, but he only mumbles that she is "pert as ever." Whatever that means!

It's true that Alma and I have chosen different paths in life. We have little in common except what we have learned from each other. She taught me so much. I can never repay her. She was my first friend when we came here, and she is the children's godmother. I must find a way to see her. I do not want her to think I have deserted her.

Yet I cannot visit her. I simply cannot bear to go near the farm! I am torn; I want to know, must know, what's happening to my husband, yet I fear he will turn me away again.

November 11

Adam came by today. I asked him, "Why does Alma not come with you?'

He shrugged and started to mumble again, but I would have none of it. "Adam, I must know. Alma is my friend. I miss her. The children miss her. You are their godparents. What is wrong?"

He avoided my eyes. "Truth is, she be ashamed," he said.

I was astounded. "Ashamed? Why? What for?"

He then told me that, since I have moved to town, put my children in school and begun giving piano lessons, Alma does not want to visit because she thinks I might not wish her to. "She be jest a farmer's wife," he said. "Not like a towny."

A towny? That's the first time I had heard such a term. So that separates me from my friend?

I told him quite firmly that I would never be ashamed to have Alma as my friend, and I would like very much to have her visit me. I issued an invitation to tea for the following Sunday after church. (Alma and Adam have chosen to attend the new Methodist church, so I do not see her on Sundays even if she comes with him.)

"You tell her I insist that she come," I repeated. He nodded and said he would.

"Has Alma told you that she knows how to read?" I asked,

breaching a confidence for the sake of a friendship.

"Long time ago," he said. "She thought I'd not like it, but I'm right proud of her. I've asked her to teach me."

Pleased, I invited him then to walk with me to the new library, housed at the school. (The Ladies' Circle raised enough money, by auctioning off our latest quilt, to add a room to the building for books. Perhaps that's where the money came from for my piano as well?) Clara greeted us at the door. I entered Alma Baumgarten as a patron and paid her fee, then selected two books for Adam to take home, *Jo's Boys* by Miss Alcott, and Mr. Hawthorne's *The Scarlet Letter*. The latter is difficult, and it has some troublesome moral content, but I have confidence that she will be able to conquer it. A few years ago for Christmas I presented her with a dictionary, which was well worn the last time I saw her. She will refer to it often as she reads Mr. Hawthorne's weighty tome.

It is my fond hope that she will become a regular patron and return frequently to deliver and select books to read. When she comes to town, I shall be sure to see her.

Before Adam and I parted company, I asked him if he had spoken with Lucas, as I have not heard from him yet. Adam's face grew sad, his voice somber.

"I'm afeard for him," he said. "He jest stays in that barn all the time."

My heart leaped into my throat.

"Is he all right? He's not—"

"He's jest there. Not harvestin', not leavin' at all."

"Does he care for the stock?"

"Far as I can tell. He gave us your cows a while ago."

He gave Adam and Alma Judy and the bull!

"Perhaps I should borrow a horse and go see him."

Adam shook his head. "I'd not do that, Hannah. Yore man is workin' somethin' out in his mind, and the best thing to do now is let him be. He'll come around soon; you'll see."

With those words I had to be content. I knew Adam was stopping by to see Lucas as often as time permitted. It would have to do for now.

November 22

Alma has been here for a delightful visit. I did not chastise her for believing I would fancy myself her superior now, but I hope she understands that I care for her as much as ever I did. The children were delighted to see her, and she took to Helene right away.

She brought cookies for the children and one of her famous burnt-sugar cakes for our tea. I told her she should enter her baked goods in the county fair, which takes place in our town, the county seat. She demurred at first, being such a modest soul, but I think I persuaded her.

Though I was fearful we would have difficulty finding topics of conversation, in the end we talked about books. She had not known of the lending library, which opened quite recently, and was delighted to learn of it. After we had tea, she went outdoors to play with Freedom and the children and revealed the treat she had brought with her in a covered basket—a kitten no more than a few weeks old. I was surprised, for the creature had made no sound while Alma was in the parlor having tea.

The little thing came to her door for food, and she decided it would be a perfect playmate for Randall and Meggie, Freedom having become somewhat less playful as he ages. Puss, too, is past the playful age and spends most of his time dozing in the sun.

They promptly named the kitten Amanda (I've no notion where they got the name), being convinced that she is a girl. Alma is uncertain. She advised confining the kitten inside when it (she?) gets a little older, just to avoid having more kittens we would need to find new homes for. Puss, she thought, was past the age where he would be interested. Randall was especially fetched with the kitten, which is orange and has very large eyes and ears. Alma estimates it to be about six weeks old.

I thanked Alma for her visit and for the kitten. " 'Tis I who should be thanking you," she replied, clutching her new books to her chest. "You've given me the best gift I ever got," she said, and hugged me quickly. Then she left before I had time to ask her about Lucas.

December 1

Georgina visited today with a distressing story. Although his teasing and bullying seem to have stopped, Hank Yarrow brought a note to school from his mother. Georgina showed it to me. It read: "Techer, my boy ain't goin' to school lessen that nigra boy stops koming. Don't never set my boy Hank alongside that filthy boy agin."

"Poor Hank has a mother who is barely literate," commented Georgina. "Moreover, she has no notion about cleanliness. Hank Yarrow's face and hands are never scrubbed, and his clothing reeks. I don't know when his hair was last washed. I suspect he has head lice."

"Poor Hank, indeed!" I said angrily. "Poor Randall!"

"Hank is the one to pity, Hannah," said my friend. "Pity him growing up in a household so full of hatred, rife with dirt and neglect. Pity him being taught the ways of the world by such parents."

"Are you acquainted with the father or mother?"

"Mr. Yarrow works at the mill. I have not met him. Hank has numerous brothers and sisters, so I imagine Mrs. Yarrow is kept busy at home."

Like Lucinda Smith, I thought. And like so many women who have more children than they can decently care for. My heart filled with gratitude for my absent husband.

"What did you do when you got the note?"

"I handed it back to Hank and told him to tell his mother to come and see me."

"Did she?"

"No, she did not, nor do I expect her to. I went to the school principal—a newcomer to town named Aaron Stimson—and told him what had occurred. I assured him that if Randall were forced to leave the school I would leave with him, and start my own private school where all children of any skin color are welcome. I reminded him of the Christian precepts by which I live. I'm afraid I seemed a little overwrought."

"And?"

"He invited me to sit down; then he told me that under no circumstances was I to expel a student for such a reason. Indeed, if any child were expelled it would more likely be Hank."

"But it's his mother, and possibly his father, who are creating the difficulty, not the boy."

"Indeed, that is true. Nevertheless, if it comes to a choice, Hank will have to go."

I was reassured by her actions and Mr. Stimson's soothing words, but I am discomfited by this blatant act of hatred. Will it never stop? Lucas and I were forced to leave the home of my birth because society would not accept us. Richards cruelly shot my husband. Now this. It is disheartening.

December 25

We went to church on Christmas Eve.

We walked the short distance. It had snowed, so the ground was covered with the dry, crunchy snow so common here. The rooftops were all white. Lighted windows, some with candles in them, winked out of the darkness. We could see the stars so clearly. The sky was perfectly clear. Meggie and Randall sat with

Georgina while I played the organ. Georgina and Herbert shared Christmas dinner with us after Herbert had conducted the services. We sang carols, and there were small gifts for the children of the church, who earlier had decorated a small, perfect blue spruce. There was a beautiful crèche next to the podium.

I was at peace for the moment, except for the absence of my husband. I miss him most acutely at such times, special occasions like this.

We have a small Christmas tree at home, too. The children have decorated it with popcorn strings and candy canes and some ornaments they made at school. I would not permit candles for fear of fire, to their disappointment. I feel full of despair. What makes me saddest of all is that Meggie and Randall did not even ask after their father today. It is as if he has died. All day I watched the door, hoping and praying Lucas would come. The children miss him so, although Randall has stopped crying himself to sleep. But on Christmas Day, why is he not with his family?

Dear God, I must not even think such thoughts.

December 31

Of all people to be destroyed by the train, the last one I would have supposed would be Peter Ferris. Yet he was killed yesterday. The engineer tried to stop when he saw a man on the track, but he could not bring the heavy locomotive to a halt in time. What was Peter doing there? Why had he stopped? It looked as though he were tying his shoe. On the tracks? People say he was a rather odd man, tending to talk to himself as he walked down the street, but I had not thought anyone to be quite that removed from the world around him. But now poor, dear Helene is without any parents at all—an orphan.

I will *not* allow that child to be sent to an orphanage! I have offered to take her into our home. I don't suppose I would be allowed to adopt her, a woman without a husband, but I shall fight fiercely to keep her from a terrible fate. Poor child, she has no one but Meggie, Randall and me. And Lucas, when he comes. He will not refuse to help this child.

Perhaps when the children go back to school, I will set out one day and go to the farm even though Adam advises against it. This has gone on so long with no changes, no resolution, and I am frightened and anxious about Lucas.

1881

January 10

Even though she seems slightly confused about the change in her life, Helene has settled in nicely. She sleeps with Meggie in her warm feather bed. She brought with her a large collection of dolls and some sweet miniatures which Randall finds entrancing.

She asked me once where her papa had gone. When I told her he was in heaven and she was going to live with us, she smiled and said, "Good." She is a child of few words, and she does not seem sad about her father's death. Perhaps she simply does not understand what's happened.

But judging from the condition of her clothing, I don't think Peter spent much time with her anyway, or paid her any attention at all. Her wardrobe is woefully inadequate, poor child. Peter had a housekeeper, but the woman evidently did not attend to Helene well, for the child's clothing is worn and far too small for her, and her underthings are a disgrace.

I shall set to work at once to remedy this situation. The bank has arranged for Helene to have an allowance to help with her care, and I intend to use it to get her new clothing and shoes. She does not seem to mind that her shoes pinch her feet, but I do.

January 12

Randall seems to be happier at school since the holiday. When I spoke to Georgina about it, she told me the Yarrow family has left town. "The father's going to try his luck in California," she reported. "He never did have a steady job here." I am thankful they have left, for even though Meggie protected her brother well enough, I'm sure the boy's mere presence was upsetting to my son.

January 16

Jacob Richards has been shot. A neighbor found him, they say, and fetched him from his pasture to town in his wagon. They took him to the Devons'.

Who could have done such a deed? I *know* it was not Lucas, although he had reason enough. He would never, could never, kill. He told me once, a long time ago, that the field hospital where he was working came under fire and one of the surgeons shot a rebel soldier who came toward the field-hospital tent, his rifle pointed straight at them. "We all shouldered our rifles," Lucas said. "The rebel fired a shot at the tent, and Dr. Black brought him down with his rifle. I was relieved that I had not had to fire that shot. I don't think I could have done it."

Richards is still alive, but he is seriously injured.

January 17

Richards was shot in the belly. The wound is festering. Lucas could help, but Richards permits no one near him except Clara. Lucas *would* help him. He'd help the devil himself if he were injured.

Could Adam have shot Richards? Impossible. Who could it have been?

January 18

The newspaper is full of speculation. Lucas's name is mentioned, since it is known that Lucas was wounded last spring, probably by Richards. Richards has shown no improvement. I fear for my husband if he dies, for he's known to have been behaving strangely these past months. People might well be tempted to blame Lucas simply because of his race. Some have been accustomed for so long to blaming the black man for every ill that befalls mankind.

January 20

Richards died today. His last words were, "This'll fix that nigger for sure." Dear God! Did he believe that Lucas shot him? What can I do?

I am terrified for Lucas. I shall get a horse and go to him tomorrow as soon as the children are off to school.

January 21

Today was the worst day of my life. My hand is shaking so that I can hardly write.

I got a horse from Owen and set out for the farm as soon as the children were gone. But I had gone no more than halfway when I met a party of horsemen coming toward town, led by the sheriff.

Lucas was on Nappy. His hands were tied to the pommel, and the sheriff was leading the horse. A deputy was on either side of him. I spurred the mare toward Lucas, but a deputy stopped me.

I turned toward Mr. Musgrave. "Why are you arresting him?" I cried. "He has done nothing wrong!"

"I'm arresting him for the murder of Jacob Richards," he replied.

"On what evidence? You can't have any evidence! You never have any evidence!" I knew I was shrieking, but I was near losing control of my faculties. I couldn't help myself. The mare began to paw the ground.

"Mr. Richards himself accused Dr. Bowman before he died, ma'am, and I have a witness."

My heart sank. "A witness? Who? Whoever it is, he's lying!"

"It will all come out at the trial, Miz Bowman. Circuit judge'll be here in a couple of weeks." With that, the men surged around me and rode toward town. Stunned, I remained motionless. What should I do? At length I decided to go to Adam first, seek his help, then get to the school before the children came out. They needed to hear this dreadful news from me, no one else.

I urged the mare on toward Adam and Alma's farm, where I found Adam in a nearby field, mending fence, and told him of the disaster. He immediately saddled his horse and headed to town with me. "Alma and I'll care for the stock," he told me. "I'm goin' to Denver to get a lawyer. I'll leave at first light."

I know I should have felt profound gratitude at having such a loyal friend, but all I felt was terror. We hurried into town, Adam heading for the jail, and I arrived at the school just as the children were coming out.

I gathered them around me.

"Darlings," I said, "a bad thing has happened, but your papa will be all right. Until this is over, I'm going to ask Georgina to care for you, because I need to be with Papa." I told them, then, that their father was in jail, but it was all a mistake. Soon, I promised, it would all be all right again. Meggie screamed, then put her hands over her ears. "It can't be true," she cried. "Papa would never do anything wrong!" Randall simply stared at me solemnly. Helene said nothing at all.

I pulled them close to me. Meggie began to beat me with her small fists. "Where is Papa? I want to see him!" she cried.

"Children aren't permitted," I told her, and I held her close to me until her wild sobs subsided. "Why don't you write him a letter?" I said as I was delivering the children into Georgina's hands—thank the Lord for another faithful friend—and went home, for I knew now what I must do. "I'll deliver it when I visit Papa today."

That cheered her up a little bit. "I'll write it in French," she announced. I promised to come back to Georgina's house before I went to the jail.

Tonight, I shall go to the jail. I've seen frontier "justice" in action before, and I do not trust Mr. Musgrave to keep my husband safe. Oh, no. I shall do it myself. Let a mob come anywhere near him and I shall shoot them all, one by one.

I have packed some cornbread and cold roast for him and filled a canteen with water. I have seen to the animals. I'm on my way.

January 22

When I first saw Lucas in the cell, I recoiled with shock. His hair, his lovely black hair, had turned completely white. I had not noticed that when the deputies were bringing him to town. He did not stand with his back straight and proud as he always had but was sitting stooped over, like an old man. When he saw me, he moved toward the front of the cell, but slowly, as if every step was an effort.

I swept past the deputy, bringing a chair toward the front of the cell over his protests. I was armed with the rifle, crooked over my arm, my food bundle in the other hand. I challenged him to stop me.

"Let me by," I said.

He stood in front of the cell, blocking my way. I jabbed the rifle into his chest and cocked it.

"Stand aside," I said. "I am not intending to free my husband, only to protect him from a violent mob. I've seen that happen here before, and I won't let it happen to Lucas."

Seeming unsure whether I would actually shoot or not, the deputy stepped aside. I reached out through the bars to touch

Lucas. He took my hand. "I did not kill him, Hannah. You must believe that." His usually deep, warm voice sounded high and harsh, scratchy.

"Of course, I believe you, Lucas. You would never kill anyone." My voice betrayed my feelings, as the words came out hoarsely. "Adam?"

"Adam was in Denver at the stockyards. Someone else killed him. I don't know who."

The sheriff came out of the back room. "What are you doing here, Miz Bowman?"

I told him why I was parked in front of the cell and what my intentions were. "A mob will have to kill me first," I informed him.

"This ain't necessary, ma'am. We'll see he comes to no harm."

"So you say. Even so, I shall stay here all night and every night until the circuit judge comes."

He must have encountered determined women before, because he did not cross me after that. "Bob here'll be awake all night," he assured me. "The doc will be safe enough." He left.

As soon as Bob began to snore loudly, I said to Lucas, "Are you all right?"

I handed him Meggie's letter. He sat down on the bed to read it. When he'd finished, he looked up at me. "*Mon dieu,* what have I done to my family?" Then—"She wrote me a letter every week, all these months. I didn't open the letters. I couldn't bear to." He began, at long last, to talk to me.

January 24

It is painful to record what my husband said to me, and I am so very fatigued, but it eases me to set it down on paper, so I shall try.

"I did not kill him, Hannah," he repeated. "I don't know who

239

did." Fear clutched my heart. Would anyone else believe in his innocence?

"Adam has gone to find an attorney, Lucas. The best."

He drew a long, deep breath and looked at me with anguished eyes sunk hollow in his face.

"Hannah, I must tell you about these last few months. I know I have not been a good husband or father since my injury.

"When you left, I barely noticed you were gone. I was obsessed with vengeance. I don't know why I felt so, but I did. I am not even certain I said farewell the day you drove away with Adam. Musgrave would do nothing, even though I appealed to him a few times, so it seemed evident to me that if justice were to be done, I would have to bring it about myself. I spent every waking hour for so long dreaming of ways to avenge myself, scheming and plotting. I became completely lost in it."

"I know," I said. "And yet you knew I would need funds, so you made an arrangement with the bank."

He nodded. "I think I was relieved you were gone, because I did not like for you and the children to see me in such a state."

He told me how he did the chores mechanically, without thought, all the while plotting schemes for revenge. Shoot Richards's cattle? No—that would be taking his anger out on innocents. Burn his fields? Worse yet—the fire might spread to Adam's fields or ours. Finally it came to him: he would wound Richards as Richards had wounded Lucas and leave him, as he left Lucas, to his fate. He convinced himself that if Richards died, it would not be his fault.

That Lucas would *consider* even wounding someone was repugnant to me. I felt ill and light in the head at those words coming from his lips.

He described spending the evening hours cleaning and oiling his army rifle over and over, practicing his aim in daylight. He drew the outline of a man on horseback on the side of the barn.

240

He planned the assault, when and where and how it would take place, rehearsed the scene again and again. He picked the exact spot. He tracked Richards, watched him at his work or riding his range, so he knew where to find him at what hour.

"Sometimes, I wanted to give it up. I knew in my heart how wrong it was. But I kept on." Perhaps, I thought but did not say aloud, all the insults and mistreatment over the years had accumulated in his mind. It was not only Richards who was the object of his vengeance.

"Just two weeks ago, I concluded the time had come to put my plan into action."

I pictured Lucas spying on Richards, hiding and peering out and carefully observing details, and my spirits fell.

"Why did it take so many months?" I asked him.

"I don't know, Hannah. I hardly knew how much time was passing." He went on.

"I prepared very carefully, making sure that all the fine points were taken care of. I had no other thoughts but revenge. After all, the Bible says, 'an eye for an eye,' I told myself. This is but justice done by one man instead of society, for I did not believe society would act justly toward a man of my race. I've seen too much in America to think that possible."

He told me that he went to the spot he had planned on. Richards came by, just as he had expected. He raised the rifle, had the man in his sights. He said he knew just where he would hit Richards—the same place where Lucas had been hit. Lucas had practiced at home a hundred times.

"When the moment came to pull the trigger, I found my finger frozen fast. It would not move. After some time, I do not recall how long, I threw down the weapon and rode away."

Tears were coursing down his cheeks. His eyes were haunted. "I am a doctor, Hannah. I heal people, not hurt them. I treated so many terrible wounds wrought by just such a weapon as I

241

held in my hands that day—how could I for even an instant have imagined I would use it on another human being, no matter what he did to me?"

I was crying, too.

He spoke, then, about his actions, so unlike the man I know and love. "Perhaps I had gone into a decline because of the wounds, and the farther I fell, the harder it was to pull myself back up. After a time, I was ashamed of what I had done, causing you and the children to leave the farm, shutting you out, but I couldn't seem to change the course of my actions. Not until I had that rifle in my hands and Richards in the sights."

How I longed to hold him in my arms! I had gone through the tortures of the damned—but then I understood that he had, too.

January 25

The children have been taunted at school, Georgina tells me. I assured them that their father is innocent and will soon be home with them. Helene, thank God, does not understand. She has never met Lucas, so this whole episode is beyond her imagining. But what can I do to protect Meggie and Randall? I feel so helpless. Meggie speaks up for herself and her brother and defends her father, I know, but the cruel words must hurt her even so.

I know Lucas is innocent, but will he be freed? Now as never before, we need the help of the Almighty.

Adam has been to visit. He is caring for the stock on our farm. He has found an attorney who will come three days before the trial. Adam is so good; I thank God for him.

February 2

A traveling judge is expected to come to Johnson City in two days, so Lucas will be tried then. The attorney has arrived and spoken with Lucas several times. He does not tell me how he plans to defend my husband, but if Adam trusts him, so will I.

My fears about a mob have been eased, since nothing has happened during these terrible days. I visit the jail daily, taking delicacies to tempt Lucas's palate. He looks so miserable. He just sits in the cell, his head in his hands. He seems to have abandoned hope. He has aged even more since the day he was put in that horrible cell.

Today I asked the sheriff again why he had arrested Lucas.

He told me that he has a witness, someone who claims to have seen Lucas kill Richards. "Who is it?" I asked.

He would not divulge the name but said it would come out at the trial.

February 3

I have learned from talk in the town that the witness is a Mrs. Henderson, a new neighbor to the south of our farm. The family came here from Louisiana. It seems probable to me that they dislike and distrust people with dark skin.

People stop talking when they see me coming, but not soon enough. I hear what they say.

Mrs. Henderson claims that she saw Lucas riding away from Richards's ranch on the day he was shot. From what Lucas has told me, she may well have seen him doing just that—a damning circumstance. It looks bad.

But is her mere word, the word of a newcomer, enough to *convict* him? Is it *evidence?* Will she lie and say she saw Lucas shoot him too?

I cannot sleep for worrying. Two of my pupils have canceled their lessons. Some of the townspeople turn their heads away when I walk by. When I was on the farm, there were days when I was in utter despair and it seemed that life has become impossible to bear, yet now it does not seem that life could become more difficult than it is now.

I thank God for dear loyal Georgina, for Clara and my other friends. I don't think I could survive without them.

The trial is tomorrow. I am in agonies of suspense. I do not sleep.

February 4

Just after I returned from seeing the children to school, Lucas came up the walk. He walked slowly, like an old man, but his head was held high.

"Are you free?" I cried. "What's happened?" I ran out to embrace him. He pulled me to him in the old familiar way. We held each other tightly for a moment before we went into the house.

The sheriff came to the cell early this morning, he said, and released him. All charges against him have been dropped. The real killer has come forward and confessed.

Thank God. We are vindicated! Sheriff Musgrave apologized to Lucas, but that does not make up for the time he spent confined in a jail cell. He could have been convicted and hanged! I shall find it very difficult to forgive Mr. Musgrave for taking the word of a stranger, using that as a reason to arrest my husband when he would never arrest Jacob Richards for all the crimes he committed.

We talked most of the day. He spoke more of the bad time on the farm, and I told him what I had done, what I had accomplished, since moving to town. I told him I do not want to go back to the farm, ever. I am happy in town, and there are so many bad memories at the farm now. He agreed. He said he'd never wanted to be a farmer; he settled on the homestead only to please me. We decided that we would sell the farm to Adam.

I confess here to considerable anxiety about the future, although I did not speak of my fears to Lucas. One day I may, but not yet. Will we ever recover the friendship and trust we had before this terrible event? Will he sink once more into gloom and take his soul away from me, from us? How will the children respond to their father, when they've been so long without him? Who is he, what has he become, these last few months since we've been apart? I still love him, oh so much, but I do not know him anymore.

Yet my heart is full and I remain hopeful for the future, for our future together. Lucas will open a medical office in town; I will continue my piano lessons. In time, I am certain, people will come to see what a marvelous healer my husband is and forget the color of his skin.

We are a family again, at last. We will begin with that.

JUNE 2000
HANNAH LOUISE PARISH

June 3, 2000

What a treasure I've found—a journal written by my great-grandmother in the 1870s. Now that I'm a lady of leisure, I have time to look for answers to some of the missing links.

A lady of leisure, thanks to Lennie. Goodness, how I miss her. My mentor, my partner, my friend. The clinic never would have happened in the first place without her, and now she's saved it thanks to the windfall her brother left her. I'd give up every cent of the money she left me to have one more day with her. But that's not possible, and I know she'd want me to enjoy having enough funds to live well, for once in my life. Imagine—no more long hours, no more scrimping and begging to keep it going. . . . Someone else is in charge now, and the clinic is sound thanks to her generosity. So I truly can begin to enjoy my life, as much as is possible without her in it.

I came here to Johnson City to bury my grandmother's ashes at last, but I'm going to stay a while to find out more about my great-grandmother, Hannah Bowman. What an extraordinary woman she was.

I've intended for so long to track down my forebears and learn about my history. There just never seemed to be any time. When my grandmother died and left me everything, I just put it all in storage in Denver, paid the fee without letting myself think about what might be in that little storage unit.

I let thirty years go by before I went to get her things. But then Lennie died and woke me up to my own mortality. Death has a way of smacking you in the face. So I went to the storage place planning to haul it all to the dump or the Goodwill, until I found that cedar chest. Once I opened it and saw those journals, I knew I had to come here even if I hadn't quite decided yet to bury Grandmother Meggie's ashes with her parents.

Each journal was carefully bound with ribbon, with the year on the outside cover. What a priceless record of Great-grandmother Hannah's life. She left some loose ends, though, so I hope I can tie most of them up while I'm here, prowling around the museum, the library newspaper archives, and the county courthouse.

June 4

My grandmother Meggie, Hannah Bowman's daughter, grew up to be an ardent suffragette. She devoted her life to her cause and neglected her only child, my mother. Meggie was probably one of those women who should never have had children (although I'm glad she did). She must have conceived my mother in a rare moment of passion. Hannah was a feminist too, to judge from her writings, before that label came along, but she didn't go out on the front lines the way her daughter did. Mom told me that her mother was right there with the women who chained themselves to things and went on hunger strikes. Imagine my grandmother being hauled off to jail!

Meggie did go to college, Mom said—the Sorbonne in Paris (glamorous!) and McGill University in Montreal, but I can't find any record of degrees. What was her work? What did she live on? Can't solve that one, but I strongly suspect that Helene Ferris's estate supported her so well that she could afford to go around saving the world.

She was fluent in French and German, Mom mentioned

once. She traveled all over Europe and lived off and on in France until just before World War I. I'm sure she faced some prejudice because of her mixed race, but maybe it was easier for her there than here, as it had been for Lucas. I picture her being ambiguous about her race, maybe even resentful.

She was a *lovely* woman, though. I found photos of her as a grown woman in some newspaper accounts she'd kept about her protests, taken sometime in the twentieth-century teens, I should judge. She had an exotic face. Her eyes were very intense. Her hair, which was thick and black, flew all around her face. She looks quite determined. She was tall, really thin, very elegant-looking, but her outfits are just kind of thrown together. She reminds me of those 1930s movie stars with the long dresses and the cloche hats and that steamy look. She didn't seem to care much about her appearance, but she was one of those women who look good even when they don't care how they dress.

After women won the vote, Meggie took up the cause of women's treatment in factories, which was pretty bad. She got involved with labor unions. Legal birth control was another of her causes. She was a peace activist, too, and continued to get into trouble until she was too old to go out and march anymore.

June 7

From newspaper accounts, I learned that Meggie's marriage was short and sad. Her husband, Ross Chandler, my grandfather, was a gambler. He was shot in New Orleans during a poker game only a few months after their marriage.

What attracted sensible, strong-willed, feminist Meggie to such a man? Quite possibly she was emotionally vulnerable after the death of her brother. According to Hannah, she loved Randall very much and protected him when they were children. She might have felt that she had somehow failed him.

She came home to give birth to my mother and left again, without her child, a few weeks later. She never used her married name. She came once in a while for short visits, but she was never a mother to my mother. They never shared a home. Meggie didn't offer to take her daughter with her on any of her travels. My mother had to see Europe on her own when she grew up, after World War I was over.

Mom never forgave her mother for abandoning her. Meggie was gone when she was a teenager, just when a girl needs her mother the most. The Bowmans raised my mom. Great-grandma Hannah did her best, so Mom often told me, but she was old and tired and probably heartsick, and she just didn't have what it takes to deal with a young, unhappy girl. As for Great-grandpa Lucas, I gather he was too busy with his medical practice to pay much attention to my mother. Mom seldom mentioned him.

I never met Meggie. Mom left Johnson City when she turned eighteen, went to college in Chicago, which is pretty far from Colorado, got married and settled down there. We never went to see my grandmother even after she got old and went to an "old folks' home" (as they called it then) in Denver. How I regret not making an effort to get to know her in spite of Mom's being so estranged from her. Even though Mom made it pretty clear she didn't want me contacting her mother, I could have gotten in touch after Mom died. Why didn't I? I guess I was too busy with the clinic to think about much else.

After she left home, Mom went to Johnson City by herself a time or two to visit Hannah and Lucas, she told me, but they were both dead by the time I came along.

Meggie outlived Mom. She was almost 100 when she died. Tough lady! And what changes she saw in her lifetime. Mind-boggling. I wonder why she kept that cedar chest of her mother's, since there was so much animosity between her and her parents.

Along with the journals, I found a gorgeous little christening dress, a Bible, some old piano music, and apple seeds. I also found a big, red, faded bow—from when they presented Hannah with the piano?—and a tuning hammer. Must have been Hannah's.

The writing in the journals is very neat, that old-fashioned, flowery script you see in museums—very pretty, very stylized, very challenging to decipher. It's readable even if the pencil writing has faded a bit. If the journals are any indication, life on the frontier was really tough for women. Hannah's writing is pretty frank; I didn't think people were so open in those days.

Mom never told me a whole lot about her family, and I didn't ask—for which I'm sorry now. Oh, she told me stories sometimes, but never anything important, no real history. I had to come here to find things out for myself.

June 10

It's beastly hot today. Imagine what this high, dry plain would have been like before air-conditioning! How did women stand it, with all those clothes they wore?

Talking to people, asking around, I've found out quite a bit. My great-grandparents left their mark on this town. People knew who they were; in fact, they were local legends. They're even mentioned in a local history book someone wrote a few years ago.

After Lucas sold the homestead, they spent the rest of their lives in Johnson City. Hannah taught piano into her eighties and played the organ in the Johnson City Community Church. Lucas practiced medicine until he died suddenly at age seventy-five of a heart attack. I *have* heard the story about how my great-grandfather carefully set his medical bag on the dining room table then collapsed on the floor, dead.

He had an office in the back of their home, the same one-story frame house Hannah moved into when she came to town—certainly not the fancy home of a wealthy doctor. They must have added the room after he came to town. Mom told me Lucas usually went on house calls rather than having patients come to him. I don't suppose he ever got rich from his doctoring, but I'm sure he was happier than on the farm. People seem to have accepted and trusted him in spite of his mixed race.

If Hannah is to be believed, and I have no reason to doubt her, he was a gifted doctor, progressive and humane. Mom thought so, too; she did tell me about some of his famous successes. Once he performed surgery on a young girl who had a cleft palate, long before plastic surgery was even thought of. Another time, he diagnosed a rare disease, some obscure condition that now is called some kind of syndrome. I probably learned about it in medical school, but I can't remember it now. He performed more than one Cesarean and quite a few emergency appendectomies, even a tracheotomy or two. He kept up with medical advances. Mom mentioned that he always had a medical journal lying around.

Wouldn't he be astounded at some of the medical advances that have come along these last few years! I can imagine his fascination with DNA and the whole genetics thing. He could have made a name for himself in the medical world if he hadn't lived in a little Colorado backwater like Johnson City and been half black. (Though it sure isn't a backwater now! It's grown to a good-sized town, and the college has become a university.)

By the time my mother was old enough to have memories, Lucas had gotten one of the first cars in town, a Stanley Steamer, to make his house calls. Mom used to laugh when she told about all his arguments with the thing. She told me people would call out, "Get a horse!" After a while he did go back to horses, and he was still riding everywhere when she left home. Later they got another car, a Ford, which worked better. But Hannah drove it, not Lucas.

June 15

I went to the house they lived in. It's still privately owned by an elderly woman and her young companion. To my surprise and delight, there's a small plaque in front of it designating it as the home of Lucas Bowman, the city's first doctor. (No mention of Hannah, though.) The woman let me in to see the place, but I'm sure it looks nothing like it did when my great-grandparents lived there.

I found the homestead, too. It's still being farmed, but now it's part of a large commercial operation. The original home-stead, the house Lucas and Adam built, still stands, but the barn's long gone. Too bad. I wonder whether the outline of Richards that Lucas drew on the wall would have survived all these years. The house is some sort of headquarters for the farming operation.

Were Hannah and Lucas happy together after the reconcilia-tion? Mom never spoke about it, but if they'd been really unhappy she would have mentioned it, I think. I'm certain, though, that Mom never knew about the whole business of the separation and the murder. The only thing Meggie knew was that her beloved father had stayed on the farm and then come to town, and Hannah evidently never told her children much more than that. Being as sharp as she was, Meggie certainly noticed that her dad's hair had turned white, but she probably didn't think it was all that unusual. She and Randall did know he was in jail for a little while, but I suppose they forgot that pretty fast when he came home again. Hannah didn't tell Mom much about it—why would she? It was a dark time in their family's history.

Mom had a photograph of her grandparents, apparently taken some time in their sixties. Hannah was a slender, rather severe-looking woman with her hair pulled back from her face. There is intelligence and compassion in her eyes. I wouldn't call her beautiful, but she is attractive. For the photo she didn't wear the glasses Mom had told me she used most of the time, so Hannah did have some feminine vanity. In her writings, she doesn't mention her personal appearance except to despair about her hair.

Lucas was incredibly handsome—fairly tall, with powerful shoulders and wonderful, keen eyes. He stands behind Hannah, one of those hands Hannah often wrote about resting on her shoulder. They look to be strong, capable hands. He has a kind face; I can see why Hannah was in love with him.

June 18

Today, I'm trying to learn what happened to Little Adam's grave. Since Adam and Alma had no children to take over their farm, they probably sold out late in their lives and moved into a nursing home. I doubt if there was one in Johnson City at the time. And that means they left town.

Hannah doesn't mention the Baumgartens much in her later entries, after she had moved to town. In those days, it would have been pretty hard for the two women to keep in touch. I couldn't find the grave at the homestead. I can't imagine Hannah would have left her dead baby there after the Baumgartens sold out, so I visited the cemetery on the grounds of the old community church. The church and grounds have been preserved as historic sites, the first burial ground in Johnson City. It's on high ground north of the river. I walked around among the headstones, found both my great-grandparents. Meggie wanted to be cremated. I had to take care of that. I'd thought I might bury her ashes in Johnson City, but I haven't done that yet. I still have them in my car. While I'm here I'm going to arrange to bury them in the new cemetery and order a headstone. The old cemetery next to the church isn't used anymore, so I can't put her next to her parents. Perhaps it's just as well.

I didn't find a headstone for Adam Bowman in the cemetery, which led me to wonder whether Hannah might have taken his coffin into her home when Adam and Alma sold the land and asked that it be buried with her when she died. Given her devotion to her children, it makes sense. Maybe she asked that his name be carved on her tombstone, but somebody forgot. Meggie could have done it later, but she didn't.

I am going to do it. I'll have a headstone made for Meggie and Little Adam together. That would please Hannah.

The Baumgartens are in the cemetery. They died within a few months of each other, in 1919 (probably during that awful flu epidemic), long after Meggie had left home, and Hannah would have moved the coffin when they sold the farm, if she moved it at all.

June 20

I found Helene Ferris's tombstone, too, but the dates had weathered. Because my mother never mentioned her as part of the Bowman household, I plowed through newspapers (quite literally; they're not even on microfilm!) for several years after 1880 and found an obituary for Helene in 1894. The address given was the Bowmans', so I assume she lived there even though they never formally adopted her as far as I know. The obituary mentioned that she had been nearly blind for some years. Poor dear, she was only twenty-one when she died. I don't have much to go on, but from the way Hannah describes her, I'm guessing she had Down syndrome. Since she'd gone blind and was rather heavy, she might have developed diabetes too, which in those days would have killed her pretty fast. She was lucky to live in a home where she was loved and encouraged instead of ignored or mistreated and could get the best medical care available at the time.

When she died, Helene had just "attained her majority," as they so quaintly phrased it in the newspaper. Since her father had owned one of the two banks in the town and she was an only child, he must have left her a fortune, probably in a trust. And she left it all to Meggie. I found her will among Meggie's papers, the signature an uneven line of large block letters.

June 22

I've been here almost a month, and most of my questions are answered. I'm going back to California soon and enjoy the cool. July will probably be unbearable here! I'll take the journal with me. Everyone will love it.

I'm so grateful that Meggie retrieved the cedar chest that had the journals in it. And grateful for that wonderful tool, the Internet. I wonder what we ever did without it.

June 24

Meggie's brother, Randall Lucas Freeman, went to the Spanish-American War as a correspondent and was killed in 1898, the same year my mother was born. Randall was still single; he was only twenty-three. Losing her son to war and her daughter to the suffrage cause must have broken Hannah's heart, though I suppose my mother was some comfort to her.

Based on the behavior Hannah describes, I've concluded that Randall was mildly autistic. Maybe he was an Asperger's. He probably never would have married. Tragic that we have learned of this condition so many years after his death, so there was no help for him. He must have been lonely, and a disappointment to Lucas. Hannah said he was not a risk-taker, yet he went off to write about a war.

All the letters to Hannah's mother are carefully folded inside the journals. Folded with them are some small, darling sketches of two children who must be Meggie and Randall.

Margaret Rose Morris Schussman, Hannah's mother, died in 1876 of some kind of "wasting disease" (probably TB). Was Margaret Rose already ill when Hannah left, ill enough that she couldn't cope with her husband and protect her daughter? As far as I can figure, she never knew where Hannah went, whether she was alive or dead. It was lots easier for people to disappear in those days before telephones and Social Security numbers and such; I'm not sure how Margaret Rose would have been able to find her children even if she'd had the money and the freedom to try.

From what Hannah wrote in her journals, I'm guessing that her hatred and fear of her stepfather were stronger than her love for her mother. Until she became a mother herself, Hannah wouldn't have understood how heartbreaking it would be to have a child disappear and never know what happened to her. But once Hannah had children of her own, it's hard to figure why she held back the letters. She must have had her reasons.

Modern psychology would no doubt say that Hannah resented her mother because Margaret Rose seemed so blind to her husband's behavior and apparently did nothing to try to stop it. Karl abused Hannah sexually, and his wife must have known, or suspected, what he was doing. Perhaps Hannah didn't mail the letters because she feared Karl so much and didn't want to put her mother in danger. That would be a charitable choice. My best guess: she had deeply ambivalent feelings toward her mother that she fed by writing letters to "Dearest Mama" on the one hand and withholding them on the other. Hannah was a woman of her time in lots of ways, even though she was so independent and frank, and she never expressed those feelings about her mother in her journal. In places, though, her writing is confused emotionally, like when she wrote about her brother's departure and Margaret Rose's stillborn baby.

Ironically, Hannah's last letter to her mother is folded neatly near the end of the 1876 pages. ESP?

Karl Schussman, Margaret's husband, died a year after she did, killed in a carriage accident. The business he had usurped from her evidently failed; I could find no trace of it. That's justice done, at least.

No trace of Lawrence Randall Morris, Hannah's brother, my great-uncle, born 1850, beyond a birth record and census records through 1860. I can only suppose he died an early death, maybe on the river he wanted to navigate. Or, based on Hannah's journals, maybe he changed his name and did play the piano in a New Orleans dance hall or on a riverboat. He apparently didn't enlist in the Union army, which would have had a record of it. But he must not have survived his escape from Karl for long, or he would have written to Hannah.

There is that one letter to Lawrence. Only the one letter, written after she moved into town.

June 26

One mystery solved. Very lucky, too, because a fire had destroyed the newspaper archives for the year Richards was killed. Folded in the last page of the journal were two faded newspaper clippings. The first headline read, "Betsy Confesses."

The story said that Old Betsy the laundress (Betsy Andrews) came to town just hours before the trial was scheduled to begin, walked into the sheriff's office, and said, "I killed him."

"Holding out her roughened, misshapen hands, she invited the sheriff to put handcuffs on her," the story said.

Betsy explained that Richards had "violated" her granddaughter Martha, who had recently given birth to a healthy boy.

When Betsy went to Richards for money and an apology, he knocked her down and told her to get off his property before he killed her. When she sought justice, the sheriff said he had only Martha's word, *no evidence,* so he couldn't charge the man. No DNA testing in those days!

Betsy took care of Martha until the baby was born, but when he came, she determined that he must not ever see or know his father. " 'You wouldn't do nothing,' " she told Sheriff Musgrave, according to the newspaper account. " 'I had to do it.' " She said she took her shotgun, walked to his property in the dark of night (it was several miles), and concealed herself in his barn overnight. When she saw her chance, she shot for the heart. She missed slightly, hitting him in the belly instead, but she said he saw her shoot him; in fact, he'd started toward her when she pulled the trigger.

He *knew* who shot him, yet he accused Lucas when he was dying! Can hatred be that strong?

Lucas had a rifle, Betsy a shotgun, but somehow nobody had looked at the type of bullet that killed Richards. Forensics wasn't much of a science then. Not only was the sheriff unwilling to go after Richards, he was obviously incompetent. They found the rifle Lucas had thrown down, and that was apparently evidence enough for the sheriff.

Betsy was a crack shot, of course. She had to be; all frontier women did. Hannah describes in detail learning to shoot a rifle, and I'm sure she would have used it to defend her children if she'd had to. That's all the old woman was doing, defending her granddaughter. Surprising that she didn't hit the heart. Maybe she wanted the old boy to suffer before he died.

The story ended by saying that Betsy had gone with her granddaughter and great-grandson to Denver to settle them there with a relative before coming to town to confess her crime. That's why she hadn't come to the sheriff sooner. She would never have let Lucas hang, she said. She was sorry "the good doctor" was put in jail.

The other article, from the next week's edition, was headlined, "Where's Betsy?" When the sheriff's wife brought Betsy's breakfast to the jail the morning after she was jailed, the cell was open and the old woman was gone. Later issues of the *Clarion* speculated for a time about where she might be, but no one ever found her. If she went to Denver to be with her grand-daughter and the child, she'd have been hard to find. I think "no evidence" Musgrave might have released her himself, since he had only her word to go on that she had done Richards in. Maybe he was even grateful to the old woman for killing the guy. At least he took her word for it and let Lucas out of jail. So different from today, with fingerprints and computers and such!

June 28

After all these weeks I've come to know my ancestors pretty well. It pleases me no end that I see bits and pieces of them in me. Lucas is the part that encouraged me to go to medical school. Hannah gave me her love of music; I started playing the piano when I was four and have never stopped, not for more than sixty years. From Meggie the rebel, my grandmother, I got courage and the passion for causes. Without the gift of her public spirit, would I have worked so hard at that inner-city clinic for so many years?

I wonder what my grandfather the riverboat gambler passed down to me—my sense of adventure, perhaps, my restlessness. I've always wanted to see what was beyond the next hill. Now, with Lennie's money, I'm finally free to roam the world. Or maybe that urge came from my great-uncle Lawrence, who ran away from home at an early age. Mom had it too, wandering all over Europe as a young woman, marrying late in life. I guess she just hated to settle down.

Mom. She gave me courage, especially after Dad was killed in the war. She just carried on—just like Hannah, now that I think of it. She was my role model long before I met Lennie and we started our practice together. Of course, I'm my own stubborn, independent self too, the woman who didn't want to get married or have children (wrapped up in my causes, I feared I might have neglected them as Meggie did my mother), the woman who wanted to be a doctor from the time she was very small. I hope they would be pleased with who I became.

June 29

I'm leaving for home in the morning. This has been a fascinating and fruitful time, and I'm so grateful to my great-grandmother for writing the journals and to my grandmother for not destroying them. What luck for me! Reading her journals brought my great-grandmother to life for me. I've come to know and admire her. She was a brave, strong, remarkable woman. Words can't begin to describe how it feels to think that her blood flows in my veins, and that I carry her name.

ABOUT THE AUTHOR

A native Coloradan, **Barbara Fleming** has long been interested in history. She writes a weekly historical newspaper column about Fort Collins, her hometown in the high plains of northern Colorado, and is the author of *Fort Collins: A Pictorial History*. Some of the incidents in *Journeying* are loosely based on real-life events in Fort Collins's past. She lives in her hometown with her husband, Tom, and their gray cat, Shadow. She is an avid reader and has always wanted to tell stories from the past from a woman's point of view. Write to her at fcwriter@frii.com or visit her Web site at www.authorBarbaraFleming.com.